NO MORE THE SWORD

DEDICATION

To Mark, whose initial hard work provided the basis for this book, and who supplied much historical information. To Sylvia, whose encouragement never faltered, and to Ted and the family for their unquestioning support.

No More the Sword

by

Marcia Treece

William Sessions Limited
York, England

ISBN 1 85072 280 3

Printed in 11 on 12 point Plantin Typeface
from Author's Disk
by Sessions of York
The Ebor Press
York, England

Prologue

SARAH LUSCOMBE turned her face to the sea and the early evening sunshine. She loved this spot on the Hoe of Plymouth sheltered by a grassy bank and with an uninterrupted view of the wide stretch of the Sound. There were not many people on the green slopes, nothing to disturb the wandering of her thoughts. They went as always to her son Thomas, her youngest, born when she was nearly forty years old, and far away now across the vast ocean. He and his young wife Priscilla had sailed aboard the *Desire* three years ago to seek with other Plymouth Quakers a new life in Pennsylvania. He had wanted her to go with them but she could not. Her other children were all hereabouts and her growing family of grandchildren and most of all, her dear husband John lay in the burial place not far from where she now sat. And too, as she moved slightly to ease an ache in her back she was conscious of the fact that it was 1690 and she would be sixty years old in the eighth month.

She was thankful to be very hearty still, but travel across the sea was not for her - if only Thomas was no further away than St. Nicholas Island. She would like to make one more journey though - north to Swarthmoor Hall to visit her dear friends Margaret and George Fox and to walk again across the Moors at Ulveston. But age was creeping up on them too, and she must wait to seek God's will for her.

A breeze had sprung up now and Sarah pushed a tendril of silver hair back beneath her white cap, knowing again with certainty that this was where she belonged. She was thankful for the fulfilling life she had had - not that it was over yet. Wasn't she awaiting even now the birth of a great grandchild, a grandchild for her daughter Elizabeth, and her heart sang as she thought of all the love and joy that this blessing would bring, for this child would surely know safety and security. Please God there would be no more wars like that in which she had grown up, with families rent apart. Though now she allowed herself a moment of most un-Quakerly pride, remembering how Plymouth had stood alone for Parliament, holding out through the dreadful years of the Siege and the Sabbath Day's Fight - and afterwards with Charles' punishment of the town. Her brothers had talked of that battle at Lipson for many a long day, especially to their father when he returned from years in Cromwell's service, saying he could no longer wear the sword. Sarah smiled to herself recalling that that moment had seen the beginning of a new life for them all, a life that was to bring their family and friends great joy, but with it much suffering and persecution. But now, the Royal house had changed once more, the Stuarts gone at last, and with the passing of last year's Act all the Friends could gather without fear, their Meetings peaceful and uninterrupted. They could go about their business unmolested, living their lives freely in the light.

Yes, this child should live with God's blessing into the new century just ten years away, and getting to her feet, Sarah smoothed down her plain, grey gown and started down the slope towards her daughter's home to see if the new young Friend had come yet into this world.

Chapter One

"MAY I GO NOW, mother, to see the ships come in? James has gone down to the Pool already and I don't want to miss everything." Sarah was hopping impatiently from one foot to another.

"Go along then, but walk child, sedately, and don't be long. Father has friends coming to talk after supper so I want to have it early this evening." Mistress Mary Jewell's tone was kind, but she shook her head in despair at the hoydenish behaviour of her only daughter. At ten years old Sarah was already tall, slightly built, but in determination and strength of will very like her father.

Now, she walked obediently a few steps down the cobbled street, but as she reached the bottom she gathered up her skirts and would run, her mother knew, around the corner and straight to the harbour. It was mid July 1640 and the first of the fishing fleet were returning from Newfoundland with, hopefully, holds full of mostly dried cod, and perhaps pilchards from nearer home. Mary turned back into the house and the preparation of the evening meal, her mind on the sewing that needed to be done and the store cupboards to be checked.

Sarah felt the sun on her face and the soft west wind as she ran to the harbour. It was a scene of noisy activity and an excited happiness filled the child as she called to friends and watched the gulls wheeling and crying before landing on their wide, webbed feet ready for any morsels that might come their way. There were four fishing ships in and groups of men gathered on the quay by each one, watching the catch as it was unloaded. There were shouts, calls, sudden guffaws of laughter and squeals from the children chasing each other around the boxes, piles of nets and coiled ropes. Sarah sniffed with pleasure the scent of fish, tar, wood and sun, smells that had been part of her life here in Plymouth for as long as she could remember. She could see her father standing with a group

1

of men against the harbour wall, taller than any of them, and the summit of her childish world. Her elder brother Francis was with him and James, three years younger than Sarah, was racing across the cobbles with other small boys. There were women too on the quay, not many, but Sarah knew that the poor would gather there in the hope of discarded fish that would help to feed their families. Suddenly there was a cry from the direction of a small vessel at the far end of the harbour. A knot of people stood there, gathered around a woman who broke away from the others and stumbled in Sarah's direction, looking wildly around her and crying desperately, a toddler clinging to her skirts. Her friends caught up with her as Sarah stood still, the day suddenly darkened and the wind cold. She caught snatches of conversation - "he was a good man", "a good father, how will she manage now" and the despairing - "drowned like a dog in the sea while I waited through the summer, the children, the poor children and me," and she collapsed onto a pile of woolsacks standing ready for shipment.

"Sarah, come along, it's time to go." She hadn't heard her father come up to her, James and Francis on either side of him. "Oh father," she caught his hand, "That poor woman, her husband's been drowned."

"Yes I know my love," he smoothed her white cap. "But don't you worry. To-morrow I'll see what I can do to help - she's better left with the women to-night." Sarah tried to match her father's long steps as he strode in cuffed leather boots across the quay. "And mother too," she said with growing confidence, "She and Betsy will take her some broth and tarts for the children, won't she?"

"She certainly will," Richard Jewell smiled at his daughter. "Your mother's broth is a cure for all ills." The four of them, waving to friends, turned the corner into Rag Street and hurried to the house half-way up which was their home, Sarah fervently glad that her father was not a fisherman but a dealer in wool who stayed safely at home, and as they opened the heavy, oak door, appetising smells of mutton stew and newly baked bread wafted out to greet them, and Sarah realised how hungry she was.

The table was already spread and the family soon gathered around it, Richard taking his place on the great, carved chair at one end and Mary on the smaller, plainer one at the other, with the children on their stools between. Betsy, a cheerful, plump young woman of about twenty, brought in the final dish of baked fish and took her seat beside Sarah. Betsy, locally born, had come as an orphan to the family to help Mary when Francis was a small boy and had stayed ever since, fulfilling every role of help and comforter, even to the burial of the babies who had died.

It was a God-fearing household and Richard gave thanks before the food was served and eaten. As they ate he told his wife the news of the fisherman who had drowned - "just fallen overboard and was gone before they could reach him." Immediately, as Sarah had known she would, Mary started to plan ways in which she could help. "We'll go and see the poor widow tomorrow, Betsy, and I'm sure some of the other wives hereabouts will do the same, she won't want to take her family to the poor-house if she can help it." [The hospital of Poors' Portion had been founded a few years previously just beyond St. Andrew's Church.]

James, as always, was the first to finish his meal and amused himself by pulling his sister's apron-strings. She tugged his hair in retaliation and their mother, exasperated, sent them both on chores, James to carry the dishes to the kitchen and Sarah to gather lavender from the little herb garden behind the house. "I need it to sweeten the linen chests," she said, then turned to her husband with a sigh. "I'm sorry, Richard, I know how you value a quiet supper-time." He caught her hand and his smile was gentle. "Leave them be my love," he said. "Childhood is short enough and who knows what lies ahead for them - or any of us for that matter," and he sighed now. Mary nodded in agreement. There was great love and understanding between these two, and what she did not understand Mary accepted with trust in her husband's judgement. She knew that Richard and many of his friends were anxious for the country at this time and Plymouth in particular, but for the moment the immediate concerns of her family and those about her were enough for her. So she, small, dark and quick of movement like her younger son James, carried on with the evening's tasks, while Richard, whose fair colouring and serious nature were reflected in Francis, sat on at the table a few minutes longer reflecting on the meeting to come.

Sarah came back to the house, her nose buried in the bunch of lavender, loving its perfume. Then she laid it on the kitchen dresser for her mother who was busy with Betsy preparing tankards of ale ready to refresh Richard and his friends. Sarah saw her father lift the big family Bible from its box and place it ready on the cleared table, and, taking her stool, she tucked it into a corner close to the wide casement window, hoping that her mother would let her stay there, quietly out of sight but able to hear the men's deliberations. She had not long to wait, for just as Mary was sending James to his bed her father was admitting the first of his friends.

They left their cloaks on the oak chest in the hall-way and took their places at the table. Sarah recognised each visitor as he arrived for they were all old friends and neighbours. Peter Perryman came first, a man of about her father's age, Sarah thought - though she could not be sure of course, and anyway, they were over thirty she knew, which was quite old. He kept a grocer's shop just two streets away, and close on his heels was the clothier, John Light. A few minutes later Jacob Thomas made a noisy entrance. Sarah thought that he always seemed to fill any room he was in - a big, black-bearded man with a ruddy complexion. He had been a seaman for many years, and was now the owner of fishing vessels, remaining himself on dry land.

As these men took their seats there were slow, shuffling foot-steps in the hall, and Richard helped Ephraim Goodyeare into the room. It was obvious by the way the others greeted the newcomer, pulling forward the best chair for him with a stool for the leg that clearly gave him pain as he leant heavily on a stout ash stick, that they held him in great esteem. Ephraim was a well-to-do woollen merchant of some standing in the town and Richard had worked for him for many years until now he virtually ran the business though the old man kept a shrewd eye on things. It seemed that the company was now assembled and ready to begin. Sarah noticed, as she looked at them, a ray of evening sunlight caressing the polished, worn surface of the old oak table, dust motes dancing along its curves and ridges. But there was a timid knock on the door and a fair head came round it blinking his fringe out of the bright, blue eyes. It was Francis. "Shall I come in father and sirs, just to listen to what you have to say?"

It was Ephraim who answered, shaking his sparse grey locks with approval as he did so.

"Yes, come along in boy, and add the weight of your thoughts to ours. You're almost a man and your father was no bigger than

4

you are now when he first came to work for me. How old are you my lad?" Francis made himself as tall as he could. "I'm thirteen, almost", he stammered, as blushing, he squeezed himself onto the end of a bench that had been placed along one side of the table. Richard opened the Bible. "We'll just have a few words from the Book." he said, turning to his favourite chapter in Isaiah, "to put us in right mind." The others, except for Jacob nodded in assent and listened quietly to the verses read. As soon as the Bible was closed Jacob got to his feet. "What's to be done about the pirates," he shouted, banging his hand on the table. "One of my ships came in yesterday, but there's no news of the other. The lads that got back said they had a hazardous run all the way, and if the other's gone that's forty men lost plus the vessel and cargo." The others joined in now, one after another - "There's a spice ship should have been back long ago," and "Yes, and one with woollen goods from Holland. 'Tis said that some men from these parts - of wealth but no morals - even help the pirates." Richard tried to calm their anger. "We'll have to petition the king."

"What's the use, we've done it before but he takes no heed." This was evidently the lead Richard was waiting for. "You are right my friends," he now said firmly. "There are too many matters that get no attention from the court. How can it be otherwise without a Parliament to negotiate for us? I suggest that we put together as good a case as we can and see our M.Ps. Thomas Sherwill and John Glanville - and John Pym for Tavistock. They're all good men and it's time that the people of Plymouth stood together."

There was quiet for a few minutes in that room in Rag Street. Sarah, from her window-seat, felt herself uplifted by her father's words, by the still warm sunshine and the heady garden scents coming through the open window, so that when her mother, realising where she was, came to collect her for bed, she went unresisting, with a curtsey to the company and a kiss for her father.

Chapter Two

SARAH WAS LONG to remember that autumn of 1640 and the winter that led into '41. She sensed that changes were afoot, strange happenings she had never known before. The ordinary facts of life and death did not disturb her greatly. The drowning of the fisherman in July had saddened her for a little, and there were others as the fleet gradually arrived back, but these things came and went as they always had.

This was different - a feeling of foreboding indicated by signs sometimes as slight as a snatch of conversation caught as she passed people in the street, or just the sight of two or three huddled together whose words she could not even hear. Her own parents would draw apart as she ran into a room where they were sitting side by side, though inevitably they would hold out welcoming hands to her. "Sarah love, come along in," or "What have you been doing child, you look as if you've been rolling along the quay."

Leaflets appeared on walls and gate-posts as presses worked hard to produce them. Sarah carried a sheet into Richard one day as he sat at the great table pouring over his accounts, preparing them for Ephraim's scrutiny. "Father, what does this mean?" He looked up from his work and took the sheet. "I can understand some of it," Sarah said, frowning, "but what are our liberties?" Richard read aloud - "Men of Plymouth, remember the Charter granted to us in 1601 by Queen Elizabeth. We must always preserve our liberties, even to the fighting for them."

Richard drew his daughter into the circle of his arm as he explained the words, but, though he seemed to be talking to her, Sarah had the strange feeling that his audience was much wider - anyone in fact who would listen. "Our liberties are our freedoms, hard-won many of them, but ones we must keep at all costs - to worship as we think best, to pay only fair taxes and to be ruled

6

justly, with a Parliament. We're a long way from London, child" and he hugged her suddenly as though remembering she was there, "but we're still part of the realm, and the people of Plymouth are becoming impatient."

"But fighting, father! Would you fight? I don't want you to, you could be killed," and she clung tightly to him. "Hush my love, these things are not for you to worry about. We'll have to hope it doesn't come to that." He smiled reassuringly at her serious expression, feeling as always, a great tenderness for this daughter of his. "We'll have another reading lesson this evening," he said, "I've been neglecting you lately with so much on my mind, but run along to mother now, I'm sure there are lots of important things for you to be doing in the kitchen." She pouted at him but ran off willingly enough to fill the carved candle-box hanging on the wall by the fire, and the salt-box below it, for a fresh supply of these and other goods had arrived at the house that morning, and the salt particularly must not be allowed to get damp.

Richard wondered suddenly whether either of his sons, even Francis, who liked to be included among the men, would have queried the wording of the leaflet. Both boys were pupils at the Grammar School in Catherine Lane, Francis in his last year, but it was Sarah who had the greatest thirst for knowledge. "Please God," he prayed now, "that she will never know war," though even as his mind shaped the words, he could not see how else the troubles of this land - of his town - could be resolved. Richard remembered then, as he often did, that terrible time fifteen years earlier when Charles, in the first year of his reign, had assembled an army of ten thousand men in Plymouth for his planned conflict with Spain. The town couldn't cope with the invasion and hunger and squalor were everywhere. When the army returned, beaten from Cadiz, ragged and starving, plague came with it and by 1627 it had spread with devastating consequences. All business in the town ceased, and two thousand people died. Richard could remember now as clearly as though it had just happened, the suffering of so many families he knew, and he clenched his hands at the still unbearable recollection that his own brother had been a victim and that the grief had killed his mother.

He put together the papers still on the table, wondering yet again at the utter ineptitude of this king and his failure to care for his people. Even that tragedy seemed to have taught him nothing, for in '28 he gathered another army in Plymouth and wintered them barefoot in tents on the Hoe, through a bitter winter, unpaid, unsupplied. He even visited the town himself at that time and borrowed - Richard smiled grimly at the term - one hundred and fifty pounds from the citizens, who had to somehow support the starving soldiers for many months, while there had been no end to the extravagances of Charles and his nobles.

Richard shook his head. No, things had not improved since then, and the people of Plymouth had little reason to love this king. But the devastating reality was that the war which probably awaited them all would not be a united assault against a common, foreign enemy, but Englishmen fighting each other, family against family, brother against brother.

Two afternoons later Sarah went into the town with Betsy. She always enjoyed such excursions, the bustle, the noise, the people, the never quite knowing what she would see around each corner that they turned. Before walking from their home down Rag Street they turned upwards to Castle Dyke Lane where some of Richard's weaver outworkers lived in a cluster of tiny cottages. The door of the first small house was open, children played on the cobbles outside. Sarah did not follow Betsy when she went in to deliver her message. She knew that the room was small, and taken up almost completely by the big loom and the bundles of yarn, and was glad that her house was roomy and comfortable, as she bent and played with the toddler who was twisting a length of wool around a stick. Betsy came out calling over her shoulder to the weaver: "The master will call in tomorrow when he's been to the yarn market," and Sarah got up from her knees to join her, giving the baby a piece of gingerbread that she took from her apron pocket.

They passed the rope-walk at the bottom of the hill. This was one of the new ones recently built - not like the great one at Teats Hill but always busy. The shoe-maker's shop was just a few yards further on, and Betsy had been instructed to check on the progress of new boots for Richard. Sarah sniffed appreciatively the smell of the leather brought in from the nearby tannery. They went then to the miller in Horsepool Lane. Betsy put a bag of flour for their immediate use into her basket and ordered more. As she waited Sarah watched the corn being ground between the great wheels until Betsy called to her, tut-tutting as she brushed flour dust from the girl's dark gown. "Come along child, we've still got several calls to make." As they got further into the town the streets were busier and several times Sarah was pushed and jostled. There had been no rain for several weeks and the roads were dusty and rubbish-laden. A horse-drawn cart went by and Betsy pulled Sarah back close to her. "You stay by me," she said, knowing Sarah's habit of wandering off when something caught her interest or curiosity.

They walked by the parish church of St. Andrew, passing the walls which shielded its extensive gardens, orchards and stables. "Aren't we going to call at the fishermen's houses?" Sarah asked now, "I thought I might see Will." The houses in which the better-off fisher folk lived were a source of great fascination to the girl with their large cellars - storage places for nets and fishing tackle, and wonderful hiding places for children. The upper floors of these houses were reached by outside stone steps, also a novelty. Will was Sarah's friend and the grandson of Jacob Thomas. He lived with his family and his mother's unmarried brother Edward who was earning a name for himself as one of the best fishermen working out of Plymouth. "No, we haven't got time to-day," and Betsy quickened her steps as she spoke. Sarah stole a quick glance at her, knowing that a blush would have heightened her already healthy colour. "Look," Betsy said now, as they reached the road leading to the Guildhall, "there's a crowd gathering already there and more joining them." The woman and girl hurried to the old market cross area, which was now a covered space where Processions to Church started from and where great events were announced. The new Council Chamber had recently been built above this, and was sup-ported by pillars.

"It's the old vicar", Betsy said. "What does he want?" Suddenly a cheer went up from the crowd. Sarah kept reaching up trying to see above the people milling in front of her. Then she caught sight of the Rev. Thomas Forde holding up his hand. "People of Plymouth," his voice was loud and clear. "I have news for you. Our petition for a second Parish Church has been answered. The King has agreed to our request." A murmur of excitement passed through the crowd. "It's to be on the north side of the town, right on the edge". He paused as everyone listened expectantly. "But we have to raise the money for it ourselves, and it's to be called

Charles Church after the King." The murmuring sounded angry now. "Who'd ever heard of a church named after a king - it should have a good saint's name." The vicar spoke again. "That's all the news I have at this moment, my friends. Go now to your homes in peace.

The people moved away, Betsy and Sarah among them, and the child heard scraps of conversation that she stored away to think about later. "He's still our real Vicar doing his best for us."

"Well, at least we're going to have another Church, and maybe we'll have more say about the preachers for this one." "Yes, we don't want the King's High Church men, almost papists some of them. Out with Wilson and Bedford I say" - a cry echoed several times. Sarah decided she'd have to ask her father about all this later.

Then, just before they turned the corner to Rag Street and home she heard her name called and, looking back, saw it was Peter Perryman, the grocer at his shop doorway. "Tell your father I'll be up to see him later," and as Sarah nodded she had the feeling that he would not be the only one.

Chapter Three

JAMES RUSHED INTO the house when he returned from school, scattering hat and books and cascades of raindrops on the way. "Mother, mother, they've started, with workmen and men measuring and they're digging already." Mary came from the kitchen wiping her hands on the hempen apron that she had tied over her white one. "What are you talking about James?" Her tone was serious but her smile indulgent. Francis, thoughtful and sober as always, had followed his younger brother in. He put down his school books as he answered their mother. "It's the new church, the one the king said could be built over on the edge of town." "But that's not on your way home from school." "Oh, all the boys went to see it," James protested, while Francis reassured Mary. "It was quite safe mother. We older ones kept an eye on the children." His emphasis on the last word caused James to reach up and tweak his brother's hair before clattering away upstairs.

Sarah was in her own small room sitting on the window seat and gazing out at the dripping garden. It had been a mild winter so far in Plymouth but a wet one, and now, at the beginning of March, the mist, sweeping in from the sea, hung in the still air, and Sarah watched the droplets of drizzle run down the windows and along the leaves and branches. Her sampler lay in her lap, but for the most part neglected. Sewing was not the child's favourite occupation, and sometimes she felt that if she held it and contributed the odd stitch she was doing all that could reasonably be asked of her. As she heard James' steps on the stairs she came back from her day-dream of going out in a boat across the Sound with Will, and ran down to her mother. "Can I go to meet father, it's his time for coming home?" "Well, all right, you've been in all day, I suppose, but fasten your cloak, the drizzle is thick now," and, as Sarah made haste to leave the house, she called after her: "Don't go any further than the bottom of the street, you can take shelter and wait for father there."

Sarah liked the feel of the rain on her face as she sped down the steps and along the narrow road. When she reached the corner she sheltered as her mother had said, where the first floor windows of the houses almost met across the street. She peeped ahead but couldn't see her father's tall figure among the hurrying crowds. Then, as she waited, she heard shouting - over and above the general noise of the town. It got louder and she could just see the head and waving arms of a man who must be standing on some sort of platform. He wasn't very far away, just on the open, cobbled space near the Customs House. She had to see what was going on. After all, it wasn't much further than mother had allowed her to go, and it was on the way that father would come. She pulled up her hood and made her way as quickly as she could towards the clamour.

There was a small crowd already there, mostly young men. She noticed, and then with a gasp she recognised, the speaker. It was Edward Curnow, her friend Will's uncle, and a member of the household of Jacob Thomas, the fishing boat owner and friend of her father. Edward looked angry as he stood on his upturned box. He was a thick-set man in his early twenties, his usually ruddy complexion rendered a deeper red by the weather and his own excitement. His head was uncovered and his long black hair clung lankly to his face and neck. Instinctively the child looked round for Betsy, knowing the off and on relationship she had with the fisherman, but realising instantly that she wasn't there. Edward started to shout again and Sarah tried to listen and to understand.

"We be better off with the King than all these Puritan merchants lording it over us. I tell you they're a miserable lot, didn't they stop our Maypole dancing on the Hoe and send the Players away, without so much as a single performance?"

There were murmurs of assent from the crowd gathered around him, some of whom were laughing and cheering and, Sarah was sure, were more than half drunk. She noticed certain of the more sober citizens hurrying past the scene, with very disapproving expressions, and then, as she thought that perhaps she should go back towards home, she felt a hand on her shoulder.

Sarah spun around peering up through the drizzle straight into her father's face.

"And what are you doing here child, on your own?" She caught hold of his hand. "I came to meet you, I was waiting on the corner of Rag Street, but I heard the noise and just came a little bit further. Do you see who it is, father, it's - it's Betsy's friend Edward." "Yes, I see, but let's get home now, we'll talk about this later, mother will be getting worried about you, and I'm later than I meant to be." Sarah hurried along beside him. "Mother will be cross that I came further than the end of the street." She looked hopefully up at Richard who patted her head. "Leave it to me," he said, knowing that there were more serious things than this to be considered.

Later that evening Sarah from her stool in the window corner watched as a visitor arrived for her father. It was Jacob Thomas, a worried expression on his face as he spoke quietly to Richard in the hallway. Richard, appearing to reassure him, ushered him in to a seat by the fire. "Do not be concerned friend Jacob, we cannot expect to have no opposition. This was just a crowd of hot-heads, all too young to understand the threats that hang over us. The older man put out a hand to the blaze and sighed heavily. "Life has been too easy for some of them. They have no memories of wars with Spain, of capture, of the Inquisition and torture, in fact of all the dangers of popery." Richard agreed. "No, we must be ever-vigilant". "'Tis hard though," Jacob persisted, "when families themselves cannot all see things through the same eyes." Richard got to his feet and gripped his friend's shoulder. "Do not be downcast Jacob, we must try to teach them that there are greater things to hold to than merriment and licentious living. Pray God we succeed so that when the time of testing comes it will find us in unity. Not forgetting too that there are some, even of our own kind, who would not deny the divine right of the king to do as he pleases. Now you rest there a moment while I have a word with Mary. Then we'll talk some more about the meeting to-morrow."

That was the last serious conversation that Sarah heard that night but it was sufficient to make her understand that the sense of foreboding she felt all around was drawing closer, even to touching those of her own household.

The next day was clear and dry, and if not really bright, yet a watery sun appeared every now and then through the clouds and people told each other that there was a feel of spring in the air. Mary had promised to take Sarah to visit a friend who worked for the Sherwill household on the Houndiscombe estate, and in anticipation the child was willingly helping Betsy clear the dinner-table, carrying the pewter tankards and trenchers carefully into the kitchen, picking up the last piece of cheese-cake and popping it into her mouth as she did so.

"Father has an important meeting to-day, hasn't he?" she said to her mother as they tidied their hair and put on their cloaks.

"Not much gets past you child, does it?" Mary put some pasties into a basket and covered them with a white cloth. "Come along then, it's a fair walk. Betsy are you ready?"

"Is Betsy coming with us to-day?" "Yes, she's not feeling very well at the moment - a little outing will do her good," and, in fact, as Betsy joined them and the three left the house together, her usual cheerfulness seemed to have quite deserted her, and she walked with bent head and downcast eyes.

Richard was already on his way to the Guildhall where the Mayor, William Byrche had, with his Corporation, called a special meeting of all merchants and concerned townspeople.

The lofty room was almost full when Richard climbed the steps to it and waved or nodded to friends and acquaintances. Ephraim Goodyeare, the wealthy woollen merchant for whom he worked indicated a vacant seat beside him in the front row, and Richard eased his way to it through the ranks of soberly clad merchants and tradesmen.

"I believe there's a lot of business to decide to-day, and much news from London," Ephraim said to Richard as the Mayor rose to his feet to open the meeting. Richard listened to the routine concerns that had to be dealt with or reported - all the time knowing that they were only the prelude to matters of much more weight.

"The next item - the annual auction will be held tomorrow on Dung Quay for the right to remove all the street sweepings collected there." This announcement was greeted with murmurs of "about time too," and "the weather's getting too mild to have all that lying about." "Still the farmers need it for the crops so good luck to whoever gets the right."

The next matter was the petition to be sent to the justices at the Quarter Sessions in Exeter about worries over the declining fish industry and concerns about the Irish rebels. This engendered a lot of discussion, but it was resolved at last.

Then there was a pause, and the Guildhall became quiet and still, and Richard could feel the tension in himself and all around him. The Mayor cleared his throat and picked up a sheaf of papers from the table. "Our correspondent" -he indicated John Collier, a wine merchant and member of the Corporation who sat beside him, "has received a newsletter from London, which brings us up to date with news from Parliament and all matters that are important to us. I will deal with these as clearly as I can, but beg your attention and patience for it is right that all of you know what the future of Plymouth may be." They waited, they listened, they argued and discussed before making their decisions and plans for the future of their town.

"Friends, neighbours and fellow townspeople", began the Mayor at this point, "I, we - ," he included the Corporation ranged around him - "feel that there is now an urgent need to assess our situation. Plymouth has been a proud and Protestant town for many years. In 1549 we stood firm against the Prayer Book rebellion and attempts to make our services Catholic. We are determined not to lose now all we have fought long and hard to obtain and maintain, both as far as our religion is concerned and our political and economic life. You will all know that Charles ruled for eleven years without a Parliament, and will know too what he did during that time to raise money - mainly for his own extravagances. He used monopolies on articles of common use like salt, starch and soap, obtained ship money, impressed seamen from Devon ports, who were badly treated and seldom paid, and all this during a time of bad harvests and a slump in the woollen industry. However" - and here the Mayor paused, looking around at his audience as though willing their support - "We now have a Parliament, and the assurance that never again can it be dissolved against its will, and my friends, we can all be very proud of the part that John Pym and other men from Plymouth and hereabouts are playing in Parliament at this very time."

There was a cheer then as this pride of which he spoke surged through the hearts of most of the men there assembled, and Richard found himself on his feet, waving his hat in the air.

15

Byrche held up his hand for quiet. "Just to clarify what's going on," he said, "As most of you will know too, the House of Commons is led by Pym, the M.P. for Tavistock, and of our M.Ps. John Glanville is the Speaker, with Thomas Sherwill also working always for our good. William Strode, the member for Bere Alston has now been freed from prison. He and Pym are two of the main thorns in the King's flesh, and when he tried to arrest them they were successfully defended by John Maynard M.P. for Totnes and Recorder for Plymouth, so you can see how well they have acquitted themselves and are an example to us all."

As he paused John Collier got to his feet. "And don't forget the other side of affairs. Through the work of our friends two of our enemies - Strafford and Laud have been impeached. Archbishop Laud and the Queen between them would have rendered us all Catholics if they had not been stopped. No friends, there is no going back now, not unless we all want to give up and follow those thousands of our fellow countrymen who have sought freedom in the New World."

There were murmurings at this and groups of men started to talk amongst themselves - some nodding in agreement over shared views and others openly hostile. Ephraim, sitting next to Richard, looked anxious. "We don't want this to get out of hand, it's too important." He banged his stick on the floor and, clutching Richard's shoulder, got slowly and painfully to his feet. "Pay attention men, we must listen to the mayor." Everyone now seemed to settle back in their seats, ready for guidance. "We - the Corporation and I - have a proposal for you," the mayor said, slowly and carefully. "I think we have brought you up to date with the situation as it is now, and I will call a meeting whenever there is more news to give you. Meanwhile, will you agree that we stand firm supporting Parliament even if" - and he straightened himself here - "even if it means defying the king? Our cause is a just one and God is with us. How vote you on this?"

The room was strangely silent for a moment. Then, one after another, merchants and leading townsmen rose to their feet. Jennings, Fownes, Eliot and Parker led the declaration. Each man raised his hand - "Aye, we're with you." Richard and his friends took their turns, and his heart warmed at their support. But the mayor needed to be fair and sure. "Some of you are clearly not yet with us," he said. "We will listen to what you have to say."

There was a stirring, a rustling in the hall, a spokesman was evidently needed for those who had not declared themselves. Suddenly an elderly man arose, his grey locks curling on his wide collar. Richard recognised him as Robert Tremayne, the owner of the largest tannery in Plymouth, and knew him to be a hard business man, but a fair and just one. "I and my friends, of whom several are present in this room to-day, agree with most of what has been said. We know that our religion has often been put at risk and all our business enterprises, and as Mayor Byrche has said, we have all worked hard to maintain those things we value. None of us would quarrel with that. But," - and here he paused and looked around at the men for whom he spoke, "but we too have searched our souls and minds and we do not want war."

Here Richard could not contain himself - "None of us wants war." He got to his feet. "But we have to accept that it may be the final choice, it may be all we can do."

Robert waved him down. "Let me finish, friend. Why can we not keep what we have without taking arms against the king? We can support ourselves - we largely do that now - with access by sea, there aren't many ports in the land greater than Plymouth, and by road. We can continue to export, and to import all we need but do not produce. Let London look to itself!"

Robert sat down then to murmurs of agreement around him. All eyes went to the Mayor as he slowly got to his feet once again. "Thank you Master Tremayne," he said. "I think I can fairly say that we understand and respect your thoughts and views, but I also have to say in all honesty that I do not think we can carry a policy of isolation for too long or too far. There are so many matters entangled and interwoven. It seems to me that all we can do for the time being is to wait and be vigilant. As I said just now, I will call you all together whenever more news reaches us, and we will make our judgements as needs dictate."

He paused, then went on, "Whatever happens my friends, we must stand together, the whole history, tradition and future of our beloved Plymouth depends on it." No arguments were raised at this, there was no dissension. The worthy townsmen and merchant venturers rose to their feet and left the Guildhall quietly, with scarcely a word passing between them, but with much to occupy their thoughts as they returned to their homes. Richard walked with Peter Perryman till they reached the grocer's shop and home, then, shaking his friend's hand, he continued alone the short remaining distance to Rag Street. He had only taken a few steps up the hill when a call behind him broke through his contemplation.

"Father, father, it's us!" He turned to see Sarah running up to him, and looking beyond her, saw Mary and Betsy just turning the corner. All three were smiling, their faces rosy in the March wind - even Betsy he noticed, looked much more like her old, cheerful self. Sarah held out a bunch of flowers - "Look, I picked these in the hedges around Houndiscombe, everything's early this year," and she sniffed the nosegay of crane's bill, vetch and milkworts, and even one or two tiny white violets. "Mother has marchpane too, in her basket, in different colours - we've had a lovely time."

As they reached the house together and Richard opened the heavy, oak front door, he wondered which was the real life - the meeting he had just left or this little family group, and it was only as he looked at Mary and saw the questioning concern in her eyes that he knew the two could not be separated.

Chapter Four

NOT ONLY HAD the winter of 1640-41 been mild but the spring that followed was warm and the summer maintained the pattern of sunshine. Some of the people of Plymouth saw this as a good sign for the harvest that year was much improved and there was the hope that Parliament would put everything to rights, and all shadows of war hanging over them would disperse and fade. But many of the artisans and workpeople, the apprentices and shop-keepers as well as the more senior townspeople, the most committed and concerned of the merchants, watched events carefully - even those that seemed trivial - and waited.

In May 1641 news came that Strafford had been executed, and there was a general sense of relief that his treacherous presence had been removed. He had been feared and hated for his ruthless putting down of all opposition in Ireland. There was a complicated two-way link between Devon and Ireland at this time for there was a threat of subversion from Irish Catholics flooding in, and also from a network of family relationships which tied together the people of Devon with the Irish protestants.

But domestic and economic life continued as usual in Plymouth and in August came the wedding of Betsy and Edward Curnow. This was a happy event for the Jewell family, and especially for Sarah, once her mother had told her why the young man - clean and tidy with hair neatly arranged and looking very serious and uncomfortable - had been closetted with Richard for the whole of one evening. "We're the only family Betsy has," Mary explained, "so we're very concerned for her welfare and happiness, and your father wanted to make sure that if they were married Edward would look after her properly."

"She seems cross with him most of the time." Sarah's comment was, to herself at least, irrefutable. Mary looked at this daughter of hers, growing up too quickly, and sighed. "That's only because she knew that some of his opinions, well, didn't agree with your father's, or Jacob's for that matter. But they've come to an understanding, and everything will be well." Then she said, more to herself than Sarah, "Our Betsy'll keep him in line and make him like it."

The young couple were going to live in one of the fishermen's cottages down near the shore and Sarah took great delight in helping get it ready for them. She and Mary went through their linen chests and sorted a good supply of blankets and other bedding, and even caps, gloves and stockings, all sweetly scented with rosemary and lavender. They put together, too, a generous collection of herbs, lotions and samples, leather bottles of cider and home made wine, and pots of honey. Then when a shipment of sugar arrived from the West Indies, some of which Richard bought, Mary selected a ten pound loaf and gave it to a delighted Betsy, together with a carved, wooden box to keep it in and a pair of iron sugar cutters.

Edward played his part too, in all these preparations. He was a good carpenter and a hard worker when his mind was set upon a project, and all the time that could be spared from the fishing that summer was spent carving, turning and producing most of the furniture they would need - stools, benches, a chest, and a bed frame ready take the rush base and feather mattress, and a sturdy joined table, one side of which was polished and the other had a working surface. Betsy was very excited when this last was finished, and she invited Mary and Sarah to come down to the cottage to view it.

"It's too fine for us really," she said, "but Edward was determined to make it. He saw one like it at Master Collier's when he delivered fish there and nothing else would do." She reverently touched the shining surface with her strong, capable hands, and looked around her new home with pride.

"I've got something for you too," Sarah remembered, and took from her pocket the sampler she'd been working on for so long. The letters were crooked and the stitches cobbled in two places, but it was finished at last, and Betsy received it with a look of great love for the child, and she wiped away a tear with the corner of her apron. "I'm so fortunate," she said, "and we'll have to find a special place for this. To think you made it for me!"

Sarah, embarrassed, kicked at the rush matting covering the hardened earth floor. "Can I go and look for Will now?" she asked her mother, and receiving permission, ran out on to the shingly beach. She found her friend, barefoot, hunting among the pools for cockles and limpets. He turned and waved to her, and Sarah, tucking up her skirts, scrambled across the rocks to meet him, happy in the sunshine, watching the gulls - and the gannets with their gleaming black wing-tips - wheeling overhead and stopping to pick up sea-shells that caught her attention with their varying shapes and irridescent colour.

After a while Sarah found a flat smooth rock to sit on, and when Will joined her they shared an apple - bite for bite - that had been tucked away deep in her pocket, and discussed the peculiarities of the grown-up world.

"I've just been to the house where Betsy and your Edward are going to live," she said. "It's looking very nice." Will was sceptical. "'Can't see why they want to bother. He seems comfortable with us, and won't you all miss Betsy?" "Oh, she's going to come up to us every day, and help mother. She says she couldn't just leave us."

"Well, there you are then." - no more needed to be said. Will picked up a flat pebble and skimmed it across the water. "I hope Ned will still take me fishing. We go out a long way in his new boat." Sarah popped the bladders on a strand of sea-weed, then dropped it into a tiny rock-pool. Will went on, as she'd known he would: "I'm going to have my own boat one day, after I've worked with the other men for a bit."

"You are lucky. I'm going home now," and turning abruptly she ran back across the shingle, leaving Will to gather up his basket of shell-fish and set off for his own home. "It's not fair." Sarah scuffed at the pebbles as she reached the end of the quay. "Boys have a wonderful life, especially when they become men, but what is there for girls? We just look after the home - and everyone else, and it's just not - important enough."

The wedding itself was a simple service held in the Parish Church and conducted by the Rev. Thomas Forde in defiance of the King's choice, High Churchman Wilson. The church was decorated with wild flowers, and the sunlight warmed like a blessing, the young couple and their families and friends come to support

21

them. After the ceremony everyone gathered for a fine meal spread on trestles in the garden of St. Andrew's, and prepared beforehand by Mary and her friends and neighbours. The children were allowed to help themselves from the overflowing dishes and to carry their wooden trenchers to favourite places in the garden, while the adults more soberly enjoyed their meal at the tables. Will and Sarah, laden with pasties, tarts, pies and various sweetmeats sat beneath the branches of a great oak-tree, leaning against its gnarled trunk.

"This is the best part of the day," said Will appreciatively, his mouth full of mutton pie, and Sarah nodded her agreement.

Perhaps Richard sensed Sarah's restlessness, for that autumn he often took her with him on visits to merchants, suppliers and outworkers, and even Mary had to admit that the girl seemed happier on these occasions than she did when occupied about the house with herself and Betsy. Francis had left school and was now apprenticed to his father. He was a biddable youth, reliable and quick to learn, but when the three of them were out together, it was Sarah who asked the questions and was interested in everyone she met.

She enjoyed best of all their excursions out into the countryside beyond the bounds of Plymouth and sometimes even on to Dartmoor where there was so much to see in the fields. There were the herds of fine Devon cattle which provided them with meat and hides and all dairy products - butter, cheese and cream - and beyond them the flocks of fat, curly-fleeced sheep from which their wool came, and the meat for their tasty pies and pasties.

Richard hired a horse and cart for these outings and Sarah, sitting beside him, felt the world was hers. He would point out to her and Francis the distant Cornish hills where the tin and lead brought to Plymouth for shipment overseas was mined, and where slate was quarried, and she realised that although her home town held at this time all that was precious to her, yet there was much beyond it, that one day perhaps she would see.

They would follow the leat that Francis Drake - ancestor of the M.P. for Plympton - had laid and Richard would explain how water was carried by it 17 miles into the town, and what a wonderful feat it had been in 1570, and what a boon to the townspeople ever since.

He took Francis and Sarah to the mills where the cloth was woven and showed them how these mills were driven by water from the leat. Back in the town, in Horsepool Lane, there were falling mills, also water driven, where cloth was cleaned and shrunk, then spread out on racks to dry and become serge.

The young people already knew many of the cottages where women and children carded, spun and knitted, and so Richard tried to instil into his son and daughter a knowledge of the roundness and inter-dependability of all aspects of their lives, and by doing so to make them realise that these lives must be protected and defended at all costs.

Chapter Five

SO PLYMOUTH WAITED, trying to maintain its economic life. The farmers outside the town produced all they could and what was not used or sent away filled the barns and store-houses. The mills were seldom silent and the outworkers never short of employment. Sarah and Will and the other children found the quay a never-ending source of entertainment for, apart from the fishing boats, there seemed to be constant landings of French and Spanish cargoes of wine, salt, paper and linen, while ingots of tin and lead and great piles of woolsacks were always wanted for shipment out. Some of the imports were re-loaded and travelled on by sea to other ports in the Kingdom for the roads out of Plymouth (especially in winter) were rough and ill-made and sometimes barely passable. It was as though the bustling trading port, already beset by pirates in the Channel and by the King's uncontrolled taxation , and not knowing what lay ahead, could not afford to slacken its efforts for a moment.

Sarah listened to her father and his friends and went with him whenever he had time to take her, but as the months went on he seemed more and more busy and preoccupied, leaving the child to her mother's care and instruction.

Then, one evening late in December '41, Richard returned to the family in great excitement. "There's news from London," he said as they gathered around the supper table. "We are to have a visit from a friend of John Pym. He cannot leave Parliament himself at this time, but is concerned about his constituents in Tavistock, so he is sending Matthew Penprase and he, from Tavistock, will come on to visit us here in Plymouth. We could not receive a better advocate of our cause." "Do you know this Master Penprase then?" asked Mary when she could stop the flow of Richard's excitement for a moment. "Why yes, he is a clothier of some repute and Master Goodyeare has often had dealings with him. The messenger said that he is coming while there is still time."

Richard pondered over those last words a great deal in the next few days as the corporation and merchants of the town prepared to receive their visitor, knowing that this was probably their last chance to learn at first hand how matters were proceeding in London.

Master Penprase was to be brought straight to the Jewells' house from Tavistock for rest and refreshment there before the meeting in the Guildhall the next morning, and afterwards his long, uncomfortable and dangerous journey back to London.

It was still early evening but wet and stormy when he arrived. Sarah had been moved to the tiny room vacated by Betsy, and had helped her mother prepare her own chamber to receive the visitor. The bed was re-made with sweet linen and the floor covered with fresh matting. A table and chair were brought in for his use as well as the carved chest and stool.

A family meal was prepared ready to be eaten as soon as the guest arrived though James and Sarah had been warned that he would be weary and travel-stained, and would probably wish to rest before eating. Sarah, supposedly helping her mother, was constantly in and out of the kitchen, listening for the knock on the door. She checked that all was ready on the long, oak table, and the big family Bible at hand in its box, for Richard had said that they might all worship together.

Mary came in carrying a copper boot-shaped container of spiced ale and bending down she pushed the toe of the boot into the fire, standing beside it the best pewter tankard with the hinged lid.

Suddenly Francis, who had been watching from the window, called out: "He is here, he's come." As Richard flung open the door in welcome, Sarah was just in time to see a tall man, enveloped in a dark cloak, descend from a farm horse and cart and take from the driver a large box. As Richard ran to help him carry the box up the steps into the hall-way, the driver with a wave of his hand and a pull on the reins, encouraged his horse down the narrow road into the driving rain.

There was a great shaking of hands amongst the grown-ups, and pats on the head for James and Sarah, and within minutes the visitor, stripped of his outer garments, was ensconced in Richard's great chair and his legs stretched out to the fire, and with the tankard of warmed ale in his hand. "That will help to drive out the cold and damp," Mary said as she gave it to him. "I'm afraid this weather is all too common, down here. It blows straight in from the sea."

"Do not be concerned, Mistress Jewell." Some of the tiredness and strain went from Matthew Penprase's face as he supped the drink. "The air here is pure and clear, not like that of London, where I fear so much is noisome and dirt-laden that it is a natural home for the plague. There are many empty benches in Parliament at the moment, where Members are afraid to return from the safety of their country seats."

Sarah sat on her stool in the corner and looked at the visitor in awe. He was indeed very tall, even without his high pointed hat, his head had almost touched the ceiling beams and his dark hair and complexion were quite frightening till he smiled and then his expression was serious but kind. He smiled at the girl now as she said excitedly: "Oh, please sir, tell us about London. I should so much like to see it and all the life that goes on there." "Hush now," her mother reproved her. "If our guest is willing, perhaps we can have our meal now. all is ready and I want him to eat in comfort, before some of your father's friends arrive to talk to him - as I'm sure they will." They all moved to the table, and Mary and Sarah brought in the dishes of hot food that had been keeping warm by the kitchen fire. Richard asked their guest to give thanks for the meal, and soon there was the warm, comforting sound of the clatter of dishes and the passing of utensils and trenchers.

Mary encouraged Matthew to partake of everything. "These are pilchards caught here in the Sound," she said, "and I think you'll like the rabbit pie." She was pleased when he admired the buttercup pattern stamped upon the new round of butter. "It's my own mould. Most housewives hereabouts like to have their own, especially if they send produce to the market. Richard carved it for me when we were first married." "I'm afraid I haven't carved much else," Richard smiled ruefully. "I'm not really much given to working with wood."

Sarah was getting impatient at all this domestic talk. "Please tell us about London," she said now, "while there is still time," (that phrase again, thought Richard, though in a different context) "and the king, is he very wicked?" Francis looked shocked, but Matthew laughed and Sarah realised he wasn't as old as she had first thought - probably only a few years older than her father.

He spread a hunk of bread thickly with honey. "I don't think he's wicked at all. He's just in the wrong place. He shouldn't be the King of a great country. He doesn't know his people, doesn't understand them. He has never walked amongst them and is probably the most sheltered and secluded of all the kings in Europe." Matthew warmed to his subject now and everyone, even James, their supper forgotten, listened and imagined and stored up his words.

"There are two worlds, you see. There is Court with its gaiety and flattery, the courtiers presided over by the Queen, and its restless search for amusement like the gaming tables of Piccadilly and the race course at Hyde Park, and the poets and writers who gather in St. James and Whitehall. It is true that the King has deeper interests, with his fine collection of works of art, and his support for the sciences. His greatest love is for horses, and it's said that being quite small, he does not burden his mounts and rides very well. But these things are all indulgences, and though I think he has a sense of duty towards his people, it is something seen from afar. He dislikes their proximity and distrusts their opinions. As I have said, he never moves amongst them and their needs mean nothing to him. In fact, he travels a great deal in Scotland, seeking support there at this time."

He paused for a moment and Richard broke in quickly. "His Divine Right is all, I suppose?" "Absolutely, and though he calls the Church Protestant because the Pope has no power over it, yet in effect it is as Catholic as ever it was. It is the Puritans upon whom he is hardest. But this is how it's been for most of his reign and we have tolerated it. Now, it has become unbearable - as you will know -" he looked at Richard, who nodded in agreement "- and where he was just, selfish and indolent, now he is using corruption to gain his ends, with never-ending monopolies and taxes, patents, extorting money wherever he can. John Pym has been doing his best against these practices since last year, trying to restore the balance and to do it without revolution, but it has gone too far. There is no turning back now."

The room was very quiet and as though realising where he was, Matthew Penprase stopped talking and looked around the table at the faces all turned to him. "I'm so sorry, Mistress Jewell, this is no talk for the dinner table. I will save the rest for the meeting tomorrow." The spell was broken, and Matthew returned to the fire where Richard joined him and they talked quietly and seriously. Sarah helped her mother clear the remnants of the meal, and soon afterwards she went up to bed without argument, quite content, for she had much to think about, and she heard the first of her father's friends arrive to discuss the next day's meeting.

The house was astir early that morning and Richard took Matthew down to the Guildhall in good time, greeting friends and neighbours on the way, and assuring his friend of the solidarity of support for Parliament that there was in Plymouth.

The rain had stopped overnight, and a grey light broke through the clouds as they mounted the steps to the Guildhall. Richard commented to Matthew on the crowds of men joining them. "You can see how concerned the people of Plymouth are, they will want to know all you can tell them and their support, once given, will not waver."

Indeed Richard had almost to clear a way for the visitor at the doorway and because of his height and presence and the fact that they knew he was not a local man, not one of them, they made way. Richard got him to the front of the hall where the Mayor was waiting, and after some words of introduction he left him there and found a seat on a bench near the front.

It was not long before the Guildhall was full to overflowing, with more crowding the entrance way. The Mayor explained briefly why they were there, and acknowledging the urgency of the situation, asked Matthew to carry straight on. This he did and as at the supper table the previous evening, his own enthusiasm and positive sureness of the cause to which he was dedicated, commanded absolute attention.

He began with a background assessment of the situation and then, as questions came at him, he answered them and moved on to explain and make clear, his eyes burning in his thin face as he willed his audience to be with him. Richard was caught up in a tide of excitement as he heard all the words that expressed his own thoughts but more clearly and succinctly than he could ever do.

Matthew told them about the new ordinance that had been passed on Sabbath-day keeping, in order to strengthen the Puritan position. There were to be no games played on the Sabbath - the merchants looked at each other in satisfaction at these words for this observance had for some time been a rule in Plymouth - but also there was to be no bowing in Church, no images, and the communion table must be moved from the Catholic eastern position to the middle of the Church. This was something different and this time the exchanged looks said: "we must remember this as Charles' Church grows", and the Mayor made a mental decision to fix a gate on the eastern side.

Then someone called out: "Tell us about the Remonstrance", and Matthew reminded them that this had been compiled some time before, setting forth in detail all the errors of the King's rule, and it was an impressive list. Recently it had been taken up again, and the Queen, frightened by Charles' absence in Scotland, tried to get him to return. There had been - and still was, Matthew informed his listeners - much chaos in London. The King left Edinburgh for the long journey south, over-confident, sure he had many new friends in both countries. The Puritans had lost some ground and Pym fought desperately to regain it - both sides using weapons of rumour and slander. Then, at last, the Remonstrance had come before Parliament, and Pym in spite of some members changing sides and joining the Royalists, had worked unceasingly to maintain the cause. He argued "the necessity of the times". Matthew's voice rose as he quoted his friend's remembered words. "It is time to speak plain English, lest posterity shall say that England was lost and no man durst speak truth."

The vote was taken, 159 members were in favour of acceptance of the Remonstrance so it had been printed and published, and was to become their Guiding Document. Cromwell said: "If the Remonstrance had been rejected, I would have sold all I had the next morning and never seen England more." "Confusion broke out, my friends," went on Matthew, and John Hampton and John Pym only with great difficulty brought calm. In addition seeing what lay ahead and anxious to have the armies with us, Cromwell asked that the Earl of Essex be given command of all the trained bands in the south."

Several burghers got to their feet at this point. Robert Tremayne attracted the Mayor's attention first. Richard waited anxiously for he knew the tanner's (erstwhile) support for the King. "Who is this Cromwell? I have heard his name often these last months but know little of him." "Ah, Oliver Cromwell." Matthew was obviously happy with this subject. "Yes, he has come to the fore of recent times and we are glad to have him. He comes from farming stock in Huntingdon and is, since 1640, now the member for Cambridge. His interests and concerns are many and any cause he espouses he does without reserve."

Tremayne did not quite give up. "I hear it said that he is indeed a country fellow, and his clothes are plain and put together without care or style."

"He certainly cares naught for fashion and his ways and manner of speech may be blunt and without affectation, but he is none the worse for that and Parliament values him greatly."

There were murmurs of support from around the hall and Tremayne resumed his seat. "Let me just bring you right up to date now," Matthew continued. "There are many genuine fears of popish plots and there are crowds of Londoners lobbying Parliament every day, and very much worse, swords were drawn in the House in mid-November, and only last week, the King tried to arrest our leaders. But it was a botched coup, our men fled to the safety of the City of London and Charles to look for support in Scotland and northern England. We have come to a stalemate my friends, neither side will back down. Maybe the King is as sure of right on his side as we are, so I cannot tell you what the next weeks and months will bring, but be assured they will be the best we can manage for our people, even if this should be a bloody war."

Matthew sat down then looking drained and exhausted, but he half-rose again almost immediately to say: "That is all I can say now in general terms, but if any of you are so desirous" (and he looked round at the Mayor and Corporation) "I will willingly stay longer to discuss practical measures with you." He sat down again and Richard, with several of his friends and other merchants, joined the group on the platform, while most of those present, who felt they had absorbed enough and must return to their own affairs, left the hall.

30

An hour or so later, Richard took Matthew back to Rag Street for refreshment before he commenced his long journey back to London, Richard's head full of facts and figures - the need to keep the ports, especially Plymouth, in Parliament's hands and that the richest areas in the country - the clothing counties of the South West, East Anglia, Yorkshire and Lancashire, all backed the Puritan cause, so that, Matthew informed them, as a source of comfort, in a long war, Parliament was sure to win.

"It makes war seem inevitable," commented Richard as the two men crossed the cobbled quay together, and he looked around at the peaceful town he loved so passionately. Matthew shook his head. "I see no other way, though I know that the aristocracy have forgotten how to fight and some do not want war. Many are even paying high taxes to save their estates from confiscation. But I care not for them. The humbler folk will support us, and the yeomen and merchants who are the backbone of England."

As winter turned to spring in 1642, news was often sparse and out of date by the time it reached Plymouth, but the townspeople knew that their leaders in London were working for their cause. Especially was Cromwell proving himself not only a promising military leader, but taking an increasingly important political role. He served on many committees, defended the commoners against enclosure, and successfully moved a resolution to permit parishioners to elect their own vicars - a means of counter-balancing the King's appointments of high church clergy. But military matters were probably his greatest concern as he realised how much did and would depend upon them. He carried many practical motions in Parliament, like that which enforced the Company of Armourers to report weekly to the House what saddles, arms and muskets were being made, and who bought them. By July 1642, this Cambridgeshire farmer was completely trusted and depended on by John Pym and John Hampden, the leaders of the Commons, so that when in August the King raised his standard in Nottingham and war had arrived, Cromwell immediately started to raise a troop of horse at Huntingdon. This by March 1643 had become a regiment - his "Ironsides" led by carefully picked men "who will stand with us for the liberty of the gospel and the law of the land. If you choose godly, honest men to be captains of horse, honest men will follow them."

And in their thousands they did.

Chapter Six

THREE EVENTS OF importance to Sarah occurred that August of '42, and sometimes looking back she wasn't sure which was of the greatest significance.

The first was the birth of a son to Betsy and Ned Curnow and a few days later Sarah held the red-faced screaming bundle for the first time in Betsy's cottage. She touched the thatch of dark hair and the smooth cheek and looked into the eyes that were very dark blue, almost black. Then, as the baby stopped crying and held her finger in his fat little fist, she looked at him in wonderment and cradled him close to her. "He knows me," she said in delight, "he's quiet for me!" "Yes, Sarah, he is indeed." Her mother took the baby and put him gently into the carved wooden crib that had once rocked to sleep Francis, Sarah and James. "Perhaps you'll be able to come and help Betsy look after little Nat Edward sometimes," Mary said as they waved goodbye to the proud new mother and walked up the hill towards their home.

The next event occurred in the middle of the month. It was Sarah's twelfth birthday, and what she was long to remember of the day was not the picnic lovingly prepared for her and her special friends, but it was the talk that she shared with her father in the early evening as they took a walk together down on to the quay. They sat for a while on Sarah's favourite smooth stone, and looked out across the Sound lit by the last rays of the sun, low in the western sky. Richard rested an arm on his daughter's slender shoulders. "You're growing up quickly, my love - almost a woman already, and I don't know what the next years have in store for you - for any of us." Sarah turned to him, anxious at the seriousness of his tone. "We'll all go on being happy here together, won't we, father?" He hugged her close. "I hope so, my child. I really do hope so, but you know that the country is in a parlous state at the moment. You have heard the talk, seen the visitors coming and going, and it seems likely that we shall have to fight. I have spoken of the probability of war to you before, have I not?" "Yes, father, you have, but I hoped..." and her voice trailed away. "We must always hope, and pray, and I pray especially that Plymouth will be safe, but I want you to know, Sarah, that I depend upon you a great deal. While I am here I will protect you all, but if I have to go away then I hope you will look after your mother and the boys for me. You are the most sensible and resolute of all my children and I pray that if the worst should happen, you will be given all the strength you need. God bless you, my very dear child." His voice broke then, and Sarah grew up in that moment, as she now held her father close, promising that she would always be his faithful daughter.

The next morning came the news that Charles had raised his standard at Nottingham, and war had arrived, the third happening in Sarah's life that August.

For the people of Plymouth, the early days and weeks of the war were strange and (sometimes) bewildering. They were conscious of being a long way from London and the heart of the conflict and yet, as plans and preparations went on all around them, they knew without doubt that they were part of the war and would continue to be so until this grievous matter was settled.

The Mayor, it was Thomas Ceely at this time, immediately assumed complete control of all civil matters, and one of his first actions was to send away the Royalist Clergymen, Wilson and Bedford, and to welcome Thomas Forde and Alexander Grosse back to St. Andrew's Church. Work on the new Charles Church soon ceased till peace came again. The partly completed building was covered by canvas and services held there later in the war.

Amongst many of the young people there was sometimes in these first days, an air of excitmenet. On the beach children played games of war with wooden weapons and "killed" each other enthusiastically, while their older brothers, and even sisters, thought of glories that might await them. It was their fathers who talked anxiously of dangers to come, and their mothers who already imagined the killed and wounded, while the elders amongst them, recalling earlier conflicts, shook their grey heads in foreboding. Groups of people were to be seen on street corners, and there were meetings everywhere, both official and spontaneous, spur of the moment. The Mayor held an open consultation each morning in the Guildhall to share information as it came in and to make plans.

The fishing fleet gradually came in from its summer season in Newfoundland, welcomed thankfully by families who feared, many of them, anything outside their home town. Betsy and Ned's reunion was especially ecstatic for there was his new son waiting for him, and for a few days the three of them delighted in each other, and in just being together.

But then, all too soon it seemed to Betsy, the war penetrated even their cosy, sturdy cottage, and she could sense a restlessness in Ned and, as she told Mary, "He seems to spend a lot of time with the young hot-heads he used to meet before we were married. I've heard them talking about following the King's standard. I am worried." She was in tears now, and Mary tried to comfort her. "It's just talk, I'm sure. He promised Richard to always be sober and sensible, didn't he?" But Betsy was not convinced.

Just a few days after this conversation, the Mayor was very relieved to tell the townsmen that Charles had sent for the Governor of Plymouth, Sir Jacob Astley, to be his Major-General of Foot, and the sober merchants, gathered in the Guildhall could not restrain a cheer at the news. Richard was there and his friends Peter Perryman and John Light, and he asked the Mayor just what the news meant. Philip Francis rose to his feet, his excitement obvious. "It means, my friends," he said, "it means that Plymouth is in our hands - Parliament's hands. The Forts on St. Nicholas Island and the Hoe, and the Castle too."

"That means the entrance to Sutton Pool is safe." This was John Light's comment and it was obvious that the relief and the hope were infectious. One after the other men rose, asking questions, offering suggestions, until at last it seemed as if the thoughts of all were drawn together in one great realisation. The harbour, the navy, the shipping were theirs. There wasn't a man there who did not realise what that meant to a port like Plymouth. It was a safe anchorage for troops - Parliamentary troops - and provisions to come in and to go out to other parts of the country.

For the rest of that day the plans went on, the Mayor closed the meeting for a short while at midday so the merchants could return to their homes for a hurried meal before they resumed their deliberations till the evening. The Mayor took over control of the castle and the town, and Sir Alexander Carew the forts on the Hoe and St Nicholas Island. "This means we will never be starved of food or munitions and there will be no sea-power hereabouts for the King." These were the closing words of the meeting and they echoed and reverberated in Richard's head as he hurried home to Mary and the children.

But he had no chance to tell them all that had happened, for he was greeted by sounds of sobbing and attempts at comfort. Sarah came into the hall-way to meet him, followed by Francis looking shocked and embarrassed. "There's trouble, father," Sarah said. "Ned's gone and Betsy's in a bad way. Come quickly," and she drew him into the living-room where Mary was trying to still Betsy's crying, rocking her as she would have one of the children.

Richard's expression was serious, and taking a chair in front of the women he exchanged glances with his wife then concentrated on their friend and servant. "Now Betsy, what's all this about. Calm yourself and tell me exactly what Ned has done." His firmness was obviously what was needed, and Betsy gulped down the last of her sobs and wiped away her tears with the corner of her apron. Then, with a great effort she looked up at Richard. "He's gone," she whispered. "Gone, to join the King's army. I knew he would." Richard didn't attempt to deny the seriousness of the situation. "When did he go - and how?" he asked. "Tell me exactly." "It was very early this morning, not really light. I tried to stop him, but I could not. I'm so sorry," and she burst into sobs again. Mary tried to comfort her but Richard knew he must get at the truth.

"Now Betsy, no-one is blaming you. Just tell me how it all came about." "It was the tanner - you know - Robert Tremayne." Richard nodded. "Well he's planned this ever since we knew for sure the war had come. He's sent a whole lot of men, young like Ned, to fight for the King, given them money and all they needed." "But how have they gone, did they get horses and ride out?" "No, they've gone by ship. Others came from Cornwall to join them. I saw them leave."

"I suppose Master Tremayne provided the ship and said they were following a glorious cause." Richard sighed. "Well, we can't stop them. There were bound to be some to take the King's side, God help them, but there won't be many more, I'll warrant, especially when we strengthen the fortifications. Let us pray that all the South West is for Parliament. We'll look after you and your son, Betsy and I expect they'll be other familes to care for. Do not fret." "Oh, Ned gave me money, all he had from the fishing. I'll be all right. He just made me promise not to tell you till this evening - to give them a chance to get away."

"Every man must follow his conscience," was Richard's comment. "It's just a pity that they didn't understand our position here in Plymouth."

Betsy insisted on going back to her own home, so Sarah fetched the baby from where it had been put to sleep on her bed and with her mother accompanied them back to the cottage, settled them in for the night, and promised to see them the next day.

Meanwhile Richard, without pausing for food, went out again to pass on the news of the escape of the King's supporters.

Chapter Seven

IT WAS AS THOUGH the town suddenly accepted the actuality of war. It was here, inescapable, and must be undertaken with precision and whole-hearted determination. Defence was Plymouth's first concern. It may send its men away to fight, but the town must be protected at all costs from an enemy whose strength was as yet unkown. There was already the Castle, and the natural defence of the sea, from where look-outs were now posted night and day, but the Mayor soon realised that fortifications were needed all around the outskirts of the town to make it as impregnable as possible. Plans were drawn up for a line of forts on a high ridge of ground and work began on them immediately with teams of masons and carpenters augmented by men from every profession and skill, and those without any, who worked willingly in shifts as labourers. Richard and his friends gave unstintingly of their time and efforts, and those, like Francis and Will, little more than boys, played their part. James begged to be allowed to "work with the men", but Mary and Richard flatly refused this and he had to be content with helping in his father's business (outside school hours) carrying messages and copying receipts, and orders, and other of the more simple jobs earlier undertaken by Francis. They did not know that before the war was over, even children not much more than toddlers would be dragging up buckets of soil to help with the earthworks.

As summer gave way to autumn and the daylight hours shortened, efforts were intensified to get all secure, though it was to be the next summer before all the new forts were finished.

Sarah with her mother and Betsy worked hard to fill their store-cupboards with every kind of food and drink, and supplies of linen and wool, the three of them taking care of baby Nathaniel between them. Sometimes when Mary thought her daughter had done enough and should get a mouthful of sea air, Sarah would carry the baby down on to the beach, and rocking him to and fro, would tell him stories of the sea and the adventures he would have when he grew to be a man. Nathaniel was a happy, contented baby and would look up into Sarah's eyes with a quizzical expression which she was sure meant he understood all she said. Sometimes Will would join her on the beach and they'd hunt for shell-fish together, but he seemed to be growing up and away from her and she knew with a sad certainty that things would never be the same again.

Betsy too had changed. She no longer sang about her work and her face had lost its round cheerfulness and ready smile. Sarah came upon her sometimes with the baby clutched to her in an almost fierce embrace, as though afraid that he too might leave her. Sarah was concerned about the change in her constant friend and confidante whom she had known all her life, and when she spoke to her mother of her concern, Mary admitted that Betsy was worried about Ned. "She'll be better," she said, "when she has news of him," but they both knew that there wasn't much likelihood of that. Sometimes Sarah saw Betsy talking to one or another of the wives and mothers of the other young men who'd gone with Ned, and it seemed to the girl that she drew some slight comfort from the shared unhappiness which Mary and Sarah could not, as yet, fully enter into.

It soon became obvious that Plymouth's position was of great strategic importance. News came through that Cornwall was firmly Royalist. But Cornishmen were reluctant to march eastwood through a Parliamentary Plymouth to join the King, so very few were able to do so at this time. For a while Devon further east either held for Parliament or was neutral, but gradually Exeter, Barnstaple and Dartmouth, the county's major towns, fell into Royalist hands, so that Plymouth was the only town to stand loyal to Parliament, remaining so throughout the conflict. This was the iron in the bones of Plymouth men and women, the fire in their bellies, and the faith in their hearts and minds.

Meanwhile, they prepared and waited - but not for long. News came through of the first engagement of the war - a drawn battle at Edgehill on October 26th 1642. Charles advanced on London, but Parliament's troops held him and he withdrew to Oxford which was now his capital. In fact Plymouth's resistance was what largely thwarted Charles' plans to take London - for to do so, it was necessary for the armies to conquer the West and march to London along the Thames. The Earl of Essex spoke of Plymouth as "a place of as great concernment as any in the kingdom next to London."

Late in the autumn, Philip Francis became Mayor of Plymouth and at the first meeting that he called he reviewed the whole situation to Richard and his fellow merchants. One matter of great importance was that the Navy had since the commencement of hostilities supported Parliament. The fleet was commanded by Vice-Admiral Batten and he came to Plymouth and to this meeting to encourage the townspeople. "We will keep this port open," he declared, "and remember it can never be totally surrounded. Remember too, my friends, that the countries of Europe, France, Spain and the Netherland, will surely support us, while we control the seas around England."

But all those men knew - the merchants, the corporation and all those who were working to defend their town - that its vulnerable areas were the plain from Plympton on the east and the north where the high ground looked down upon the town, so they could not relax their efforts.

It wasn't long before fear crept in as the Royalists began to move large concentrations of troops into the neighbourhood. Soon, meeting with no resistance, they had taken all the surrounding towns and villages, including some important positions on the Tamar at Saltash, and especially Mount Edgcumbe House, which was converted into a Royalist fortress. Parliament was aware of Plymouth's danger and of her strategic position, so sent Colonel Ruthven to command the Plymouth forces. The townspeople were glad and relieved to welcome him, for his reputation was high and his judgement reliable.

Events moved quickly now. In November '42 Sir Ralph Hopton, the King's General in the West, advanced to Tavistock, then came on towards Plymouth with a force of 2,500 horse and foot. As he marched across Dartmoor, he cut off Drake's Leat - the town's water supply, sure that this would bring the inhabitants to their knees, but they were made of sterner stuff and used instead the wells, of which there were many in the town, praying that rain would soon come to replenish and that the still water would not bring disease. Plymouth had placed a garrison at its outpost in

Plympton. Hopton drove the troops from there and withdrew to Modury where he established his Headquarters, attacking next Ruthven's outposts at Laira, but the attack was beaten off and Hopton fell back. A few days later the Colonel, with a force raised from Kingsbridge and Plymouth, attacked Modbury, defeated the Royalists and forced Hopton to march away, giving up any idea of taking Plymouth at this time.

There was great rejoicing within the town and a dinner was held for Ruthven and his officers. The Corporation allowed £20 to provide for this and the women of the town took from their own precious stores to augment what this would buy, and prepared the meal to be held in the Guildhall. As she assisted in this work with Betsy carrying trenchers and cutlery across the paved Square to the Guildhall, Mary felt fingers of fear clutch at her breast and glancing at Betsy realised what she must have felt when it first become obvious that Ned wanted to leave home and fight. Richard had expressed great admiration for Colonel Ruthven, and she had come across him in their own living room, in conversation with John Light and two other friends just the previous evening.

"There's still much fighting to come," she heard Richard say. "Hopton will not have given up for long. Do you not think, friends, that the time is coming when we should think about being part of that fighting? Perhaps we can best protect our town by helping to keep the enemy from it."

She had returned to her kitchen and her cooking then with shaking hands.

Never before had she turned from her husband, afraid to discuss a problem with him, but she would not ask him about this for fear of what he would say. Instead she caught Sarah, who was helping her, in a sudden embrace so that the girl felt the fear through her mother's arms and remembered how Betsy had clutched at Nathaniel with the same desperation.

The meal was served by the women amidst much loud talk and drinking of ale and wine and great relief after the fighting, and Mary's eyes strayed constantly to Richard sitting with his friends at one end of a long table, seeing how eagerly he listened to all that was said, especially to the speech of thanks and encouragement that Colonel Ruthven gave at the close of the meal.

It was late when Mary and Richard and many others of their friends and neighbours retired to their beds, and nothing was said by either of them of the dread in Mary's heart, nor was it mentioned during the next few days though Richard spent more and more time with the army. But a week later Mary heard from Francis who had hurried home from a Guildhall meeting, that Ruthven had decided to take the fight into the enemy's territory and was to head immediately for Cornwall. Then she could wait no longer and when her husband returned exhausted that evening from work on the fortifications, she managed, but only just, to restrain herself while they ate their meal, but immediately afterwards she sent the children from the room and moved close to Richard who now sat by the fire, his eyes closed in weariness.

She gently took the tankard of ale from his hand and placed it in the hearth. He roused himself at her touch, and some of the strain left his eyes as he smiled at her. "I must speak to you, husband," she said, laying a hand on his arm. "But of course, my love. I fear I have been neglecting you of late. Tell me what troubles you," and he pulled himself upright in his chair.

"I have to ask you about - about any plans you may have. You have spent so much time with the military lately, and I am fearful that perhaps," she could not finish but covered her face with her hands. "Mary, my dear," he reached up and taking her hands held them tightly in his own. "Do not fret, as I would never do anything without consulting you, but knowing the times you will realise how my thoughts are jumping and chasing themselves like rabbits in the fold." She nodded, unable to speak for a moment, and Richard continued. "Perhaps it is as well for us to have this talk now. You have heard doubtless that Ruthven intends to head for Cornwall. He has hopes of securing at most the county for us. I was not tempted to join him, though no doubt many from Plymouth will do so. But now there is the other news." Mary looked at him questioningly, and he went on more excitement in his voice now, and Mary could see that his tiredness was forgotten. "We expect the arrival of Lord Robartes, with a great force of three regiments of foot and 1,000 dragoons. A messenger has come today, and the news is that Robartes cannot be more than a day's march away. Parliament has given him command of the whole west. Plymouth will be well protected if Hopton attacks again, and it may be, my dear wife," he paused and they looked at each other, each reading the other's thoughts. Mary found her voice first, though it was hardly more than a whisper. "What may it be, Richard?" "It may be," he repeated, "that I shall no longer be able to let others fight for me and mine without playing my part." He caught her as she fell forward into his arms, and so they sat without saying more, till the candles burnt low and, flickering, cast shadows across their entwined stillness.

Chapter Eight

WHEN SARAH AWOKE two mornings later, she found the house a hubbub of activity. There were voices, more than was customary, doors banging, feet on the stairs, and overall as she opened her chamber door, a sense of urgency. She ran down to the kitchen where her mother was filling a leather bag with food wrapped in a white cloth. Betsy came in behind the girl, carrying a pair of thick long-cuffed boots and a black cloak and leather gauntlets. "Why, those are father's, surely?" Sarah cried, the surprise in her eyes increasing as she saw the tears in Betsy's. She looked from her to Mary, thoroughly alarmed now. "What's happening, where is father?" Her mother reached out her hand and caught the girl to her. "We have got to be brave, Sarah. Father is going away, with some of our friends - John Light and Peter Perryman, and others. He feels it is right to go with Colonel Ruthven." Sarah drew away from her mother in horror. "But he can't be, he would have told me."

She turned and ran across the hall-way into the living room. Richard was on his knees, sorting through a pile of papers. He turned to Sarah and wordlessly held out his arms to her. He held her for a moment stroking her hair, then he sat her down on her stool and looked at her with seriousness and love."

"This has all happened sooner than I expected, my dear child," he said gently, "but things are now as I told you they might become. Ruthven marches into Cornwall this day, and I must go with him. Come, we will breakfast together, and I will tell you all I can."

They ate their bread and honey, Mary continually coming into the room, and plying Richard with more food, butter and cheese, and bringing extra shirts and stockings that she insisted he must take with him. He tried to laugh gently at his wife. "I shall be too weighed down to march," he said, "let alone fight." His voice trailed away on the last word as he saw fear in both Sarah and Mary's eyes.

"But, come," he said briskly. "The time is pressing and I must join the others." He stopped then and looked from one to the other anxious face, for the boys had now come into the room and all eyes were fixed on husband and father.

Richard drew James towards him first. "I know you will be my obedient and hard-working son," he said, "and do as your mother and the older ones say. I'm sure I shall not be away from home for long, and it will help me to know all is well here." James, his usual cheeky grin gone, clung to his father.

Richard turned next to Francis and gripped his arm. "You are the man of the family now and I'm sure I can rely on you to do your best. I know too how much you wanted to come with me," and indeed there was a droop to the boy's mouth, "but you are needed much more here, my son, to help Master Goodyeare keep the business going and look after the family." "Yes, father," Francis stood straight, trying to look as responsible as his father wished him to be.

Richard's smile was tender as he held out his arms to Sarah. "What more can I say, my dearest daughter, except God bless you - and all of you," and he looked at each one in turn, his eyes finally coming to rest on his wife, and as the children saw them embrace, they turned and quietly left the room. Sarah gently closed the door behind them, knowing that this was a momentous day in all their lives, and that their parents desperately needed this last few minutes together.

A short while later they were all hurrying down into the town. Richard had gone ahead to join first his friends and then Colonel Ruthven's troops assembling in front of the Guildhall, but Mary and the children were not far behind, determined to catch the last possible glimpse of him. Sarah had never seen the town so crowded - so full of noise and activity. Shopkeepers stood in their doorways, small boys ran everywhere, provoking more shouts and cuffs from those who almost tripped over them. They had to keep close together so as not be separated or to be jostled by men - many with women still clinging to them - or run down by horses. Some of these had already had their baptism of fire and were reined in by experienced hands, while others were not much more than farm

44

horses, brought in from the fields, and though powerful beasts were still frightened by so much noise which was everywhere. The smells too were almost overwhelming, even to a child like Sarah, used to the quay and streets which contained so much of the rawness of life - humanity en masse, the sweat of horses, and all the accoutrements of men preparing for battle.

Ruthven's captains were trying to deal with the local men like Richard, recruits to the cause who were arriving in motley attire. Many wore the only clothes they possessed, long boots that mostly reached over their stockings to their doublets and above shirts and tunics, some with cloaks and tall hats and others without. In the baggage carts were piles of yellow sashes which were soon to become the distinctive mark of the Parliamentary armies, a bright splash of colour amidst the blacks, greys and browns, and the armour of breast-plate and helmet. These were to be distributed as far as possible when the march out started, together with pikes and muskets.

Sarah had never seen such weapons before and exclaimed to Francis at the size of the sixteen foot long spear-headed pikes. "How can father carry that?" "Of course he can," her brother scoffed, "and wield it well, I warrant."

Food carts were trundled up now and Sarah saw their friend the miller load on sacks of flour. The children had to step back quickly as a company of dragoons formed up ready to lead off. These were experienced soldiers who had arrived only the previous day with Robartes, and some of them regarded the new recruits as country bumpkins, though as Peter Perryman muttered to Richard while they waited in line pointing to the short muskets they carried, "they're only mounted dragoons, infantry men, and will be fighting on foot like the rest of us before long."

It was the presence of Robartes' troops as well as Ruthven's that caused such chaos in the town, but Sarah gave no attention to them while she could still see her father's tall figure near the front of the column, and squashed against a pillar of the Guildhall, she stood on tip-toe with her mother and brothers watching, as the line, surprisingly orderly after its raggle-taggle assembly, moved out to the shouts and cheers of the crowd and the beat of the drums. An enormous man whom Sarah knew to be a blacksmith in the town, had lifted James on to his broad shoulders, and as he lowered the excited boy to the ground, he said to Mary, weeping now while trying to comfort Elizabeth, Peter Perryman's young wife, "don't fret, mistresses, they'll give a good account of themselves and show those Cornishmen the right way to go, and be home again before you know it, and we've got Robartes and his troops to defend us now, so all will be well."

Slowing, pushing their way through the jostling throng, the Jewell family made its way homeward - to a house which they all knew would be very lonely without its master.

It was long before Sarah fell asleep that night, sounds and images chasing themselves across her mind, together with some realisation of her mother's loneliness and that of Betsy, for this is how she must have felt the night that Ned went away. The noise and clamour in the town had heightened the girl's senses, and though with the night there had come a lessening of activity, her head still held the sounds, especially the beat of the great drum, and the rattle of the feet of the men marching to it, and she wondered whether this town, her town, would ever be again as she had known it throughout her childhood, or was it changed for ever as she was sure her own life would be.

That much quickly became obvious, for it seemed that as the days went by, Mary clung more and more to the girl and did not like her to be far from home. Sarah helped her mother in the house all she could and looked after Nathaniel when Besty brought him to Rag Street, but she missed her erstwhile freedom to run down to the beach when her chores were done and she envied James who had quickly regained his usual high spirits. Francis took his duties and responsibilities very seriously, worked hard at his father's business, and was content to do just this, but it was Sarah who seemed to have lost her youth. When her mother did send her on an errand, she made the most of it, rushed through her task and stole a few extra precious minutes to mingle with all the activities now in the town. She noted and listened to all she could

Lord Robartes' troops were everywhere, and it was obvious that Plymothians had great faith in this new Commander. "He's a Cornishman," was a comment Sarah often heard on the streets, "a man from the west and he fought at Edgehill in Essex's army."

Many of his men were quartered in tents on the Hoe, some within the castle, and others billeted on houses in the town, though there were not many at first to offer such accommodation.

But over all the talk was of the work to be done to improve the defences of Plymouth. At first the 15th Century wall which encircled it had to be quickly improved and extended. Then more important defences were constructed, reaching out into the county beyond. News came also to the Jewell family, when friends of Richard's who had not marched out with Ruthven, arrived from Guildhall meetings to keep them informed. Chief among these was Master Goodyeare, who had promised Richard to keep a watch on Mary and the children, and who also came to rely more and more on Francis to keep the woollen business still flourishing.

It was Ephraim who told them that to pay for all the work of defence, it had been decided that the townspeople "be rated and assessed according to their respective estates and substance."

Ephraim paid them one such visit a week after Richard's departure, and at Mary's invitation joined the family for their evening meal. The children were no longer shy of this guest, even James realising that his gruff voice hid a kind heart, and Sarah sensed quickly that he was a lonely old man. He was in fact a childless widower, looked after by an almost equally elderly housekeeper who kept a clean but cold and cheerless house.

Mary helped him now to another portion of mutton stew, and drew her chair closer to his. "Do you know - is there any news of Colonel Ruthven's troops?" "I'm afraid not, my dear," he shook his head, "but it's early days yet. We believe they were making for Bude. It's a long march towards the Cornish border, but they'll send a messenger back as soon as there's anything to report." He broke off a piece of bread and dipped it in his stew. "And don't forget, they're only a unit raised for the one purpose of gaining Cornwall for us. Richard and the others should soon be back with us again. Just you keep your spirits up," and with this Mary had to be content.

The next few days saw great activity in the town as all the work of defence gained pace. Another complete wall was built stretching from the castle right down to the Barbican. There were two creeks at Stonehouse and Lipson and the sides of the valley were so steep that outworks were constructed along the high ground between them. A great ditch was dug and the earth from it used to form a wall. This ditch and earthworks followed the line of the forts already being constructed and all efforts now concentrated on completing them. There were five forts, triangular-shaped, between Lipson and Pennycomequick, the one at Lipson commanding the London road, then Holiwell, Maudlyn (on the site of the old leper or Maudlyn House), Eldad and Pennycomequick itself. The only other ways into Plymouth were by water, and one other fort was built in a key position, commanding the Cattewater and the entrance to Sutton Pool. This was known as Mount Stamford. It was the Earl of Stamford's troops that helped Plymouth to raise these defences.

Sarah's memories of this time were to be of noise, bustle and urgency. She had never seen the narrow streets so crowded with men, horses, carts and rubbish and dust everywhere. Her mother spent much time preparing food for the men and boys working on the fortifications and Sarah, with James, was sent to and fro with heavy baskets to the works.

Just two days after Ephraim Goodyear's last visit, the children were making their way homewards after one of these trips, when their path was barred by crowds surrounding a group of men holding between them a ragged figure. James wriggled his way through men's legs to see the little procession pass, then darted quickly back to Sarah with the news that "he's all bloody, his head and arm and -" he pulled at Sarah. "I'm sure it's father's friend, Master Perryman." "Are there any others with him?" Sarah looked anxiously back through the jostling throng but there seemed to be no one else - no other wounded soldiers, no Richard.

"We must hurry back to mother," she grabbed her brother's hand, "and she'll know what to do." They ran as fast as they could, pushing their way through the crowds and arrived at the house in Rag Street. A few minutes later, and after two voices trying to explain at once, and Mary only hearing the one fact that one of Richard's comrades was back, the three of them were hurrying to the grocer's shop two streets away. They found three soldiers guarding the doorway, armed with pikes and swords hanging from their waist belts, and effectively keeping at bay the mob around the doorway. Mary, nothing daunted where possible news of Richard was concerned, reached up and spoke to one of the men. He looked behind him into the shop, and called to someone there. Mary recognised the man who came out as one of Robartes' captains, and as he beckoned her forward, she and the children followed him anxiously into the dark interior of the shop and the house beyond.

Chapter Nine

MARY, SARAH AND JAMES hurried after the Captain through the passage behind the shop to the spiral staircase beyond. Mary, holding to the rope guide-rail, tried to keep up with the soldier's heavy tread as the climbed the stairs. They crossed the landing to the bed-chamber, and to the little group around the four-poster bed. Although it was a summer evening, the room was dim while candles cast a flickering light. Even lavender and rosemary could not completely hide the smell of blood and injured flesh.

Elizabeth Perryman and two other women were gently bathing the wounded man's injuries, stripping from him the bloodied rags and torn clothing. On the threshold the Captain stood aside for Mary to enter and this she did. Very quietly, as though already in the presence of death, Elizabeth turned and came to her quickly, the two women weeping in each other's arms.

"He is alive," Elizabeth said, "and, please God, with care and rest he will recover." "The others, is there news of them?" Mary spoke in no more than a whisper but the soldier, alert in the doorway heard her and stepped forward. "Your pardon, mistresses, but this is something I must ask, as soon as he is able to speak. You will appreciate that we must know what is happening beyond our boundaries."

All eyes were now on the man lying on the bed and he, waving away the neighbour who was attending to him, struggled to raise himself. Elizabeth, kneeling by the bed, lifted the pillows higher and supported her husband with her arm around him. "Things have gone badly for us," he managed to say, in a low, hoarse voice. "We were defeated at Braddock Down, almost in Liskeard and then at Saltash, and our losses were heavy. It was a rout, bodies everywhere, men and horses screaming," and he started to shake uncontrollably. Elizabeth held him tightly, trying to soothe him. The soldier came closer waiting for the spasm to pass. As soon as Peter seemed a little calmer, he bent twards him. "What happened to our troops? Did they get away? Have they formed up again? We need to know." Peter's face twisted in pain, and in an almost wry amusement. "I don't know who got away. We couldn't even tell, most of the time, whose side every man was on. We looked alike and even spoke the same language, and our weapons were the same, even to drawing the same blood. I came to myself close to a hedge, the battle long finished, for it was dark.." He sank back on his pillows then his eyes closed, scarcely breathing. The Captain, seeing he would get no more information for the time being, turned on his heel and marched quickly from the room and the house, while the women directed all their attention to the wounded man. Then, as his eyes fluttered open again, and Mary saw a little colour come into his white face, she remembered her children waiting below. She embraced Elizabeth and hurried down the stairs.

Most of the crowd had dispersed but Sarah and James, standing close together waited patiently in the shop. Mary, an arm around each of them led them home to Rag Street.

Sarah could not wait to question her. "Father, what news is there of father? Is he coming back?" Mary tried to make her voice sound reassuring. "We - we don't know, my dear. Master Perryman got separated from the rest and managed to get back to the town. He said General Hopton's men are massed outside, so your father and the others will be hiding till they can get back too. We must be patient and carry on as he would wish. Come now, Sarah, and help me with the supper."

Francis arrived home soon after, and it was a subdued little family who sat together to try to share a meal - each of them encouraging the others to swallow food they could not themselves manage. Sarah, in particular, feeling very protective towards her mother, with a responsibility that she was sure would not leave her for a very long time.

The next day a great meeting was held in the Guildhall, addressed by Lord Robartes himself, and to this came not only the merchants and responsible men of the town, but also a number of women and even children. It was as though it was accepted that in this struggle now upon them, there was no difference of gender or age, all would be called upon to suffer and to fight so with so

50

many men already away, their places must be taken, in every sense, by whoever remained.

Thus it was that Mary, Sarah, Francis and even James, took their places in good time.

The general exhorted them all to brave endurance and promised that never would the town be left unprotected. "We have more troops arriving by sea, for Parliament realises the importance of Plymouth - strategic and economic, and they will bring what supplies they can. But I know all these extra men will mean a careful conserving of all we have and a sharing of all our resources. But do not despair. Together we can survive to a great victory, for God will support our cause. However," - and here he paused, looking at all the faces turned towards him, strong Devon faces their expressions expectant, serious, frightened, but overall trusting - "we are now in a state of seige and Royalist forces are massed against us. We shall drive them back to the best of our ability, and prevent the Cornish traitors from joining them. Even now news has come Sir George Chudley has won a victory at Bodmin. So with that information, be of good cheer and firm hearts and I will speak to you again when matters dictate."

It happened that the summer of '43 was a quiet time for the Plymouth garrison with skirmishes outside its walls but no major battles. The work of fortifications continued and it was estimated that the Plymouth garrison had 9,000 men at that time. The Royalist forces did not attempt to attack the town, though there were five regiments encamped around it. It was believed that they still felt too weak to attack without the Cornish, who would not cross the Tamar. In August, however, there was a sudden surge of activity, felt throughout the town so that even in the cottages and houses there was a sense of foreboding among the old, and almost excitement - certainly anticipation - whenever young people got together.

There were 900 Royalist troops under Colonel Digby based at Plymstock and news filtered through of a vast army approaching Plymouth led by Prince Maurice himself. He had taken Exeter and was about to lay siege to Dartmouth. Then, just as a decision was being taken by Robartes to attack Digby, there was a great commotion within the town for the Mayor, Philip Francis, discovered a greater danger - a group of secret Royalist supporters led by

51

Sir Alexander Carew, the officer in charge of the Hoe Fort and Drake's Island, and secretly in league with the Cornish Cavaliers. Carew was captured by Drake's Island's own force amidst great pandemonium. The townspeople, especially the women, cried for his blood and wanted to hang him without trial from the great tree in the centre of the town. Francis rescued him from this, and sent him to London. Here he was tried, found guilty and beheaded a year later on Tower Hill. Had Carew not been discovered and caught, Plymouth's supply line from the sea would have been cut and defeat inevitable.

That incident was safely concluded, but it caused the townspeople to be very jumpy and sometimes suspicious of their own neighbours, especially where it was known that some members of a family had earlier gone to join the Royalists. Betsy suffered to a degree from this, and for a time the ship-master, Jacob Thomas, sent one of his men to spend time in her cottage and let it be known that the young woman was not unprotected. Sarah, too, was worried for Betsy and for Nathaniel, for she had seen how cruel people could be to those who had different beliefs from their own. Although she never for an instant doubted the Parliamentary cause - the fact that her father supported it would have been enough conviction without her own growing understanding - yet her innate sense of justice made her realise that everyone's conscience is their own and must be allowed.

Perhaps it was because in the weeks leading up to August Sarah had had a little more time for thought and to wander down to the quay - though her mother always worried about this and the great numbers of troops milling about - that her thoughts went, first as always to her father and to wondering where he was, and then to this cause which she knew had rent the country in two. There had been no news of Richard nor of any others of Ruthven's men. As Peter Perryman recovered she and Mary often visited him, hoping that he would remember some detail, anything about Richard and what had happened to him. But he could not, his answer always was: "Some escaped north, I know, they will have joined up with other bands to move towards London, but many were killed, so many, it was just all confusion. When I came to I was alone with the dead and dying. But do not despair, Richard had so much to live for, he would not have given up without a struggle." With this they had to be content.

Then Sarah's birthday arrived - her 13th (and little Nathaniel's first) and she remembered her last one, the happy meal they'd all had together, and most of all, the talk she and her father had shared and the trust he'd placed in her to look after the others whatever befell. She hoped she was fulfilling this trust. She had tried, but it wasn't always easy.

Then, just a week after Sarah's birthday and when news had come that Prince Maurice was only a few days' march away, two experienced Parliamentary commanders, Colonel Wardlaw and Colonel Gould, arrived by sea with 600 trained soldiers. Although each fresh contingent of troops coming to Plymouth gave new heart to the townspeople, it also added to the problems of those trying to feed and quarter them. These soldiers came with a particular (small) blaze of glory, for they made two successful attacks - one on a small Royalist fort at Hooe across the Cattewater, where they captured urgently needed guns and ammunition, and another a few days later at Knackersknowle. Both of these commanders were superb officers and trained and drilled the troops to a very high standard.

There was a sense of expectancy in the town as the days went by, Sarah could feel it in the air, in the sound of the gulls scream-ing in from the sea, and in the quiet persistence of her mother at work. As she watched the gulls on this particular day just three after Wardlaw and Gould arrived, sitting on her favourite stone on the beach, she envied their freedom to fly out to sea whenever they liked, for in spite of being out of doors with a gentle breeze cool-ing her face, she felt claustrophobic. The people had been told that they must stay well within the town's boundaries for certain death faced them if they tried to leave, and she thought with fear of friends who lived in farms on the moors, and of whom nothing had been heard since the Royalist camps were set up.

She was worried too about Will, of whom she had heard noth-ing for more than a week. She'd looked for him at his cottage, and some of the others which seemed strangely empty, but no one admitted to knowing where he was, and more strangely still, were not worried. Ephraim Thomas had patted her on the head, and said, "He'll be all right, my child, do not fear. Now get along home to your mother," and she had done so, remembering as she went how Ned had disappeared, though at least Betsy had known how and why he had gone. Mary too had told Sarah not to worry. "We have enough to be concerned with," she had said. "The King's supporters must look after themselves."

She sighed and knew it was time to turn for home. There seemed more troops than ever in the town today, and as she started up Rag Street she saw that there was a group of soldiers going from house to house. Sarah quickened her steps. What new event was this?

Chapter Ten

SARAH RAN UP RAG Street as fast as she could. What were the soldiers doing so close to her home? Then as she saw her mother in the doorway of their house - nodding her head - she felt some of her anxiety, so easily roused these days, drain away. She reached the steps in time to hear Mary say: "That'll be all right, Sergeant," and the reply, "Thank you, mistress, we're very grateful. I'll send the men along tomorrow. They'll be no trouble, I'll warrant. They'll look after themselves and do any work for you too."

Sarah watched the sergeant in his coat and breeches of fitted woollen cloth, grey knitted stockings and worn leather shoes, and the montero that he wore on his head, like a peaked balaclava rolled back from his head. He marched quickly down the steps, and smiled at her. "Good evening, young mistress."

She followed her mother inside, still breathless from her run up the hill. "What did he want? Is there news of father and the others?" Mary put an arm around her daughter's shoulders, knowing that the thoughts of the girl were always with Richard, as were her own, no matter how busy she kept herself. "No, my love, nothing yet, I'm afraid, but God will take care of him, do not fear. No, the sergeant is looking for billets for as many of the men as possible. The camps and forts are overcrowded and they know that bigger houses, like this, are likely to have room to spare. I've told him we can take two now - we may have to squeeze more in later if things get worse. Please God they won't," and she sighed. "Come along now, and help me get things ready." They worked hard that evening, Francis helping them when he returned to move his things into the little room that had been Betsy's.

"Yes, that should be comfortable enough." Mary stood at last in the low doorway of what had been Francis' room, with its mullioned window and wide window seat, and the ceiling high and plastered, crossed by oak beams. She loved this house of hers, though it needed Richard back to make it a real home again.. Now she surveyed the results of their labours. "The bed is roomy and there's the press for whatever clothes they have." Francis laughed - which was unusual for him, especially these days. "They'll have no more than they stand up in, mother, and as for comfort, they'll think they're in heaven here after camp life." Mary was not to be put off. "I'd like to think that someone might be granting a little ease to your father at this time," and she turned away to hide a tear.

Then recovering herself she said briskly: "Now, come along. Bed for us all. It'll be a busy day tomorrow and I have bread to make and much baking to do tomorrow." She paused and then followed Francis who was putting a pile of papers on his table. "Will you be comfortable in this little chamber, my son? I thought you'd prefer it to sharing with James. I know how you value peace and quiet." She reached up to ruffle his fair hair. "You get more like your father every day, and you're working so hard. Ephraim tells me frequently how he couldn't manage without you." Francis blushed uncomfortably. "'Tis little enough, mother, not like father and the troops. I often think I should be with them." His mother clasped his hands in hers. "Do not speak so, my son. You are doing more good here. Your father left us in your care, and the business too. Pray God it will soon be over and we shall all lead normal lives again." It was not Francis' way to argue, so kissing his mother good-night, he prepared himself for bed.

The next day was full of activity from the moment Sarah awoke, and the family had scarcely finished breakfast before a knocking on the front door announced the arrival of the new - albeit temporary - members of the household. Sarah opened the door to them but stood for a moment on the threshold looking at the two men who were to share her home, the first outside her family ever to have done so. Then suddenly remembering her manners, Sarah asked the soldiers to come inside, and waited as her mother briskly greeted them, showed them the kitchen, explaining its various uses, and finally led them to the bed-chamber they would occupy. From their brief conversation with Mary, the girl soon learnt that the elder man was a corporal in the infantry, serving as a pikeman, and was a farm worker without any family who had volunteered more than a year ago and come west from Bristol with Robartes. His name was Matt Bovey and he told them he was 35 years old and had enlisted for the duration of the war. He was dressed much as the sergeant had been the day before, and carried a snapsack on his back. Sarah remembered how her brother had said they wouldn't carry much baggage.

Then at last, as they came down the stairs to where Sarah waited in the hall, she allowed herself to look at the other trooper. They had exchanged brief glances when she had opened the door to them and she had an impression of very dark eyes in a youthful face, eyes that looked right into hers, then a blush that crept over his face - and they both looked away. While she felt her own cheeks warm, Sarah had a brief thought that it must be unusual for a soldier to blush!

Her mother introduced them now. "This is John Luscombe," she said. "He's serving in the same company as Matt, and he comes from a farm out near Horrabridge. He left his family and came into Plymouth with Colonel Gould's forces." She led Matt away then to the back of the house, leaving John to follow. But he did not, right away, and the two young people stood looking at each other. Sarah was long to remember this first meeting with the tall, slender boy (he was fifteen, she discovered later), his black hair falling into his eyes. His thin wrists and long bony hands protruded from the sleeves of the coat that was much too small for him. He spoke first. "I have seen you before," his voice, still not completely broken, was low with the soft Devon burr, "when you've brought food to the men working on the barricades," and his sudden smile warmed her young heart.

But any blossoming friendship between the two young people had to wait, for two days later Prince Maurice finally arrived on the northern outskirts of Plymouth. He brought a large army, five Regiments of horse and nine of foot soldiers, and set up his head-quarters at the country house of Widey (which became known as Widey Court after Charles later stayed on a visit and held court there). The people did not know what to expect when from the town they saw the smoke of the camp-fires. Gould posted troops on the walls and wherever there were vantage positions, and reports came back into the town which were quickly passed from street to street, from house to house, some of course badly distorted.

Francis usually kept his family informed, for Ephraim seemed to have contacts everywhere and knew many of the Parliamentary officers. It was he who passed the information that there was now a tight half circle of Royalist troops all the way from Cawsands right up the Tamar, across Roborough and down to Plymstock, with the town's outpost at Mount Stamford an obvious target.

There was now in the town a sense not of panic, but of tenseness, of waiting, of life suspended yet caught up in activity. As Sarah had thought so many times before, they were held within the town, had been for so long because the enemy was out there - somewhere - but now the net was closing in and they were at the enemy's mercy or lack of it.

Matt and John came back to the house in Rag Street whenever they had a few hours off duty, though that wasn't often as the days wore on. Sarah found herself looking out for them, especially John, and was always relieved when he came striding up the hill with his odd, half-running gait, and then she'd go to the kitchen to make sure there was plenty to eat, for although he was so thin he had an enormous appetite, and she was thankful that as yet there was sufficient food.

They all knew that the outpost at Stamford was very vulnerable and it was proved so, for by night, and using typical siege-breaking tactics, the Royalists raised a small fortification close to the fort itself and dug an approach trench to encircle it. It took them nine days and a night to reduce the small Parliamentary garrison in the fort to a very few men, but still the Royalists could not force their way in. The Stamford Fort was not of much use in defending Plymouth for it was difficult to supply with food and ammunition, but the fear had always been that from this piece of high ground the Royalist cannon could fire down into the town itself, across the water. In fact, on 5th November, cannon shot rained down on the fort from the enemy positions. During the night the Roundheads worked desperately to repair the gaps in the fortification, but they could not withstand the all-out attack by the enemy's cavalry, musketeers and pikemen on the newly built bank and ditch at each end of the Stamford ridge. The Parliamentary forces fell back on the fort (now cut off from the town) many brought down in their panic to get to safety. But later that day the Captain of the fort agreed to an honourable surrender and was allowed to march the remnants of his troops out, taking their colours and weapons with them, and that: "the enemy should exchange all the prisoners they had taken of ours that day, being about forty, for the like number of their prisoners with us."

The townspeople and the garrison were in despair, for they had seen enough of what was going on to fear that this was the end of all their efforts. Indeed, Digby - the Royalist commander at Plymstock - called upon the townspeople to surrender. Many, confused and frightened, wanted to comply, but before surrender would even be seriously considered, Colonel Wardlaw imposed full military control over the town and its fortifications and declared that the militia would burn the town rather than hand it over to the enemy. One attempt to bombard Plymouth from Stamford was made, but the only damage was to the Windmill on the Hoe, which lost an arm, and a woman who also received an arm wound.

As it happened, the loss of Mount Stamford proved somewhat of a blessing to Plymouth, for the garrison now had one less fort to man. All shipping came into Millbay which became, for the first time in history, the harbour of Plymouth. A battery at Oreston had already closed Sutton Harbour, and Stonehouse Creek was closed by the guns at Mount Edgcumbe. With the lead from Colonel Gould and Colonel Wardlaw, the townspeople drew together in a great surge of activity. The quarrelling and bickering which had been growing between the people of Plymouth and the imported military, ceased. The Mayor and Corporation drew up a Solemn Vow and Covenant, and every man and woman had to take this vow. "I, in the presence of Almighty God, do vow and protest that I shall to the utmost of my power, faithfully to maintain and defend the towns of Plymouth and Stonehouse, the fort and the Island, neither have I accepted any pardon or protection, nor will accept any protection from the enemy."

People gained new hope from this declaration. They met in the streets with smiles and firm handshakes. Even the early November days, dark and dreary with clinging mists and heavier showers, could not make them lose heart. They shared meals, were concerned as to how neighbours were managing, and comforted those whose homes had empty chairs.

Mary, after talking to Richard in her head and heart as she so often did, and feeling sure that he would wish it, opened her house to family and friends, and welcomed all who would join them in a

59

thanksgiving meal, and she and Sarah provided of their best. Those who came brought contributions from their precious stores, and cupboards were carefully checked to see what could be spared. This was not done thoughtlessly for warnings were constantly being given of the need to conserve all stocks with the future still so uncertain - but even the authorities realised that one occasional relief could go a long way in strengthening resolve.

So it was a thankful gathering that sat at Mary's long oak table and at the extra benches fitted in somehow. There was a great pot of rabbit stew, mutton pasties and beef pies, for the miller had produced an extra sack of flour and the soldiers had brought beef from the army stores. There was cheese and honey and butter, though not much of these, so the bread had to be carefully spread and of cider and ale there was more than enough. As well as Mary, Sarah and the boys, Matt and John, there was Betsy and Nathaniel, John Light the clothier and his mother, old Ephraim Goodyeare and Elizabeth and Peter Perryman. Peter was recovering from his wounds and was anxious to get back into the fight, though Elizabeth confessed to Mary that she would rather have him wrapped in bandages for the rest of the conflict than to send him out again. Francis, as the man of the household, offered thanks before they ate, and read from the great Bible the Old Testament story of the deliverance of the Israelites from their enemies, though as Ephraim whispered to John Light, "we're not delivered yet, by a long way."

In the early evening, when the guests had gone and the clearing up done, Sarah stood outside the back door, seeking fresh air, for the house was stuffy. Suddenly John was behind her, and together they moved out into the garden. The rain had cleared and a fresh breeze blew in from the sea. They didn't say much, but Mary, watching from the window, could see the comfort they took from each other, and sighed at the realisation that her daughter was growing up. She must watch her carefully, she knew, but somehow she felt that John was a lad to be trusted, and they all needed something to cling to, so as they turned back into the house, she smiled and laid a hand on each of their shoulders.

It was as well that this sense of unity had been restored to the town, for within three weeks of the taking of the Vow and two of the gathering at Rag Street, the storm broke, a campaign began which was to live for ever in the history of this country and of Plymouth in particular.

Chapter Eleven

IN AFTER YEARS IT was the tiny, seemingly insignificant incidents that Sarah remembered about the events of December 1643. On the first day of the month when she took Nathaniel for a walk on the beach in a welcome respite between chores, she saw two men in close conversation under an overhanging jagged rock that made a natural cave below. She was mildly surprised, as they moved away when she passed, that she knew neither of them. There weren't many strangers around these days except for the military. By then her attention was diverted by Nat who sat down heavily on a big flat stone and proceeded to put a shiny pebble into his mouth. She took him back to Betsy's cottage soon after, and in the darkening early evening, almost bumped into a cloaked figure hurrying past the doorway.

She had forgotten both these incidents by the next morning as she helped her mother to pack food for Matthew and John, who were going on guard duty at the small fortification commanding the swamps of Lipson Creek that lay on Plymouth's eastern side that was difficult to defend. It was only as she stood for a moment at the door with John, telling him "God be with you", and watching the two men march off down the street, that Sarah suddenly felt her whole body shiver. She went back into the house and Mary, calling her, came into the hall-way. "There you are. Are you all right, child? You look very pale." "Yes, mother, I'm all right. Well, I just felt frightened for a moment. I hope... I hope the men will be safe." Her mother shook her head. "In time of war we don't know that anyone will be safe. We must just hope and pray. Now, come along, Sarah, there's work to be done, and that's the best cure for all concerns."

Sarah followed Mary into the kitchen. "Is there any new danger we have not been told about, even inside the town? I thought that with the taking of the Vow, everyone had become united," and there came back to her the two men on the beach and the cloaked figure near Betsy's cottage. Her mother looked thoughtful. "No one can be sure of everyone's loyalty," she said after a moment. "In a struggle like this one, there are bound to be some who do not share the general view. Why do you ask, child?" Sarah described what she had seen, knowing as she did so that it sounded little enough. Her mother put an arm around the girl's shoulder, and nodded. "There's no great surprise in these happenings," she said. "We know that there are those in the fishing community, especially, who still stand for the King. Remember how Ned and Will and others were, and I know that Jacob is given to plotting. You didn't say anything of this to Betsy, I trust?" "No mother, I thought it might frighten her." "You did right. I can tell you, Sarah, that Betsy does not feel a part of that community now. Jacob sees that she and the child are provided for but that is all. So she knows nothing of what goes on amongst them." "But she has us, mother, does she not?" "She does indeed, my love, and she will be here in a moment to help us, so come along. We've talked enough."

The rest of that day was busy but without incident, and by the time Sarah and her family went to bed, she was beginning to feel that her worries were all in her imagination.

Then in the dark hours of the early morning of 3rd December, she woke to the sound of cannon-fire, shouts and running feet. The boys and Mary had been awakened too, and they all rushed to their top casement window looking out towards the sea.

It was too dark to see much though there was a redness in the sky like the streaks of an early dawn, and occasionally a spurt of flame. Francis wanted to go out to see what news there was, and Sarah would go with him for she was sure that John must be in danger, but Mary was adamant that no one leave the house until daylight. "We all stay together within doors where it's safe," she said. "Your father would insist on it if he were here," and the children knew there was no argument against that.

Only James, still yawning, went back to his bed. The others could not, so they dressed and Mary made them an early breakfast, and then - and only then - did she allow Francis and Sarah, warmly wrapped, to go out to see what had happened.

Sarah did not heed their mother's injunction to "stay together" for she was too impatient for news and, her cloak gathered to her and leaving Francis behind, she ran down into the town determined to miss nothing. There was noise and confusion everywhere as more and more people were taking to the streets, wanting to be part of whatever was happening to their town. It was only just becoming light on this overcast December morning, and the smell of musket smoke hung in the damp air, mingling with that of the many flickering torches. Sarah drew back from the cobbles near the candle chandlers as a troop of pikemen marched quickly by, their stern expressions inviting no interruption or question. Then she saw John Light running from the direction of the Guildhall. "What has happened?" she called to him. "What news is there?" Master Light crossed the road to Sarah. "I daren't stop," he said, gasping for breath. "There are many people to tell, but it's serious and treacherous - it's the fort at Laira Point," and he was gone. Sarah's heart beat wildly as she looked frantically around her for someone to tell her what had happened to the garrison, and what to John, who was part of that defence. Odd words reached her - "It was attacked - the fort." "Someone escaped to raise the alarm." "'Tis treachery, treachery." "They must all be dead."

Then she heard her name called above the general clamour, and looking saw it was Peter Perryman crossing from his grocer's shop, limping still and with one arm hanging loosely at his side, but hurrying none the less. "You shouldn't be out on your own, child," he greeted her. "Where is your mother?" "I - and Francis came out to find out what was happening. Have you heard, it's the small fort at Laira." "Yes, I know, it was attacked in the darkest hours this morning, when the tide was high and trouble least expected." "But the men who defended it," Sarah caught his arm, "What of them?" Peter shook his head. "We are not sure yet, but one man escaped to tell the town while the defenders quickly gathered a force who streamed out to drive the Royalists back." "Then all is well?" "I do not yet know, but Prince Maurice would not have given up as easily as that. We are hoping to have news as the day moves on, and be sure it will be passed to the townspeople as quickly as possible. Now you haste away, and let your family and neighbours know." And as Sarah turned and sped back to Rag Lane, Peter shook his head. "If the town is not completely taken by noon," he muttered.

When Sarah ran up the road to her house she saw Ephraim talking to her mother at their front door. "Where have you been, Sarah? Francis has been back a while and Ephraim's come to tell us what he knows. Come in, both of you." She prepared refreshments for them all and they listened closely to Ephraim's information. "It's not much, I'm afraid. We know the defenders bravely pushed back the Royalists, but they couldn't drive them away altogether and we believe our troops have settled just above Tothill. The last news was that Prince Maurice is moving his main force down the slopes from Eggbuckland and Compton, but we're not sure. There are so many stories and rumours." "And the defenders?" Sarah had to ask again. "Did - were many hurt or killed?" Mary looked at her daughter, then back at Ephraim. "It's the two men who are billeted with us - Matthew and John - she's worried about them, as we all are." Ephraim shook his head. "There's been too much confusion, we just don't know. The fighting is going on at this very moment, right on the outskirts of our town. I must go, but I'll see you at church later this morning."

Mary saw him to the door, then came back to find Sarah sitting crouched over the fire, her cloak still wrapped around her. "Now, my love," she said, gathering her daughter into her arms. "We've just got to keep going, it's the only way. I've had to all this time with your father away, and Betsy without Ned." "Or Will," Sarah whispered, "and now - " She didn't finish her sentence but at least she stood up and straightened her cap. "Yes, you're right, mother. Do you know, I had forgotten it was the Sabbath. Where are the boys, we don't want to be late for church."

St. Andrew's was crowded well before the time for the service. It was as though everyone needed to be together and to seek strength and comfort in God's house. There was worry on every face and many of the women were in tears. The Reverend Thomas Forde mounted the steps to the pulpit, and stretching out his hands as though to embrace all his flock, led them in prayers - for the protection of their troops, and for the safe deliverance of their town. Suddenly the stillness was broken by the opening of the great door and the marching of boots on stone flags as Mayor Philip Francis walked swiftly down the aisle followed by the tall figure of a Roundhead officer. Sarah, like the rest of the congregation, turned to watch the newcomer, seeing his boots and tunic splashed with mud, his yellow sash torn and bloodied, a bandage around his head and a scar reaching from his forehead right down his right cheek. The Mayor mounted the pulpit steps, exchanged a few words with Reverend Forde, then came quickly down again, motioning the soldier to take his place. All eyes were fixed in this man's direction, all ears strained to hear his news.

"My friends," his voice rang through the church, "you can be very proud of those defending you this day. We were outnumbered ten to one, but our line held for over an hour until finally a group of Royalist cavalry broke through and raced for the town walls, unfortunately as yet unfinished. Thankfully they were cut down, mainly by a gun which we manned above them, giving us time to re-form into a tight line of defence. I have to emphasise that for the town to be saved, that line against Lipson has to be held. The other outworks all expect attack, so we stand alone."

As apprehension shivered through the congregation, the officer held up his hand. "There are two matters for which we can be thankful. One is, as I have said before, the courage and determination of our men. Their cry is 'God with us, God with us' and we know that even now Colonel Wardlaw is gathering more troops. And the other is that more than an hour ago the Royalists stopped fighting and just remained holed up, though why we are not sure. It has given us a breathing space and I must go back now to make the most use of it." As he walked back through the church there were cries of "well done, God bless you, the Lord be with you," and when the great door closed behind him, the Reverend Forde came back to the front of the pulpit.

"Friends," he said, "Let us meet here again this evening at five o'clock to see what has happened by then. Now go in peace, and be of good courage, for God is with us and our cause."

"It's fortunate it is the Sabbath," Mary said, as they left the church, "for I'm sure that not much work or business would be conducted today." And so it was. All that afternoon people stood about in groups, quiet, seeking comfort from each other, looking towards the fort where the fighting had started. There was troop movement in the town, but no-one knew what that meant. Mary insisted her family tried to eat a meal, though no-one had much appetite, and well before five o'clock they joined their friends and neighbours in the church.

The Reverend Forde began the service and as every heart was united in prayer, once more the great door opened, and a

Parliamentary officer marched up the aisle. It was not the same man who had addressed them earlier, and no mayor came with him, but the way he mounted the pulpit steps and spoke to the vicar, showed he had been told exactly what to do. He was a short, broad man and though his uniform was battle-stained, he showed no signs of injury.

"Well friends," he started, "Time is important so I'll give you what news there is and get back to my men. Our line of defence was thin and much earlier today Prince Maurice called upon us to surrender. But that was never something to even consider. Colonel Wardlaw hurried from the town with 200 trained soldiers and others from wherever they could be spared. They formed up and the whole Parliamentary line rolled forward into the packed mass of the Royalist army." The officer was excited now, reliving the earlier action. "We forced our way through; the Royalist line broke and their soldiers turned and ran down the slopes to the Creek now full of water. They could not find a way out and many men and horses drowned. Even now the Royalist cavalry who are trying to form a wall to hold up the attack are being cut down by fire from the guns of ships anchored off Laira Point. Prisoners have been taken and barrels of powder, and two teams of horses with their gun-carriages. We have casualties too, of course, but for the time being at any rate, I can tell you the town is safe."

A great surge of thankfulness went up from every member of that congregation, and as the officer marched back through the church, those nearest reached out their hands to touch him. Once the doors had closed behind him, the vicar spoke again. "I'm sure that the Mayor will agree that this day henceforth be appointed a day of thanksgiving for our deliverance. Now go to your homes and seek your rest, for this has been a long Sabbath Day for us all."

Mary hurried her family out of the church and as the rest of the congregation they made their way home. Sarah's mind was still fearfully on the casualties among their troops, and longed to hear that all was well with Matthew and John.

Then as they started up Rag Street, she could see a figure - no two - crouched on the top step of their house. One seemed to be supporting the other. She could not make out who they were but, her feet hardly touching the ground, she flew the remaining distance, calling their names as she went.

66

Chapter Twelve

THE FIRST THING THAT Sarah saw, or at least recognised, as she ran up the steps, was the white face of John, the dark eyes, wide and appealing. Then relief flooded through her as he rose from his knees and seemed to her to be unharmed. "John, John," she cried and without waiting threw her arms around him, almost crushing his thin body, which seemed to be more bony than ever. She drew back shyly as her mother, hurrying up behind her, took charge.

"It's Matthew," Mary said, crouching beside the still figure huddled on the step. "What has happened to him, John?" The boy dropped down beside her. "He was wounded by a pike thrust in the shoulder. It tore him badly and he's lost a lot of blood. He wanted to come back here, and I knew I had to get him home, but I didn't think we'd ever get up this hill."

"Well done, lad. Now, there's no time to be lost." Mary had the door open. "Francis and James, both of you help me to get him inside. No, not you, John, you've done enough. Come in, rest yourself till we can take a look at you, and Sarah, go and fetch Betsy."

Sarah flew to obey, with a last look at John, as though afraid he would disappear again. The others got Matthew to his feet, half carrying, half dragging him into the house and on to a hastily gathered pile of blankets in front of the fire. He was drifting in and out of consciousness, and it was obvious that he was not in a fit state to tell them anything. John, meanwhile, fell exhausted into Richard's big chair. Mary turned to him for a moment. "I trust you're not injured, lad, under all that grime." Her tone was brusque but her smile, concerned and kind, and, startled, the boy opened his eyes. "No, no, I'm all right, just see to Matthew. He knew the lad who did it to him. I heard him say: 'Wouldst kill me, Jamie, as we used to kill rabbits together?' and then he fell too." Mary shook her head and turned back to her patient.

Once the remnants of his uniform had been cut away and the wound gently bathed, the lines of worry on Mary's face eased a little, and when Betsy arrived soon after, between them they applied ointments and pads of clean linen and then, with the wound dressed and hopefully the bleeding staunched, took off his boots and made the rest of him as clean and comfortable as they could. "I think we'll leave him here for tonight. He seems to be sleeping peacefully now." The two women cleared away the water bowl, towels and linen, then Mary turned her attention to John, whom Sarah had been tempting with a tankard of mulled ale and some hot soup. "It's mostly potatoes," she said, "but it will do you good," and the boy tried to obey though he didn't even touch the new bread that Sarah knew he loved, and indeed aware of his usual appetite, it pained her to see him refuse food.

"I can't believe," she said to her mother, "that it's such a short time since they set out. Such a lot has happened." John had lain back in the chair and seemed to be dozing, then, as Sarah bent to gather up his platter, he started up. "He's down, the Captain's down," he shouted. "Look out, lads, they're upon us, they've taken the flag, take cover," and he fell to the floor covering his head with his hands, his shoulders shaking. Betsy and Sarah were in tears to see him so, but Mary, ever practical, said to the others: "Come on, now. It's time this lad was in bed." They got him back into the chair to do his dreaming there, and brought clean water and washed the obvious dirt from him, putting ointment on the cuts and scratches he had sustained. Then, calling Francis to help, they got him up to his room and into bed. Sarah kept watch for a while - "in case he wakes and needs something," she said, though her mother was sure he'd sleep soundly now.

Francis saw Betsy back to her cottage, and when Sarah finally went back downstairs, she found Mary sitting by the embers where she'd placed a tankard of spiced ale in case Matthew woke, her eyes closed. Sarah felt a great compassion for her mother, who kept them all going, maintained the home, was always ready to help and succour all who needed it, and had her own private anxieties as well, and as she crossed the room to her, she thought of all the other women who filled just such roles in this town alone, and she felt very grown up and protective as she gently roused Mary now and led her away to bed.

The next few days were mainly occupied for Sarah with helping her mother with Matthew. He developed a fever, and Betsy spent most of her time in the house at Rag Street, to take turns with him. John insisted on reporting for duty the very next day, though Sarah was sure he shouldn't have.

"We don't know what may happen next," he said as he left the house, "and they need me. I'll fight for Matthew too." But for a few days all was peaceful. The fort and other outposts were manned, but the Royalists remained in their camp at Widey Court. John returned home whenever he could and an uneasy calm seemed to settle on the town.

Then after three days, to the relief of the family, when Matthew's fever broke and he began to recover, the Mayor called a Meeting in the Guildhall. Sarah, Francis and Mary attended, leaving Matthew in Betsy's capable hands.

The meeting was short, but it gave the townspeople new heart, for as well as designating December 3rd, the Day of the Great Deliverance, as a public holiday, a motto was adopted for the town. "Turris fortissima est nomen Jehova" - "Our strong tower is the name of the Lord". As they walked home, Mary put an arm around Sarah. "Your Father would have been proud tonight." "Yes, mother, he would, and he will be when he gets back again."

It was two weeks later that Prince Maurice attacked again, between Maudlyn and Pennycomequick. He tried to break the defence lines at night, and it took three bloody assaults by the Parliamentarians to drive him back with many casualties. The attack was made by men already weakened by wounds and disease, so it was no wonder that it failed. It was the end for Prince Maurice and on Christmas Day he marched his troops away, the very day by which he had promised them that Plymouth would be taken.

As the next days passed and the year drew to a close, more details of the fighting were revealed, and John was able to tell the family, after a remustering of the troops, that their well-liked Captain Wansey had been killed on December 3rd, plus twelve troopers, while one hundred were wounded and forty-three taken prisoner.

However, although everyone was relieved that the fighting had stopped, inside the walls of the town things were getting very bad.

In the thick of the battle, concentration had been fixed on the ramparts and those who were defending them, but it was becoming obvious that the siege was now deepening. The wells were drying up and it hadn't yet been possible to repair the leat. There was little food and housewives anxiously examined flour barrels and honey jars, scraping them for everything that could be eaten, using bread that would once have been thrown out, cutting off mould and mixing what was left with a watery broth or weak porridge. The shops were empty and closed, men like Peter Perryman had dispersed their goods, dividing them out as fairly and as widespread as they could. Some of the poorest of the townspeople came to these shops in angry mood, refusing to believe that they were empty. Soldiers had to be posted to keep them from breaking in and burning houses down. But generally people were too weak to put up much of a protest, and brought their containers to the miller's, where they were filled from the last sacks of flour he had - again under military guard. The Royalists had earlier driven off all the cattle in the surrounding countryside, hoping to starve Plymouth out. Although men crept out now to search for rabbits and hares, there were few to be found. The December weather was cold and disease spread. Many died, and every day there were hasty burials in St. Andrew's churchyard.

Those in authority, the Mayor, the Vicars, and even military leaders, did their best to encourage the people, telling them not to give up after their great victory, though the troops knew that they were short of powder, shot and weapons, realising that if the enemy came back to the attack, the defenders would have no chance. Mary, like other housewives, used all the ingenuity she possessed to keep them all fed as best she could, though as she looked at her family, thin and pale, her heart smote her. Betsy and Nathaniel moved into the house with them so that everything could be shared, and Sarah saw how often her mother would say she wasn't hungry and put part of her share on to the boys' plates, while Betsy did the same for Nathaniel. Sarah herself added little titbits to John's meal, while they all tried to make sure that Matthew's gradually returning strength was encouraged. Betsy spent a lot of her time with Matthew, piling covers upon him as he sat by the fire, for there was little fuel left and people had burnt all the wood they could possibly spare.

Sarah, coming in one day from a forage for shell-fish on the beach, and with a few winkles and cockles in her bag, stopped at the living room door, as she heard Betsy and Matthew in what seemed a serious discussion. "I cannot but have doubts about this war," Matthew was saying. "I keep thinking of the boy who stabbed me. I knew him and his family well, and now we're fighting each other, and many others are doing the same. I have never doubted the cause, but now..." Betsy put a restraining hand on his shoulder. "Calm yourself, Matthew, or your fever will return. But I know how you feel, with my Ned on the other side," and they both fell silent.

Sarah went on through to the kitchen, her mind in a whirl, and she lay awake long that night, wishing with a yearning need that her father's calm reason was there to comfort her.

Then the next morning, she and the whole household were wakened by shouts in the streets, and hurrying down they heard the cries of "Fish, fish". Everyone rushed to the beach and could see a great shoal of pilchards swimming into the harbour, so many that people were gathering them in buckets as she tucked up her skirts and waded out with the others to collect all the fish she could.

"It's a miracle," was the shout everywhere, and Sarah knew without any doubt that God was still with them.

Chapter Thirteen

THE GREAT SHOAL OF fish proved more than just a miracu-
lous life-saving blessing to the people of Plymouth. It gave them
new heart and encouragement and the assurance, especially for the
faint-hearted - the numbers of these had increased in these last
months - that God was still with them and their cause. The train-
bands, unaccustomed to the rigours of war, suffered greatly as did
the women who brought to the forts "strong waters and all kinds
of provisions" for their men's refreshment, often going without
themselves in order to do so.

There were still many sick with various diseases, and the
wounded to be tended, and at the end of January 1644, Ephraim
Goodyeare died. In addition to all her other duties Mary had been
helping his housekeeper to look after him, and sat with the old man
wiping his brow as he slipped out of this world. "He looked so
small in the big bed," she said to Sarah who had waited up for her
after the rest of the household had gone to bed, "so thin, he was
too old and frail to fight any more," and wearily she pushed back
a tendril of hair under her cap. "Never mind, mother, you did your
best, I know. Come along to bed now, you look exhausted." "You're
a good girl, Sarah. I don't know how I'd manage without you,"
and she leant on the girl as they climbed the stairs together.

"What will happen to the business now?" Sarah asked. "Well,"
her mother paused at the door of her own room, "Francis will have
to keep it going as best he can. Ephraim hasn't had much to do
with it these last months anyhow - not that there is much business
now, but I just hope there'll be something for your father to come
home to," and she reached up to kiss her daughter. "Good-night."

Sarah lay sleepless for a long time that night, thinking as she
often did of her family and how much life had changed for them
all since this dreadful war had come upon them. She remembered
how she had played with Will on the beach, happily hunting among

the rock pools, carefree, her only complaint being the dullness of life for girls. She needn't have worried about that. And Will, where was he now, was he still alive? She thought of her brothers - Francis, grown more serious than ever, trying to keep the accounts in what little business they still had, while James - and Sarah smiled in spite of herself - he was growing up rapidly, working at his studies whenever someone stood over him, but there had been no school these last months and he ran about the town with his friends most of the time, always hungry and growing out of his clothes so rapidly that it took all his mother's ingenuity - with help from Sarah - to patch and darn and let down old clothes of his brother.

Sarah thought of her mother, how thin she had become, her soft comeliness gone and lines etching her once smooth brow, her struggles for them all and how often she had heard her crying in the night - crying, she knew, for Richard. There was nothing she, Sarah, could do to comfort her for there had been no news of Richard and she herself missed her father so much. He had always made things clear for her, sensible and reasonable, though she doubted there could be much reason in this siege, and she realised with a sudden clarity that her childhood days were over and her father could no longer put everything right for her. She had to be strong, as he had told her, and look after the others, and this she had tried to do. And then, as always of recent times, her thoughts moved to John, and it was with these thoughts that she would fall asleep.

She got out of bed now and crossed to her window. She could not see the fort from here, but just to look towards it gave her comfort. John had told her that he looked towards Rag Street every night that he was on duty and thought of her, and with the comfort of that knowledge, Sarah crept back to the warmth of her bed and gradually she fell asleep.

When John came back to the house next day, he had news to give them. "Colonel Gould is now in charge of all the defences," he said, sitting down at the table. Sarah gave him his porridge and bread, shaking her head over the latter's dryness and tastelessness, and giving the porridge pan to Nat to scrape out. "Colonel Wardlaw is ill and 'tis not expected that he will fight again." He ate his porridge hungrily for a few minutes, then looked up suddenly as if just remembering. "Oh, it seems the Royalists have changes too. We've heard that Colonel Digby has been wounded, and a new commander has arrived - a Richard Grenville - and I could hear the men muttering when they heard his name."

There was an exclamation from the other side of the room where Betsy was putting a clean dressing on Matthew's shoulder. "I should think they would mutter," he said angrily. "'Skellum' Grenville they call him, and he's known on all sides for his cruel and vicious deeds, and a turncoat too, for he deserted the Parliamentary cause for the Royalist one, and they're welcome to him. He's a disgrace to his grandfathers. Well, that settles it." Matthew stood up now and pulled his shirt over his shoulder, which he moved carefully. "I thank you, ladies, for all your care of me, but it's time I was back on duty. I'll away to the Fort now and see where I'm needed most." Mary and Betsy looked at each other as he made for the door. They knew that he was still far from fit, but that he would not stay any longer away from the troops.

John, meanwhile, as he wiped his bowl with the last crust of bread, could not suppress a yawn. Sarah was quick to see this and was at his side in a moment. "Come on, lad," she said, in a tone so like her mother's that Betsy's mouth twitched in a smile. "To bed with you. Your next spell of duty will come quickly enough." John obediently got up from the table, flicking his dark hair back from his eyes, and smiled at the girl. Their glances held, just for a moment, and Mary recognised what passed between them and hoped that all would go well for these young people, but who could tell in such times.

The household went about its business, but it was to be a day for news, for just as they had finished their frugal mid-day meal, there was a knock on the front door. Sarah hurried to answer it and Peter Perryman limped through to the living-room. Mary saw at once how weary he looked, and ushered him into the big chair. "Rest yourself," she said and poured ale for him. "This hill of ours is getting steeper, I sometimes think." "My thanks to you," he said, taking a sip of the drink. "Yes," he paused and then went on, "I have unhappily had several calls to make this day." He stopped again, as though searching for words, and it was obvious to the three women watching him that the news was not good. "You know I spend a good deal of time at the forts these days, helping to organise food for the troops - little enough though it is. I'm useless for fighting and have nothing to sell in the shop, so it's the best I can do." His listeners nodded, waiting for what would come next.

"This morning I was down near where the prisoners are quartered, when one of our men, a sergeant, came rushing out. He stopped when he saw me. 'You're a local man, I believe,' I said I was, and he hurried me back inside trying to explain as he went. It seemed that there was this young prisoner, badly wounded, and who had been unconscious ever since he was brought in. Only now had he opened his eyes and tried to speak - though he would not last long, the sergeant said. He wanted to give a message to someone who knew the fishing people of Plymouth and when they told him that he was in fact within that very town he became very agitated. By now," Peter continued, "we were in the - the room where the sick prisoners lay." He did not add to the women's distress by describing the foul stench of the place, or the cries and screams of badly injured men for whom little could be done.

"The sergeant took me to a corner where a young lad lay, on a kind of litter, his face and head so bandaged that I could only see one eye, and told me to bend down as he he could barely speak. This I did and the boy caught my arm. 'Do you know the family of -'" At this point Betsy, who had been standing motionless, her face drained of all colour, swayed and clutched the table. Mary quickly placed a stool beneath her and guided her on to it. Peter went on - "'The family of Will Thomas?'" Now there was a cry from Sarah, and the three women clung together almost afraid to breathe. "I said I did, and what could he tell me about him. He fell, at (I think he said) Exeter, but he was rambling again then. 'You're sure he's - he's dead?' 'Yes. He was my friend, I held him, but he'd asked me to tell his family if anything...' The weak voice faded to nothingness, and the sergeant, stepping forward, closed the boy's one visible eye and pulled up the blood-stained sheet. 'I'll try to find out if anyone knows where this one comes from, but I doubt it.'"

Peter took a mouthful of ale now, as Mary and Sarah sobbed in each other's arms, and Betsy, picking up a startled Nat, rocked the startled child in her arms and called for "Ned!"

Mary recovered first, and asked Peter: "There's no news of any other local men, I suppose - like Ned?" "No, nothing," he shook his head. "I must go now, I've been to Jacob Thomas and the others of Will's family, but I knew I should tell you next."

Mary showed him to the door and when she came back Sarah was putting her cloak round her. "I must go out, just for a little, by myself," and Mary did not try to stop her.

She ran blindly down the hill, across the cobbles to the beach, and finding the big, flat stone where she and Will had sat so often, sharing thoughts, complaints and sometimes an apple or a crust of bread, gave herself up to her grief.

John found her there just as the light was fading. Mary had told him where she would probably be, and that she would need him. When he sat down beside her and put an arm around her, she turned wordlessly to him, and they sat for several minutes without speaking. Then Sarah pulled herself upright and straightened her cap. "Thank you for coming," she said, quietly. "Was he very important to you?" John asked, and Sarah, thinking for a moment, replied, "Yes, but only because we were children together and had played and shared things until he went away," and she looked right into John's dark eyes. "Not like you and me," and their lips met in a kiss that was comforting each to the other, but nothing demanding, nothing selfish.

Looking at her daughter sometimes, in the weeks and months that followed, Mary felt saddened at the way in which she had moved so quickly from childhood to womanhood. She was proud of how practical she had become, how reliable, but sighed for the impatient girl with her unquenchable thirst for knowledge and often rebel behaviour, and wondered how Richard would view this change in his only daughter. She was much quieter now in habits and demeanour and Mary sensed, with gratitude, that Sarah tried to lift as much of the burden of caring from her mother's shoulders as she could.

There were marked changes too in Betsy. Not only was she thinner and more careworn but it was as if with the news of the death of Will her hopes of Ned's return had vanished, and she clung to the rapidly growing Nathaniel with fierce love as though determined that he should not be taken from her too.

Mary's sensitivity to the feelings of others, was heightened by her own loneliness and anxiety, and she saw how Betsy seemed to find comfort in the time she spent with Matthew. Even though his wound was healed and he did not need her nursing, yet her eyes lightened whenever he came back to the house, as did Sarah's when

John returned, and Mary was thankful in both cases, knowing that for her there would be no release until Richard himself came through the door again, ducking his head where the beams were lowest. Of the alternative she refused to even think.

As the evenings gradually lengthened and spring approached, the town tried to shake off the despond of winter and rouse itself to practical activities. For the Plymouth garrison there was some respite from assaults, and so the troops seized the opportunity to repair their defences and expand the fortifications. They even sent raiding parties out to harrass the Royalists outposts and, what was of more interest to the townspeople, foraging raids went out as far as Roborough and there was always great relief when cattle were brought in or sheep, or even rabbits and hares. Reports came in that 'Skellum' Grenville had boasted - like others before him - that he would starve the people of Plymouth into submission, and he might have done so had not the sea route remained throughout in Parliamentarian hands, so that some supplies - albeit very limited - got in to feed the troops and help the townsfolk.

Sarah would often round up a group of children to go on a hunt for shell-fish on her beloved beach, and even young ones like Nat got quite adept at knocking the limpets off the rocks with a sharp stone, and with their sharp eyes finding the winkles and cock-les in the small pools. Sarah would organise competitions to encourage them, finding a small prize for the one who collected the most, always something to eat, an apple, or the end of a loaf with a scraping of honey.

Sometimes when the work was finished, all the children at home, and John had a precious hour or so off duty, he and Sarah would find their way again to the beach, content in each other's company. John would skim pebbles across the surface of the water (as Will had once done) while Sarah, her arms hugging her knees, admired his straight, tall body and the skill of his long arms, shiv-ering as she thought of those same arms wielding a pike or defend-ing himself from an enemy weapon. Then he would join her on the great flat stone, and they would talk about 'when the war is over'. This was a hazy time, that neither of them could quite imagine, but they knew it would be wonderful - all their soldiers home, not having to look fearfully and suspiciously at any strangers, and having plenty to eat.

But Sarah had a worry about this and mentioned it as they sat one bright afternoon when even the breeze from the sea was soft. "But what will you do when peace comes, John, and you leave the army and here?" "I have been thinking about that." The boy poked at the pebbles at his feet with a piece of stick.

"I don't want to go back to the farm. It's not big enough for us all anyway - though I'll go and see them of course." Sarah held her breath and waited. "I'd like to stay here in the town. I talk to Master Perryman sometimes down in the fort and he says there'll be lots of work to build things up again. He'll want help in his grocer's shop, his wounds still trouble him and he gets very tired." "Oh, yes," Sarah was fired with enthusiasm now. "My father will need help too when he comes back. Francis says there'll be much work to do, everyone will need blankets and clothes."

"I've been wondering too," John's voice was low now, and he dropped his eyes shyly so that Sarah, looking at him, could see the sweep of his dark lashes on his pale cheek. "If Francis would show me how he keeps accounts. I've watched him do it sometimes in the evenings." "I'm sure he would." Sarah's hope to keep John with her was limitless. "We'll ask him tonight. You don't have to go on duty till the morning, do you?" John hugged her to him. "And then," he said, "then we would be together..." "For ever," Sarah finished triumphantly as they got to their feet and walked with light steps back to Rag Street.

Francis, though a shy lad, seemed quite willing to initiate John into the intricacies of simple book-keeping, and John, being a quick learner, after an early struggle with the columns and adjustments, the two of them worked together two or three times a week, Sarah watching the new pupil with pride.

On 18th March, Grenville wrote to the Plymouth authorities, explaining at great length the reasons for his change of front, and trying to convince them that they had no chance of success so should surrender to the Royalists. Gould replied with great indignation: "You might well," he wrote, "have spared us the accounts of your dissimulation with Parliament. We account ourselves safer to have you an enemy abroad than a pretended friend at home. As for proposing conditions of peace, we shall most gladly do it when it may advance the public service. The same God is still our rock and refuge." At the same time a pamphlet, 'The Iniquity of the Covenant' which Grenville had enclosed, was taken by the public hangman to the market place and burnt in the sight of assembled Plymouth.

But in spite of this defiant spirit, Plymouth was still internally in a poor condition, with quarrels and suspicions abundant, and provisions very limited, and of course the strain of not knowing how long these stressful conditions would continue. Sometimes Sarah thought this last was the worst, it was as though they were all held in a state of limbo and would be in it for ever, just growing older and more weary.

But when she was with John and they talked of the future, she was able to convince herself that one day the war would end.

In mid-April events suddenly hotted up, putting the whole town on its weary toes. Colonel Wardlaw died of his injuries, and Colonel Gould was killed in a skirmish. The new Commander of defences was Lieutenant Colonel Martin and he believed in attacking the enemy as often and as hard as possible. That meant that off-duty time was cut to a minimum and the men rested briefly in the forts before the next campaign.

St Budeaux's Church Tower was attacked with six hundred men, then Pomphlett and Plympton, and Martin took badly needed arms and ammunition from all these places.

In the next few weeks Martin crossed by the Cremyll Ferry, making for Mount Edgecumbe. He took Cawsand Fort and Maker Church, but could not take Mount Edgecumbe itself, but set fire to the house. On the way back to Cremyll the troops attacked the Royalists trenches at Millbrook and pressed on towards Saltash. But the Lynher river was too wide to cross without boats and the forces holding Saltash were too strong. So Martin decided he had done enough for the time being and with captured guns, powder, shot, muskets, pistols and two hundred prisoners, he returned to Plymouth.

Meanwhile at home Sarah had her own worries, for Mary, weakened by lack of good food, overwork, and so many anxieties, became ill. She collapsed as she was putting together a mid-day meal, and Sarah, finding her, called frantically to Francis and James, and between them they carried her up to bed, Sarah weeping over the thin-ness of the well-loved form and praying that God would give her strength to cope with this new crisis, for this time there would be no mother to turn to for guidance.

Chapter Fourteen

FROM THAT MOMENT of finding her mother collapsed, Sarah's life seemed to change. For the most part it was centred around her home and especially the bed-chamber where Mary lay, with the rest of the family a background to this, sometimes sharing the nursing with her and at others being cared for themselves by Sarah. Her moments spent with John were still precious, but they were snatched and brief, and often the garden was the only place where for a few moments they could sit or walk.

She knew that in that year of 1644 there was much activity within the town's walls and without, but she felt somehow apart from all of this and when Francis, John and Matthew brought news home, she could not quite comprehend it, the perimeter of her life had shrunk to the house in Rag Street.

Mary's collapse had been complete and for many weeks she lay still and almost lifeless, her eyes flicking open for a few minutes before closing in weariness. Both Betsy and Elizabeth Perryman, who came to help, could find no specific malady, and it soon became clear that it was not the plague, which all at first had feared, for no symptoms developed and though she was feverish, there was no rash or tell-tale marks or swellings.

Betsy shook her head as she and Sarah washed her and changed her sheets one day. "My poor lamb," she said, brushing the dark hair back from the thin face. "She's just worn out, with all the work and worry, and there's no end of it in sight." Sarah opened the small casement window as far as it would go, for the air was mild and sweet, and the room within stuffy with the odour of sickness. Then, turning to the bed, smooth and cool now, she tried to raise her mother on the pillows, and taking the dish of gruel from Betsy, encouraged a spoonful between Mary's pinched lips. "Come along, my dear," she said gently, "there's good milk in this and it will give you strength. We managed to get a little, thanks to Betsy - " She whispered this last to her friend, for it had been what was allowed for Nat. "Nat's doing fine. He's a big strong lad," and Betsy wiped the corner of Mary's mouth. They managed to get her to swallow a little more, though the brown eyes never opened, and then she shook her head once and fell back on the pillow.

The two women gathered up the washing utensils and bed linen and slipped from the room.

"Now I'm going to make a good beef stew," Betsy said comfortingly as they got back to the kitchen. "Young John managed to get some pieces from Master Perryman. He's a good lad, that," and Sarah blushed in agreement.

The girl then stole a few moments to gather a nose-gay for her mother's room, and in the garden found lavender, stitch-wort and campions, and carrying them upstairs placed the small jar on the window sill. Her mother was still as she had left her, and Sarah, sitting on the stool by the bed, took the wasted hand that lay on the covers in her own and smoothed the workworn fingers. "Oh, Mother," she whispered, "please get better soon. We all need you so much."

John and Matthew came back that night with stories of Colonel Martin's continuing achievements and skirmishes that had gone in Parliament's favour, so it was a surprise to everyone when a few days later he was suddenly replaced by Colonel James Kerr, and Sir John Bampfield was placed in charge of Drake's Island. Both Prince Maurice and Grenville were badly beaten at Marsh Mills, and hearing that the chief Roundhead prisoners were being taken to Lydford Castle, plans were made by the Plymouth troops to attack this. At first under Kerr Plymouth's problems were greatly eased, for the Earl of Essex with half of the Parliamentary main army camped outside the town before marching into Cornwall.

His presence caused the temporary lifting of the blockade of the town, and there was great excitement, for many foraging trips were made and even the women ventured just outside the stockade to gather what they could, so there was almost a holiday feeling in the air and the mild weather added to this. Betsy and Elizabeth took Nat one afternoon and came back with eggs and a great bunch of wild flowers, and more colour in their cheeks than there had been for a very long time.

"Why don't you go out tomorrow while there is still time. It will do you good, my love?" Betsy looked with concern at Sarah's pale face when she and Nat got back to the house, but Sarah shook her head. "Not till mother's better. I'm all right, and we can do a lot with the eggs, and the flowers are lovely too," and she buried her face in the bouquet.

John came from his guard duty that night with more news. "Essex moves to Cornwall tomorrow." His voice was excited as he rushed through to the kitchen where he knew Sarah would be. "He's taking a lot of the garrison with him - more than two thousand, it's said. We shall defeat the Royalists now for sure."

"We?" Sarah stopped, her hands in a bowl of flour. "You're not going, are you?" "If I'm ordered to, I must, of course. We all have to report tomorrow prepared to march, so I'll have to pack my bag tonight."

He went forward and tentatively put his arm around Sarah's shoulders. "I don't want to leave you when you've so many worries, but if I'm sent..." Sarah looked into his eyes and could see the conflicting emotions there - concern for her, but also excitement at the chance of a great campaign. She sighed. "After supper I'll help you put your things together."

Matthew came home some time later, full of more news that many of Essex's troops had brought with them, of battles, attacks and skirmishes, especially of a great battle just waged in the north. "Yorkshire, I think it was," Matthew tried to remember. "Somewhere called Marston - Marston Moor, somewhere near Skipton. Prince Rupert was thoroughly routed there."

It was quite late that night when Sarah and John stole into the garden for a few minutes quiet together. They sat on the weathered stone seat, Sarah trying desperately not to cry. John, sensing this, held her tight. "If - if I do have to go, it won't be for long, I'm sure, and I'll think of you all the time. Wherever I am, I'll think of you every evening and you think of me at the same time. It'll bring us close together."

Sarah nodded her head dumbly. Then she said to him: "Since you've been here, you know, things have been easier for us all. Even James takes notice of you. It's as though you came when father went, and now I'm going to have to manage without either of you, and I don't know if I can."

"You will, I know you will. You've been so strong for us all, and then when all this is over, perhaps we can start our own lives. Anyhow," he added as they rose to go indoors, "I may not be needed after all." But Sarah knew that he would, and was already thinking of what food could be spared to go into his knapsack.

Early the next morning she and Betsy stood at the front door seeing Matthew and John on their way. Sarah had repaired John's uniform as best she could, but it was much too small for him and there was no more to be had. She had even found him a pair of Richard's warm socks, old but still with much wear in them. Both men wore sprigs of lavender in their hats and as they turned at the bottom of the steps, John called back: "We'll be back tonight. I'm sure we will, but if not - " and he stretched out his long thin arm towards Sarah as though to reach and hold her. Then they were gone and the women went back into the house.

"Come on, my dear, let's get on with the cleaning and washing. It's a lovely day and work the best cure for worry that I know," and Betsy squeezed Sarah's arm. "Shall we go down into the town?" Sarah suggested. "We may find out something and Francis is at home this morning, he'll look after mother for an hour or two." "Oh, no, my love. I don't think we should. It's crowded already with so many soldiers, you can hear the shouting from here. No, we're best to stay at home."

The day dragged for Sarah. James had run off towards the barracks. She knew he was too young to be hanging around the troops, but she didn't know how to stop him. She'd try to talk to him this evening.

Mary seemed a little better that day, and Sarah managed to spoon some of the beef soup into her. She did not immediately slip back into her usual drowsiness, and Sarah, encouraged, brought her a thin slice of new bread spread with butter. "Look, mother, old Ephraim's housekeeper sent a pat of her butter. People have been very kind, just as you were to so many," and she could not keep the tears from her eyes. Mary managed two small pieces before smiling at Sarah and murmuring: "You're a good girl." Then she fell asleep holding Sarah's hand. It was little enough but it gave the girl new hope.

She set about preparing their supper and determinedly laid a place for both the men. The warm July day was drawing to a close and the two women in the kitchen kept busy until Francis came into the room. "Is it time the others were home?" He hesitated. "You haven't heard anything?"

They both shook their heads, then suddenly there was a knock on the front door. Sarah reached it first, then stopped, afraid to open it. Finally she threw it open, one man stood there. It was Matthew. He looked almost guilty as he gazed at Sarah. "I'm sorry, my dear, he had to go. I'd have willingly gone in his place, but there was no chance. They've just left us older ones behind to man the forts," and he went to Betsy who was waiting just behind.

Sarah thought that the next few days were amongst the worst she had ever known. Even Mary's slight improvement seemed to have given her a hope that was false, for she did not rouse again.

And then, after a week, there came devastating news, brought by a trooper who crawled back to the stockades and was let in by guards who carried him, more dead than alive, to the captain in charge. Soon the whole town knew that Essex and his army had been defeated by Prince Maurice and the King who had joined him at Boconnoc, between Fowey and Par. The Governor and Mayor, between whom there had been many arguments recently, knew that the town was now in a parlous position and must be told of the situation. The best soldiers had gone with Essex, and the garrison was down to eight hundred men who had to defend a line of fortifications four miles long.

Francis came from the Meeting in the Guildhall to tell the news to Betsy and Sarah, and the three of them sat together, trying to imagine what would now happen. Matthew was obviously held at the stockades and they knew there would be little time off duty for him.

There was no answer to the one question crying out within Sarah's heart. What had happened to John?

All the soldier who had got back could say was that there were many killed and wounded, and that when he had crawled away and got a ride in an old farm cart, nothing more could be seen through the melee of men and horses, flames and smoke.

When the others went to bed, Sarah sat on in her father's great chair. It would be August tomorrow, and her 14th birthday in a week. But her strength was gone and her despair absolute. How could she go on any longer? She realised suddenly that there had been knocking on the front door for several minutes and it was growing more insistent. She dragged herself along the hall-way too tired to even hope a miracle had sent John back to her. Then she opened the door, looking at the tall figure who stood there.

It was not quite dark and she could see he was in uniform, with a yellow sash across his tunic.

"Yes?" she said wearily. "Who is it, can I help you?"

The figure stepped over the threshold and swung Sarah up in strong arms."What, does not know me, my love?" and she looked down into the dear face she had feared never to see again.

Chapter Fifteen

AS HE LOWERED HER to the ground, Sarah stared and stared at Richard as though her eyes could not get enough of him. Then she flung her arms around him and held him as tightly as she could while he said her name over and over again. They were both laughing and crying at the same time.

"Oh, father, I was afraid I'd never see you again, and everything's gone wrong and..." "Hush, m;y love. I'm here now. All will be well. Are the family all in bed?" But before Sarah could reply there were voices from the stairs and Francis and Betsy were running down. "Who is it - what is happening?" Even a tousled, sleepy James appeared looking over the bannister rail. Richard greeted them all as they hurried down, gathering up James in his arms, hugging Francis, and embracing Betsy. As they all moved into the living-room, Richard looked from one face to he other. "Where's Mary? Where's your mother?"

"Sit down, father, and I'll explain." Even in that moment of anxiety, Richard saw how his daughter, the little girl he had left behind, took charge of the situation.

"Mother's here - she's upstairs in bed, she couldn't have heard you. But she's ill." Richard was already on his feet and rushing through the hall to the stairway. "Gently, father," Sarah called as she followed closely behind him, "don't frighten her."

He stopped at the bedroom door, then opened it and crept into the room, dark now. Sarah placed a candle beside the bed and looked at the still figure. Then, as Richard approached the bed and knelt beside it, whispering his wife's name, Mary opened her eyes and looked up at him. "Richard," the words were hardly audible, "is it you?" She tried to raise a hand to him, but it fell back on the cover. Richard gathered her up in his arms, lifting her from the pillows, rocking her to and fro as though she were a child. Betsy, who had followed Sarah into the room, touched her arm. "Come on, my love, let's leave them together for a little."

The boys were waiting on the landing and together the four of them went downstairs, where Sarah and Betsy set about preparing food for the returned soldier, stopping every few minutes to hug each other in delight.

Then, "he's coming down," Sarah cried, and ran out to welcome him all over again. They all hung upon him, asking him questions, then remembering news of their own to tell him before he could answer.

Richard's greatest concern was for Mary, and he listened in sorrow as Sarah and Betsy explained how she had gradually got weaker and more frail. "She kept us all going," Sarah said, "then suddenly it was as though she'd left us," and the ready tears came to her eyes.

"But you took her place," Betsy put in quickly. "She's been really good, Master Richard, you can be very proud of her." "And you too, Betsy. I couldn't have managed on my own." "I'm proud of you both," Richard said. "I'm just so sorry that I had to leave you all," and he looked from one face to the other, distressed at their thin-ness.

But now James was yawning openly and Francis behind his hand. "Bed, boys, I think now," Richard said. "It's getting very late. We'll talk more tomorrow. I want to hear all about the business, Francis, and what you've been doing, my lad," he tousled James's hair, and with a hug sent the two of them upstairs.

"I'd better go too," Betsy got up from her stool. "Morning will come soon enough. But Richard stopped her. "Will you wait a moment, Betsy, I've something to tell you - and Sarah, stay with her."

As she looked up at the tall man, with the strong serious face, a little lined now, his hair starting to go grey, she knew why he wore an officer's sash and was utterly thankful that he was back with them. She looked trustingly at him, wondering what news he had to give now, but Betsy seemed to have a sense of what was to come, for she sat quite still, her hands clasped together in her lap.

"Is it about Ned?" she asked quietly.

"Yes, my dear, it is," and he moved closer to her. "You must be very brave, and proud of Ned too. Yes, you can be that." He paused, looking with great compassion at the bent head before him.

"Please tell me," Betsy whispered, while Sarah reached out and covered the clasped hands with one of her own.

"It was at Marston Moor. There was a great confusion, the fighting was thick, smoke and flames were everywhere, and it was difficult to distinguish between our troops and theirs. I suddenly heard my name called, and turned in time to avoid a pike thrust, and recognised Ned and rushed towards him, but not quickly enough to pull him out of the firing range of a musket ball."

There was a gasp from Betsy, and Sarah's grip on her hands tightened. Richard went on: "I managed to drag Ned to a comparatively quiet spot under a hedge, but there was nothing I could do to save him. I held him and tried to comfort him, and his last words were to you. 'Tell Betsy,' he said, 'that I love her and that I'm sorry,' that was all. But I put him with some of our lads who'd been killed, and gave orders for his burial with them. You can be sure that you and Nat will always have a home with us, so have no worries on that score." Betsy was crying silently now. "I knew," she said, "I knew when Will died that Ned wouldn't be back either. Those fishermen who went to help the king - they should not have gone." Richard turned to Sarah. "What's that about young Will?" She told him, then helped Betsy to her feet. "Come along," she said, "sleep in my bed tonight," and the two of them went up the stairs, with Richard close behind.

When Sarah woke the next morning, even before she opened her eyes, she felt a great sense of relief, of a burden lifted, and so, remembering the events of the previous night, she jumped out of bed, made her simple toilet, and ran down the stairs. But Richard was there before her, standing at the back door and looking out at the garden. The day was already warm and Richard sniffed the air appreciatively.

The next few weeks went very quickly for Sarah, and happily after so much despair, with only the absence of John causing her heartache and faithfully, each evening, either in the garden or at the casement of her own room, she looked towards Cornwall and thought of him, hoping that she was equally in his mind.

Richard was able to spend the next few days with the family, then he had to report for duty at the barracks, still coming home when he could. On the first occasion he brought Mark Penprase, now a fellow officer, with him, and as she prepared a meal, Sarah was surprised that he didn't seem at all frightening now as he had when he came from Tavistock to tell how matters in London were progressing, a visit that seemed so long ago now.

It was Mark who told Sarah how highly thought of Richard was, and especially was his advice sought now on the defence of Plymouth.

The next day Matthew got home for a few hours and Sarah explained to her father, how friendly he and Betsy had become and how she was sure he would help her over this difficult time, and what a comfort and help both the billeted men had been.

"Tell me about this John, that I hear so much about," Richard said when they snatched a few quiet moments together one evening soon after his return, and watching his beloved daughter, and the changes of expression in her face with the love and anxiety shining from her eyes, he promised to find out anything he could about the casualties of that battle and prisoners taken, and he thought, as Mary had done, with both pride and regret that Sarah's youth had indeed gone.

But it was in the progress of Mary herself that Richard's presence made the greatest impact. From her first sight of him she seemed to take new heart. He encouraged her to eat the tastiest morsels they could find for her, and within a few days he was able to carry her downstairs, saying almost in tears to Sarah afterwards, that she weighed no more than a bird, and he wouldn't be happy till he had his plump, comely wife back again.

The summer was a very warm one and, well-wrapped, Mary was able to sit in the garden, where the light breeze brought colour to the pale cheeks, and where her eyes searched, constantly for Richard.

Now that the running of the home was easier for Sarah, she became more aware of the situation outside it, and listened to her father and his friends, for once again groups of them met at the house in Rag Street.

Richard came home one day at the end of August with important news. "At last," he said, banging his hand on the great table in excitement, "Parliament seems to be realising our parlous state and is sending Lord Robartes to take command, and eight ships to be under the orders of Admiral Batten."

"That's good, surely, father?" "It helps, but it's not enough. We know that Royalist armies are gathering all around us, an attack cannot be far away, and men and supplies are desperately short should there be another full siege."

Sarah's heart sank - not another siege, the town tightly blockaded, that awful sense of being enclosed, shut in, and there were no stores to see them through this time - they were all just eating what they could get and grateful for it.

Then as August gave way to September, Parliament sent fifteen hundred extra men and ordered that all provisions en route to Cornwall for Essex's use were to be diverted to Plymouth. As the news circulated amongst the townspeople, their spirits rose, only to fall with the most startling event yet.

It appeared that the King himself had decided to take over the attack on Plymouth, and had chosen Widey Court as his Headquarters, handed over to him by its loyal owner, Yeoman Heale. However he seemed in no hurry to make his attack, but each morning rode down the hill with his staff and generals to be received with much ceremony on the southern slopes. He would watch as his guns pounded the town's outworks, but little damage was done and the defenders began to laugh at this daily bombardment, and the King's constant calls on the town to surrender.

The hill from which the guns fired was nicknamed 'Vapouring Hill' after the 'vapourings' of the enemy's guns and the camp fires, and Charles' ceremonial greetings.

But Richard and the commanders did not share in the derision, for they knew that the Royalist forces really outnumbered Plymouth's defenders, and that moreover there was a general weariness in the town, and even the soldiers, many unpaid for a long time, were discontented. Everyone would need to summon all their strength for whatever lay ahead.

Chapter Sixteen

FOR THE NEXT FORTNIGHT it was as though the town held its breath and waited - waited with the knowledge that there were two thousand, five hundred defenders, while outside the walls the king had fifteen thousand men.

The family at Rag Street continued to live as best they could, Mary gradually gaining some strength. She even managed a few light household tasks with Betsy and Sarah hovering protectively near - crying to each other afterwards at the weakness which still beset her. "Never mind, my love," Betsy comforted the girl. "You can't rush these things. Your mother's done well, thanks to your father's return," and with that Sarah had to be content.

Then on 14th September, the Royalists launched an attack between Stonehouse and Pennycomequick forts. It was a furious battle raging from dawn till nightfall, the townspeople watching fearfully from every possible vantage point. Robartes sent out every man he could spare and sailors from the fleet took an important role in the defence of the line which was never overcome, never broken, in spite of ceaseless assaults. The next morning Charles and Maurice rode away, and the town thankfully accepted a comparative lull in the enemy's activities.

They were all too weary by now for the general rejoicing that had followed previous victories or escapes, and, after so long, everyone knew that lulls were simply that, not the end of hostilities. Conditions were still bad, and food very scarce, and getting by day to day took up most of everyone's energy. But those in command knew that efforts must be made while there was a chance of success and on October 4th, a small force was sent into Cornwall to make an onslaught first on the enemy-held Saltash then, if this was successful, on to Millbrook. Richard was placed in charge of these troops and comforted his family by telling them how slight a battle it would be.

"I'll be back before you have time to miss me," he said, as they all gathered round him on the evening of the 3rd. Betsy and Sarah were ensuring that his clothes and accoutrements were in as good an order as they could make them, while he was talking seriously to both his sons. "Remember, Francis, I'm proud of the way you're keeping the business going, though I know it's shrunk to almost nothing at the moment, and, James, no more wildness. Do as your mother bids you, and your sister too." Richard knew, as did they all, that Mary still hadn't the strength to exert her will on an unruly boy, and it was Sarah upon whom the burden would fall while her father was away.

The next morning they were all up early to watch the men march off. Mary seemed to accept, with Sarah supporting her without demur, all that was told to her, which worried Richard more than any pleading with him to stay would have done. Sarah's own plea had been the one she always made - "Please, father, listen and watch for any news of John," and she knew he would do this to the best of his ability, so her prayer went silently with him as she waved to the column of men led by the tall figures of Richard and his friend, Mark Penprase.

These two stepped out firm and straight, Mark with a slight limp from an earlier wound. There was only one baggage wagon because the force was small, and Sarah knew it was loaded with powder, match and shot, the tools of the pioneers, and food reserves. She knew too that her father was as well dressed as the family could make him, his long "bucket-top" boots well cleaned and his grey stockings washed and mended, while his shirt, jacket and breeches, were brushed and darned. The army's clothing issue had grown as the years of war went on, but it was piecemeal and some of the veterans were virtually in rags. Sarah knew too, thankfully, for he had told her so, that there was armour in the wagon, back and breast plates and open iron helmets with sliding bars to protect the face. Although food was scarce there would be bread or hard tack, cheese, dried pease and fish in his bag, and maybe even dried beef if the barracks rations ran to it.

So, having watched the column of men out of sight, Sarah and the others turned back to home and endeavoured to carry on with their lives. Everyone was concerned for Mary, trying to protect and encourage her. But that day Sarah felt another anxiety creep into her heart. This was for Betsy. She followed her up Rag Street and realised suddenly how thin and bowed she had become, more than the lack of food and rest should have entailed. She watched her all that day, and in the quiet, dusk-laden evening, she called her out into the garden.

"Let's sit here for a few minutes. It's so peaceful," and when they sat together on the stone seat, she put an arm around Betsy's shoulders. "I've been neglecting you," she said gently, "with everything else to think about. You've been so brave coping with Ned's death, and we all rely on you so much."

Suddenly she realised that Betsy was crying, quietly but with such tearing sobs, that Sarah was frightened. "Oh, please," she said, "I'm so sorry. I didn't mean to upset you," and she repeated, "You've been so brave."

"But I'm not," Betsy shook her head. "I told you I knew Ned was dead long before the news came, and now, now he's slipping from my mind. Sometimes I can hardly remember his face." Sarah tightened her arm around Betsy while she struggled to think of the right thing to say, and as always at times like this wished her father was here with his sound common-sense. Please God he wouldn't be away long, and she knew she mustn't worry her mother.

"You have to get on with your life, and look after Nat," she said after a pause. "That's why we're glad that Matthew can help you." Betsy's sobs increased rather than eased at these words. "But I feel so bad, that I - I care for Matthew so soon." Poor Sarah really felt out of her depth now, nothing in her short life had prepared her for this. "Try not to worry, my love. Just take things as they come. I'm sure it will all be all right. Now, come along to bed. It's getting late."

Sarah lay awake for a long time that night, thinking as she always did of John and trying to imagine - without success - a time when if he should not return to her she would not be able to remember his beloved face. But just before she fell asleep, she recalled overhearing her mother talking to her father before the war, when one of his outworkers had died suddenly leaving a widow and five children. Mary had said: "It's to be hoped that she'll soon find another pair of hands to work for her and provide for them all," and at the time Sarah had not really understood her father's answer, given with a sigh. "Yes, feelings have to be suppressed in the need for survival, but it would be good if there's room for some happiness." She understood now and she'd tell Betsy as soon as they had a few quiet minutes together.

No news came into the town for the next few days, till early one morning Sarah was wakened by a loud knocking on the front door. She jumped out of bed and ran down the stairs, shivering in the chilly air, for autumn had come early that year. Betsy was not far behind her as she opened the heavy door, and for the second time in recent months, Sarah did not at first recognise who was standing on the threshold - not until he stretched out long, thin arms to her.

Then, with a cry - part joy, part fear - Sarah caught him as John fell forward across the doorway, and without a word she and Betsy half-dragged, half-carried him through to the living-room, as they had Matthew not long before. Although deathly pale, he had only fainted for a moment, and was able to fall back into Richard's great chair with help from the two women. Betsy, ever practical, ran experienced eyes over the boy, and saw that although dirty and ragged, there was no sign of bleeding or of broken limbs. She hurried to the kitchen to fetch water and cloths, while Sarah, now that she had him safe, knelt beside him, cradling him in her arms, shocked at how thin and gaunt he was. She had not thought he could get thinner when he had marched out of Plymouth, but the bones of his wrists seemed almost to protrude through the skin, and she saw an angry black bruise reaching right down one arm.

"Was it very bad?" she whispered, gently pushing the lank dark hair back from his face. His eyes did not leave hers.

"Sarah, Sarah," he said, his voice hoarse and dry, "I had not thought to see you again. Those they took prisoner, including me, were thrown into Saltash fort, where Skellum Grenville took pleasure in seeing us ill-treated," and his lips tightened at the memory. Betsy had returned now, and Mary hurried into the room at the same time. She carried a tray with ale, bread, cheese and porridge, and set it down beside John. "I think he needs this before we make him clean," she said, with something of her old authority and the boy ate and drank hungrily.

94

Later when they had made him comfortable, all the family gathered around John's chair eagerly questioning him. The boys had joined them now, and James especially wanted to hear all about the fighting. But Mary had more particular concerns. How were you freed?" she asked. "Did you see your rescuers?" John sat forward, his eyes alight. "Oh yes," he said, excitedly. "We could hear the fighting outside then after what seemed a long time it went quiet, and suddenly the door of the cellar where we were was flung open and a Roundhead officer stood there. He was tall and had a look of command and never was I so glad to see anyone. Then he said, loud and clear: 'Is there a John Luscombe here?' I moved forward, and he examined me. 'I have been instructed to look for you, Master Luscombe - my daughter's orders were precise,' and though his face was stern his eyes were smiling."

"It was father," and "It was Richard." Sarah and Mary spoke together. "Yes, it was, and he organised an escort back for all the prisoners, while he and the troop went on."

He sank back in his chair now, exhausted. Mary thought he should go to his bed to rest properly, but he insisted that was not necessary. "Let me stay amongst you all," he pleaded. "I am not hurt, only weary, and I want to feel you all around me for this day. Tomorrow I must go back to the barracks." So it was, and the family paid him visits all that day, while Sarah found so many reasons to linger there that her mother said at last: "Stay with him, child, for a while at least, for you're no use to me today." Apart from her own happiness, Sarah was glad to see the increasing strength her mother seemed to have acquired.

Matthew came home for a few hours that evening, so John's story had to be told again, and it wasn't till later that Sarah and he shared a few quiet minutes before they went to bed. Mary had already said to her daughter: "Now, Sarah, it's getting late and John needs a good night's sleep. There'll be plenty of time to talk later." But John caught Sarah's hand as they sat close together on the long bench in the living room. It was too chilly for the garden now, and fuel was short so fires had to be saved for the really cold weather. But the young people's thoughts were not on the weather or the temperature.

For a moment neither of them spoke, then John said, his eyes serious, "You know Sarah, it wasn't what I expected." "You couldn't have known how awful it would be, but you're safe home now," Sarah tried to comfort him. But he looked straight at her. "No, it's not that. It's just that I've thought till now this war was a great adventure, a good cause. Oh, I'm not doubting the importance of the cause, but it's war itself, especially a war like this - it's cruel and savage and people just destroy each other, even some they know. I'll be glad when it's over. I'll never enlist again." Sarah was surprised at the vehemence of his words. "But there was nothing else to be done. Father was very sure - he would not have gone otherwise." "Oh yes, I know, it's - it's just the way I feel and I wanted to tell you."

Charles had left Skellum Grenville behind to command all the Royalist troops in the area and for the last two months of 1644 he harried Plymouth continually, so that the townspeople were constantly on the alert. On one occasion he tried to set fire to the town, and on another to bribe discontented soldiers within the garrison to blow up the magazine. Both attempts failed.

The winter that led into '45 was severe, and food became very scarce, both for the townspeople and the garrison and their horses. Then the navy captured two Royalist ships bound for Topsham and Exeter and their cargoes provided the town with desperately needed money and food. "It's another miracle," the people said, "like the shoal of fish. God has not forsaken us."

Throughout the early months of '45, it was evident that Grenville was determined to break through Plymouth's defences. The townspeople watched fearfully as more Royalist troops joined him and made their preparations outside the walls. The family in Rag Street were as concerned as all their friends and neighbours. Matthew and John scarcely ever got home for a break. Every able man was called to work on the defences, and to man them, and even the not so able were given tasks to do. Francis set aside the work of the family business and joined the band of labourers, while even James and his friends carried baskets of stones to the ramparts, their energies finding new outlets. Mary was worried about him, but Sarah persuaded her that the work was necessary and that in fact he was less likely to get into trouble there.

The women themselves took what food they could to the walls, little enough though it was, and Sarah knew that her mother thought constantly as she did herself of Richard, wishing he were there, but hoping at the same time that he was safe, and out of Grenville's grasp.

There had recently been established a Plymouth Committee of Defence, led by Lord Robartes and this Committee organised the resistence against the fierce assaults of these months.

Then in early March, after a week of quiet, Grenville made a sudden assault on Plymouth's line of fortifications, throwing six thousand men into the attack. The Maudlyn Fort was captured for a short while, but eventually the Royalists were thrown back down the hill. The next day, Grenville took Mount Stamford, but the Plymouth authorities realising the danger to the town's shipping, reinforced the nearby Fort Batten garrison. From here and from the ships in the Cattewater, the Parliamentary artillery pounded the new Royalist position all day, and at last Stamford was stormed and recaptured.

This success gave the people new heart and a welcome respite from attack. It was on one of those few nights of quiet that Richard and his men got back through the fortifications into the town.

John was on look-out duty near the main gate, and gave the warning as he saw shadowy figures moving outside. As the men of the guard waited, arms at the ready, a voice was heard giving the password - "God be with us - God save Parliament." "It's Captain Jewell and his men." They were identified and quickly admitted, John very pleased to say, "Welcome back, Captain. They'll all be pleased to see you."

This was an understatement, for a few hours later there was great relief in the house in Rag Street. Richard was home - safe and unscathed, "with few casualties," he said thankfully, "and we accomplished what we set out to do and I've sent men further into Cornwall."

John and Matthew got home too for a few hours. It was midday and they all sat round the great table enjoying the best meal that the women could put together, frugal though it was.

The room was shabby, the heavy furniture dull, for there was no beeswax left, but Sarah looked from one smiling face to another. They were all together for this day at any rate, and that was really all that mattered.

Chapter Seventeen

AS THE MONTHS OF 1645 moved on, it became evident to the Plymouth Committee of Defence that the course of the war was gradually improving for the Roundheads, for Parliament became more able and willing to provide the town with funds. Shortage of money had been a difficulty all through the fighting. Constantly the Council had been forced to borrow from loyal supporters within the town to pay labourers and soldiers, who threatened to withdraw their services if payment was not forthcoming. It was always a struggle to pay for goods and repairs, but now creditors had only to wait for the next ship carrying suppplies and money to arrive from London to be reimbursed.

As far as attacks from the Royalists occurred though, they, strangely enough, increased with the Roundhead successes, for more and more Royalist troops were falling back to the west. The assaults on the town were not much more than skirmishes, but the defenders could not relax, for they never knew what lay ahead. Yet there seemed a glimmer of hope in people's hearts, and for the Jewell family particularly, for all their members were within reach, and whenever duties allowed, were altogether under one roof. They even dared to hope that the war would soon be over.

Sarah and John talked of this in the garden as the evenings got longer and milder. "I shall be fifteen in August," Sarah said on one such day. "Mother was just that age when she and father were married." John stroked her hands that lay in her lap. "How old was your father?" She didn't look at him. "He was eighteen, I think." "I shall be eighteen in September. Do you think we could be married this summer, or at least some time this year?"

Sarah did glance at him then - shyly at first, but as he smiled at her and reached out to take her in his arms, she went to him as willingly as he to her.

Richard was on duty that night, but the next evening, when supper was over, Sarah and John stood close together by the great table.

"Can we talk to you, father, and mother too?" Her parents looked at each other, exchanging a glance that held little of surprise in it.

The boys were both out and with Nat safely tucked up in bed, Betsy had gone for a walk along the beach with Matthew. "We'll never get a better time," thought Sarah. Mary lay aside her pile of mending, and Richard the papers about the business that he had been working on in a rare few minutes taken from the affairs of war.

"Come and sit down," he said now to the young people, "and tell us what this is about."

They obeyed, still looking very self-conscious and nervous. Richard smiled at them. "This must be serious," he said, his tone teasing. "I've never known my daughter at a loss for words before." Sarah stood up quickly, ready to speak, but John put a restraining hand on her shoulder and got to his own feet. He cleared his throat.

"Yes, sir, this is a serious matter for both of us, of great importance in fact. We want to ask your permission to be married."

Sarah couldn't hold back any longer. "Yes, as soon as possible, please, father, do say 'yes'." "I wish you'd both sit down," Richard said again, "we can talk much more comfortably that way." He sat back in his chair and looked at them for a moment without speaking.

Then it was Mary's turn to show impatience. "Richard, don't keep them waiting. They have suffered enough this last year." "I know, my dear, but this is a serious matter." He turned again to the young people. "I do not doubt that you care for each other." Sarah recovered her voice at this. "Oh yes, we do, very much," and the look that passed between her and John then brought tears to Mary's own eyes.

"But," Richard continued, "you are both very young." "Not much younger than you and mother were when you married," Sarah interrupted again, and Richar's expression became stern.

"Please let me finish. This is not a time for idle chat. Conditions were different when we married. There was no war which had taken over our lives. Things seemed settled. I was already working with Ephraim Goodyeare in a good business. We had planned our life together."

He turned to John now. "You have served well as a soldier, and Mistress Jewell and I have both grown very fond of you. I know too that you have been studying accounting with Francis, but I would say that your future is very uncertain, and I - both of us - need to know that Sarah will be well looked after before we agree to your marriage."

John's dark eyes were serious now. "I do respect all you say, sir, and I will always look after Sarah. We've thought a lot about what we'll do - what we'd like to do - after the war. Master Perryman has offered me a chance to work with him, to rebuild his grocery business. As you know, he is not fit and cannot manage alone. I think I could make a success of it."

Richard seemed pleased at his reply. "That sounds most admirable," he said, "and I'm sure I could help you with affairs of that nature." He turned to Sarah now. "I presume this would all meet with your approval?" "Oh, yes, father, it would, and I would work very hard too. And do you think the war will soon be over? People seem to be talking as though it might." Richard nodded. "There are signs of hope, but I fear there may still be much fighting yet. We only see what goes on in our corner of the Kingdom, but I do know that many miles away a campaign is building up. Still, we have to plan for happier times, and I am glad that you are both so doing. However," and he paused, so that both the young people looked at him in concern, wondering what dire decision awaited them. "However," and he turned to Mary for confirmation, "I think we both feel that it would be prudent to wait, just for a while, to ensure that the turn of events is in the right direction, and meanwhile you can both make plans - and that can be very satisfying."

Sarah's frown seemed to doubt this, but she knew there was a limit to which she could push her father, and was very relieved at the progress they had made. "When do you think," she asked tentatively.

"Shall we set our minds towards the year's end, or perhaps next year's beginning?" And at the look of pure joy that illumined both their faces, he picked up his papers again, smiled at them both and held out a hand to Sarah. "Come and kiss me, my child, and say you're happy to stay with us a bit longer." There was a sudden surge of movement. Sarah, crying and laughing together, had her arms around both her parents, while Mary, her tears too mingling with her laughter, kissed them both, John having to bend down to allow her to reach him and then finding his hand shaken in Richard's strong grip.

With Betsy and Matthew to tell, plus Francis and James when they all came home soon afterwards, it was late before the household finally settled for sleep that night.

A few days after this momentous evening, Robartes was recalled to London, although Plymouth protested, praising him for his defence of the town. A Committee of five were appointed to replace him, with Colonel Kerr in complete military control, and Richard was elected to be one of the five. This meant that he was away from home even more often, but Mary accepted this thankfully, knowing that he was still within the walls of the town.

Sarah was deliriously happy at this time, and in spite of increasing shortages, she seemed to bloom. No job was too tiring or exacting for her, and although there was, by now, little to spare in household linen or utensils, yet with her mother's help, she altered and mended, embroidered and knitted, watching with great delight as the pile in the beautiful carved oak chest that Mary had given her, slowly grew. Her time spent with John was precious, and full of plans, and indeed one of her few fears was that he would be sent out on a campaign from the town before the war could end. Sometimes, though not very often, for seldom were both home at the same time, John and Richard would talk together and Sarah would delight in this, knowing that it was business affairs they were discussing and matters that would prove to be part of her future life. She was glad, too, that the two men got on so well, their mutual respect and liking developing as the months went by.

There was however a tiny cloud on Sarah's horizon, which she tried not to let develop into anything more. This was concerning her mother, for although Mary's health had rapidly improved from the day Richard returned home, her strength was still limited and she tired easily. Sarah often saw Richard looking at her with concern, and one lovely day, towards the end of May, when Sarah was sorting a basket of laundry in the kitchen, Richard came in looking for his wife. Sarah said, to relieve the anxiety she could see in his eyes, "She's resting for a little, father. We've had a busy morning and I persuaded her to lie on her bed, but she's not ill."

"You're a good little maid, we seem to rely on you more and more. Your mother's strength has never really come back, has it?" "I'm sure it will when the warm weather arrives," Sarah tried to comfort her father. "She always seems better when it's hot and sunny," and then, as he turned away to put down the books he was carrying, Sarah went on: "Do not worry about what will happen when I am married. John and I have talked about it, and if we have a little house of our own, I will always come back for part of each day to help out here, like Betsy did when she married Ned."

"Bless you, my love," and with a sigh he laid an affectionate hand on her shoulder. To divert him from the concern she saw was still in his eyes, Sarah continued: "I wonder if there'll be another wedding later this year. Betsy and Matthew seem very close." "Yes, I had noticed," Richard observed, "another change to contemplate," and Sarah wondered if she should have mentioned this.

In June news trickled through to the town of the engagement mentioned earlier by Richard. It was far off, right at the centre of the country, near Leicester, came one message, between Market Harborough and Northampton, said another. In fact this great battle took place at Naseby, on June 14th, and it was a great victory for Cromwell's New Model Army, led by Colonel Ireton and General Fairfax, with cavalry and foot soldiers utterly destroying the Royalist troops, and it was said the king fled to Wales or Scotland, seeking to raise another army.

Richard brought all this news home to the family as it was received by the Committee, and now within the town there was a feeling of waiting, just as there had been before the siege - so long ago it seemed now. Fairfax moved west, and in July took the important town of Bridgwater. Surely it would not be long before he reached Devon and Plymouth and all would finally be well.

The people waited as Autumn approached, defending the town against assaults, trying to keep their spirits light, making do with what supplies they had, and dreading the approach of another winter. Even Sarah and John, with the brightness of their future to sustain them found it hard to be cheerful.

Then new hope came, for a message had been sent to Parliament asking for help and, especially, that Fairfax should come to them. Early November brought the reply. The Committee received it with mixed reactions, for while a grant of £10,000 was agreed for the immediate relief of the town, Fairfax (under winter conditions) was to come no futher west than Exeter, and with that they had to be content.

December passed almost peacefully, and Christmas services were held in the partially constructed new parish church. The tar-paulins were removed and the people's own vicar, Reverend Forde, led the worship. As they stood together, Sarah whispered to John: "I should like to be married here," and he nodded and squeezed her hand in agreement.

The wedding was finally arranged for the end of January. "Come what may," Richard said, and they all echoed "Come what may."

Look-outs still kept constant watch along the Plymouth walls, but more to search for approaching Parliamentary troops now than enemy Royalist ones, and on January 16th their patience was rewarded. Clouds of dust, then drum beats and marching feet, and Parliament's army had arrived.

The news spread like wild-fire, gates were flung open, and the troops were welcomed until the town could contain no more, and camps were set up outside the walls.

Rejoicing was great, treasured food stores were willingly brought out and added to the supplies the army provided, so that celebratory meals were shared by all.

The long siege was over at last and thanksgiving and relief flooded through every household - weakness, sickness and hunger forgotten for these first few days.

Richard and the rest of the Committee welcomed their res-cuers and had long meetings with the Commanders. These were disappointed that Fairfax was not with them, but the news was that he would arrive within weeks with Oliver Cromwell himself, so great plans were made to entertain them both.

A few days after the final relief of the town, John and Sarah walked across the beach and in spite of the damp wind blowing from the sea, they sat together on the great flat stone, Sarah's cloak wrapped around them both for John's coat was thin and skimpy. They sighed in contentment.

"This is going to be a good year, I am sure," Sarah said. "We shall remember 1646 for a long time to come," and John, his arm about her waist nodded in fervent agreement. "It'll be our year," he said, "beginning with our wedding in just one week's time," and the kiss they exchanged was a benediction of hope.

Chapter Eighteen

IT WAS LATE MAY in 1660, fine, but still cold. St.Andrew's Church seemed to Sarah more chilly than she could ever remember it, even in winter. It was true that she had seldom entered the Church for several years, not since Friends had first come to Plymouth, and John, her husband, had had to wrestle with his conscience to cross the threshold of a steeple-house to-day. But this was a special - special and very sad occasion, for it was the funeral of Richard Jewell - Sarah's beloved father. He had sometimes accompanied them to Quaker meetings, but his heart never really left the Presbyterian religion in which he had spent his life and in support of which he had followed Cromwell.

He and his dear Mary had been married in this Church, and she had lain buried in the churchyard beyond since 1650. So, in his last days, with his family gathered around him, Richard had said that this was where he wanted to be mourned and laid to rest. Sarah glanced up at John, her husband of fourteen years, standing straight and tall beside her, and then at their children on either side of them - John Richard, twelve years old and already tall and thin like his father had been as he had grown into manhood; Elizabeth at nine giving promise of Sarah's own slim fairness, which had hardly changed over the years; William six years old, as dark as his father, but in his mischievous escapades reminding Sarah of her own younger brother James, while Mary, just two and holding tightly now to her mother's hand, had such a look of that other Mary, with her brown hair and bonny plumpness that Sarah's heart was often touched as she watched her trotting busily about the house, eager to help in all that went on.

The service finished, the mourners, with downcast faces, walked quietly out into the churchyard, and to the open grave. A feeble sun appeared through the clouds, and Sarah, looking up at the great oak tree, its leaves fresh and green, felt comforted as though her father was smiling down on them. Even the children were subdued as they waited for everyone to gather and the vicar to prepare himself for the committal. Sarah was grateful to see how many of the townspeople had come to say farewell to Richard. He had lived all of his fifty-three years in Plymouth and had served it well in war and in peace as a leading businessman and a councillor for many years. He had worked hard to rebuild the trade of the town after the war, and to make provision for those who suffered the greatest misery, and he was greatly loved for it.

Some of their neighbours and friends greeted Sarah and John with respectful sympathy but others avoided them, huddling together at the other side of the grave. Sarah and John had become used to this treatment, for there was much opposition to Friends in the town. There were so many sects now, thought Sarah, not just the two divided by the war, there were Independents, Fifth Monarchists, and strongest of all as the years of the Commonwealth proceeded, the Baptists. But the Quakers, from the arrival of the first two Friends, with strange Northern accents, in 1654, had drawn much hostility from the other churches and the town leaders. As Sarah watched the coffin lowered slowly into the ground, and scattered earth upon it, she wondered with a sigh why it was that all the other religious groups seemed to agree in a common dislike of Quakers. Then, as she gathered the children together, she said a silent prayer for her father's spirit, and for those of her first two babies who had been stillborn and were buried in the same grave, and taking John's arm, led the family and closest friends back to Rag Street, and she remembered that as John had often reminded her, the whole way of life of Friends, as they sought to "follow the light in everyone" was a threat to the established social hierarchy of all other groups and cut right through their strict moral code, and rigid disciplines.

As they climbed the hill to the house in Rag Street, to the home that she had never left, for first Mary and then Richard had needed caring for, Sarah saw that Betsy and Matthew were there ahead of them. They had been married the year after Sarah and John in 1647, and had two growing girls of their own - Margaret and Joan, while Nat was a fine, broad-shouldered young man, soon to be married himself and working, as did Matthew, in the family business, headed now by Francis. Betsy had grown stout and short of breath, but she worked as hard and as cheerfully as ever, both in

106

her own home - one of the outworkers' cottages - and in helping Sarah at Rag Street.

She was already carrying a great jug of ale from the kitchen, and checking that all was ready on the long oak table for the refreshment of the mourners. Sarah went to her and put her arms around her, and the two women took comfort from each other. "I shall miss him, Betsy," and her old friend wiped away Sarah's tears with the corner of her apron as she had done so often when Sarah was a little girl. "So shall we all, my dear, but he had a good life and you looked after him well, and now he's with your dear mother," and with a final hug they straightened their caps and turned to welcome their friends.

The room was becoming crowded. As many as could sat on stools and benches around the long table, while latecomers were found places against the walls. Francis and James had carried down chairs and stools from the upper rooms and the children took their trenchers of food into the kitchen and garden. Sarah and Betsy attended to everyone's needs while John had a word of welcome for each visitor, his dark eyes wise and kind, now turning constantly to his wife, and she, feeling his gaze upon her, would return it with a smile. People spoke warmly of Richard and many men stood in tribute to him, promising that all the efforts he had made for the good of the town would not be allowed to go to waste. John Light, grey-haired and a little bent now, praised the way in which Richard had struggled to rebuild the woollen trade, which like most industries, had been virtually destroyed by the war. "He gave his life for Plymouth and its people," he said, and many heads nodded in agreement. Sarah knew this was true for she had often tried, without success, to make him rest, until that dreadful day when she had found him collapsed on his bed. A week later he was dead. She felt the tears spring to her eyes now, and was glad of John's comforting arm around he. "Art thou all right, my love? Come and sit down. Everyone is taken care of." But she just patted his hand. "Don't worry, I'm managing very well" and she continued to move among the guests, passing bread, cheese, and slices of pie. Gradually people took their leave, until just the family, and those who were almost so, remained. Betsy brought in another pitcher of ale, and everyone sat thankfully, glad to rest after all the stress of the day. Elizabeth Perryman took a seat beside Sarah on the long bench. Peter had died some years earlier, and his widow had become very close to the family in Rag Street, spending much time with them and helping to look after the children whom she loved dearly, for she had none of her own. She looked upon John almost as a son too, for he had taken over the grocery business and was building it into a thriving concern preparing his son John-Richard to join him there in a few years

Suddenly there was the sound of young voices and William and Mary ran into the room, together with a medley of children, all shepherded by Elizabeth, conscious of the responsibility her nine years gave her. They all sought their parents, two small boys with straight fair hair and serious expressions finding Francis and his wife, Ann, while a dark little lad with the roguish expression his father had once had and a small girl about a year younger, ran to James and Rachel. Francis' children were Joshua and Thomas, and those of James were Oliver and Katherine - usually known as Kate. Matthew joined them with Nat and Margaret and Joan, almost grown-up at ten and eleven, and Sarah, looking around the room, felt that the family was as complete as it could be with the loss now of its beloved head. As though following her thoughts, John looked across at Francis. "Thou art the head of the family now, brother, and I know that we will all look to thee for leadership in family matters." Everyone murmured agreement and Francis, who had become no more self-assured over the years, blushed and answered quietly: "Thank you, brother. I shall do my best." Joshua's expression changed from serious to playful and he looked up at his father. "Why does Uncle John say 'thee' and 'thou' when he speaks to us. That's usually the way we speak to servants or workpeople, and I heard him say it to the Mayor the other day." John smiled at the boy. "That's precisely why we do it. Quakers believe in the equality of all men - and women - so we try to remember this at all times." "I have tried to explain this," Francis defended his son, "but it's hard for the young to remember sometimes." "I remember, I remember," called out Oliver proudly, and James ruffled his hair affectionately. As Sarah looked at her brothers, the one who surprised her the most was this same James. Once he had shed his wild ways, he had settled into a life of serious service. He had become a miller and had brought many new methods and improvements to that industry at which he worked hard, but his real love was for politics. He was a member of the Council, and already at twenty-seven his opinion was sought and respected.

As with the rest of the family, except for Francis who was still wary of change, John was already a deeply committed Quaker, and now looking around the room he said quietly: "Shall we go into Meeting, Friends?" and moving their stools as far as possible into a circle, with the children sitting on the floor in the middle, the Meeting for Worship began. Gradually as silence and then a stillness settled on the little group, and it became a deep, shared experience, Sarah felt the grief lift a little from her heart and a peace enter it. The children were very quiet, even the little ones, as though they knew that the Meeting was for them too. Elizabeth Perryman had a message to give, followed by Matthew and finally John, and then after a few minutes more, the shaking of hands closed the meeting.

Later that evening, when their friends had gone and the children were in bed, Sarah and John took their customary few moments together in the garden. However busy they were, they had always through the years tried to save this time for themselves and it was very precious to them both.

"To-night I feel as if the world - or my part of it - is turned upside down. Father's dying seems to mark the end of an era even more than the war itself." Sarah reached out her hand to John, drawing closer to him on the stone seat. He nodded in agreement. "A lot has happened to us and there's more to come. It cannot be long now before we have another Charles as king over us." "Will things be worse then for our people? So many are in prison at the moment?" John put his arm around his wife. "I cannot see, my love, that it will be, for we suffer as much from the Puritans and the Baptists as we do from Royalists and High Church men. But we are growing and the light is being spread. I think sometimes just how much strength we have gained since John Audland and Thomas Arey first came to publish the truth in Plymouth - and it was only six years ago."

Sarah's eyes shone. "Yes, and that wonderful visit from George Fox the next year, even if it ended for him in Launceston gaol," and they both fell silent with their memories, till they rose a few minutes later, and with arms entwined walked back into the house.

Chapter Nineteen

SARAH'S FEELING OF everything in the world changing stayed with her at this time. As she worked about the house and tended to the family's needs, she thought how different her town was now from the days of her childhood, the days before the war. She knew that many thousands of people had died during and after the siege, both townspeople and soldiers, for disease had been rife and the people were weakened by hunger and scarcities of all kinds. As for the garrison, at the worst times, many were buried where they fell. The countryside around Plymouth suffered as well, stripped as it had been by the besieging forces , it was long before many farms were able to produce crops again. Sarah, as far as her numerous duties allowed, absorbed and tried to understand all that went on around her, and John - together with James - would share with her what they knew of happenings in Plymouth at this time and of national events. Cromwell had died in 1658 and Sarah often thought that the arrival of this news had perhaps hastened her father's death, for Richard had come to know the Protector over the years and to hold him in great esteem, whereas his son, another Richard, never fulfilled his father's hopes for him and could not hold the country together. He retired into obscurity in May 1659 and the new Parliament elected after many struggles in April 1660, had restored the House of Lords and agreed to the return of Charles II.

As she waited for John to return from work on an evening in early June, Sarah expected that he would have news of this event, and knew too that he would say - for he often had of late - that Plymouth had felt let down many times by Parliament during the war and afterwards, and so many people were prepared to accept a new monarch. With William Morice newly appointed Governor of Plymouth, already a Knight and an M.P., and, it was said, a friend of John Grenville, emissary of the King in exile, perhaps the scene was set. In addition, many old Parliamentary men of property, like Robartes in Cornwall, preferred the idea of a King to an England controlled by radical sects.

But as she tucked little Mary into bed, and smoothed the soft brown curls from the clear brow, Sarah thought most of the Friends and how they were coping, and how, in spite of all the dangers and difficulties, the blessings that had come with this new faith, were beyond price. She looked out of the chamber window for a moment (stolen from her duties) across the Sound, remembering how she had gazed in that direction, into Cornwall, each evening when John was away fighting, knowing that he would be thinking of her as well. So much had happened since then, and especially since the arrival of those first two Friends - part of the "publishers of the truth" who had been sent out to do just that, and she remembered how John Audland had gone into St.Andrew's Church and testified against the preaching there and the ills of the day, while Thomas Arey had done the same thing in the Baptist meeting house, and the people had turned upon them. Yet, though they stayed less than a week in Plymouth, they gained many faithful followers - the merchant Arthur Cotton, John Harris, who farmed at Pennycross, and shopkeeper Robert Cary, all of whom were now close friends of Sarah and John.

The early summer evening was becoming dim, and Sarah was getting anxious as she did whenever John was late. Although she tried to remain calm, it was difficult for there were so many dangers that could overtake him, and not only from the enemies of the Quakers, for the town was full of beggars, desperate in their need, but even as she sat quietly for a moment on the window seat trying to hold her whole being in stillness, she heard the front door open, and hurried to the hall to greet John. Robert Cary was with him, and the two men had serious faces. Robert apologised for disturbing Sarah at such a late hour but she quickly led them both to the table and plied them with food and drink.

"We have had news," John said to his wife, "of more Friends held in Exeter Bridewell. There will be families to care for, I am sure. And more than that Priscilla Cotton is being held to-night in the cells under the town hall, and you know how much we all owe to her and to Arthur. We can do nothing to-night, but will meet early tomorrow."

John showed Robert to the door, and came back to Sarah who was clearing away the remains of their supper. Then, before seeking their bed, they sat together quietly looking for guidance. "It is good," John said with a sigh, "that our dear Friend Thomas Salthouse returns to-morrow from Cornwall. We have much need of his wisdom and guidance."

So it was that the next morning the Friends gathered in the room behind Robert Cary's shop. By now, and after so many arrests, the Quakers were as well organised as they could be. They shared each other's work and responsibilities, between them kept their shops open and businesses running, though often with great difficulties.

Sarah had stayed in Rag Street this morning with her own children and those of other Friends who had hurried to the Meeting. James arrived with Mary Cole. "We have come straight from the Mayor, Friends, but he would not listen. Mary has offered to take Priscilla's place so that she can nurse Arthur but he will not allow it." "Our women will look after Arthur," was John's quick reply, "but what of Priscilla? Those cells are noisome and filthy." James shook his head. "She is to go to Exeter to-morrow, to await the assizes. She was taken without a cloak or shoes. We must see that she has them and food at any rate for a few days. Her spirit is unbreakable but we can ensure that her earthly needs are tended to, as far as possible." The Meeting closed, and the Friends departed on their various duties, Sarah, handing the care of the children to Elizabeth Perryman, hurried to the Cotton's house to care for Arthur for the first part of the day. He had a recurring fever and a heart weakened by overwork and bad conditions. As Sarah bathed his thin body and tried to feed him honeyed gruel, she marvelled, as did all the Friends, at the unquenchable spirit of this man and his wife, undoubted leaders of Plymouth Meeting. Arthur was a man of substance, most of which he spent on caring for the needy, and his education and intellect made him the natural ambassador between those who suffered and those in authority. By afternoon he seemed better again, thanking Sarah for her nursing of him. "If thou will care for my dear wife, I shall be grateful," he said. "And God will be with us all," and then as Robert Cary's wife came to relieve Sarah, he slipped into a peaceful sleep.

That evening there was a meeting in the Rag Street house, and the Friends took stock of their position, and expressed what needed to be done for the relief of all local Quakers. John Harris led the plans that were made. At last the Friends thankfully shared a short time of worship, satisfied that they had done all they could for the moment, and must leave the rest to God. Then, as the visitors were preparing to leave for their own homes, some already in the hallway, there was an urgent knocking on the front door and John, opening it, admitted James. "We wondered why thou didst not join us at Meeting." "I'm sorry, Friend, but I have been at the Council and have come straight from there. There is news that I was anxious to tell you all as soon as possible. We now have a King on the throne of England. There seems to be much rejoicing but I like it not. 'Tis said that wine will flow in the water pipes in celebration, but there is more to life than wine." The Friends turned back into the living-room, trying to imagine how life might be for them all and for Plymouth in the days that lay ahead. Even amongst their own small group, opinions differed, but none could deny that Plymouth's fortunes in the later days of the Commonwealth had suffered greatly. "We heard to-day that those six ships in the Sound are in a parlous state, the crews starving and more ships are expected soon whose conditions will be no better." "They cannot buy food for the navy has been paid no wages for several years," Robert Cary took up the story. "There'll be great need for Friends to collect what provisions we can and go to their aid." "I'll attend to that as early as possible tomorrow.," John was swift to offer his services, "and we'll borrow a boat from the fishermen to get to the ships, for many of those stand idle at this time." Sarah, hearing these words, thought again of her childhood, and of her friend Will, whose ambition it had been to sail to Newfoundland with the fleet and return at the end of the summer, loaded down with cod and herring, and she sighed for the freedom from care, or so it seemed at this distance of time away, of those days.

After this second meeting it was late before Sarah and John finally climbed the stairs to bed, and even then Sarah could see that John's mind was going over plans for the next day, saying as he bid her a fond good-night: "All needs are bound together, my love, whether it is the sustaining of Friends or the succouring of the poor and distressed, there is much for us to do for all the people of this town."

113

Chapter Twenty

IF JOHN'S THOUGHTS were mainly concerned with help for the needy and the persecuted, it was James who sought to right the wrongs that caused much of this suffering. But as the days of the monarchy continued the people's wave of hope and expectancy gradually faded, and James realised that this was to be no easy task. Charles had been in the west-country during the last months of the year, and knew just what part the town had played in his father's defeat, and the celebrations with which they had greeted his arrival did not wipe out what he saw as their past treason.

Indeed, the events of the next few years fulfilled the worst forebodings of James and his fellow councillors, for Plymouth was singled out for special punishment, and in a campaign which became known as the Plymouth Bartholomew (for much of it took place on St. Bartholomew's Day), he took his vengeance.

But now it was still 1660, and Sarah and the others were more concerned with the lives of those immediately around them, and with caring for their own families and neighbours. Friends were much exercised about where to hold their Meetings. During the Commonwealth period, though there was no legal obstacle against it, Quakers could not afford to provide a regular Meeting House, but met in each other's homes, but now the reaction against all dissenters that came with the Restoration made matters more difficult, while in 1664 the passing of the Conventicle Act was to render illegal all religious meetings of more than five people, except within the Church of England.

However, from 1660 meetings were held in a house owned by John Harris of Pennycross and situated almost on the Hoe itself, with a graveyard adjacent to it. All the Friends contributed benches and stools to the Meeting House to refurbish it and they kept it neat and clean, so that in its quiet simplicity it soon became a place of peace and renewal. Sarah valued it greatly and it was her delight to ensure that a jar of fresh flowers - either from her own garden or from the fields and hedgerows just outside the town always brightened the sturdy oak table which had been carved with loving care by John. His skill with wood had slowly developed after he and Sarah were married, when he had attempted, at first with diffidence, and then with growing interest and confidence, items for the house and for Sarah's personal use. She had been greatly pleased by his first gift to her - a butter mould, ornamented with tiny carved sea-shells, and it occupied pride of place in her dairy, beside that made for Mary so long ago by Richard. John had also made attractive containers for many of the goods he sold in the grocer's shop, and a special stool for each new child as it arrived, the name carefully cut into the wood of one of the legs. The cradle, though, which had rocked to sleep Sarah and her brothers as well as her own children, was as strong and comfortable as ever it had been, its surface worn smooth and shining by much polishing by hands that were gentle but firm in their care and concern. So it was that 1660 was a year of comparative quiet and safety for the Quakers and townspeople of Plymouth in general, and the Friends began to feel that perhaps they had nothing to fear from Charles II, for they had never been actively disloyal to the monarchy.

Francis, James and John all had thriving businesses, and were able to help the poor and needy while the children of each family grew strong and bonny. John-Richard was quick at his lessons, and was already beginning to master simple basics of his father's trade, spending spare time in the shop and delighting to fetch culinary items for his mother, especially when deliberately she entrusted choice and quality to him. William and Mary were happy children, loving to go, as Sarah had herself, to the beach to look for shell fish and attractive pebbles. Sarah would sit on the same big, flat stone, watching them and delighting in each new discovery they made. But it was probably her elder daughter, Elizabeth, who was the closest to her heart, for she could see again in her development, her own life as it had unfolded, and she prayed and fervently hoped that some day Elizabeth would find the happiness that she herself knew. She was glad too, remembering how important Richard had been to her, that her daughter had the same kind of closeness with John, and rejoiced in the time they were able to spend together, and whenever in the evenings she saw John lay aside his accounts and welcome Elizabeth who came to him with some question or problem and with a smile reach out a hand to this tall, fair daughter, her own heart warmed with thankfulness.

Betsy's son Nat was married that summer to Jane, from one of the fishing families, and the sun shone through the windows of the new Meeting House on the simple ceremony, the first to be held there, and on the young couple, surrounded by family and friends. The women prepared a meal in the garden of the Meeting House, and Sarah smiled to see the children (as she and Will once had) take their trenchers of pasties and tarts and find places to sit under the spreading oak trees. She did not hear John come to her across the grass, and turned quickly as she felt his arm on her shoulder. "Is that a secret smile, my love?" he asked her and she, remembering how he had comforted her when Will was killed, lovingly returned his smile. "Just a fleeting moment of my youth returned," she said. "Now come and have something to eat."

But this time of peace was short-lived for the King, dependent on his Anglican supporters, was nervous, and a Fifth Monarchy uprising in London in June 1661 resulted in all dissenters, including Quakers, being regarded as a danger to the state, and a campaign was instigated to destroy them, and on the tenth of the month the Government issued a proclamation prohibiting their meetings.

The news reached Plymouth almost immediately through a net-work of Friends, and a special meeting was called for to seek guidance as to what should be done. Sarah, John and the children hurried to the Meeting House, joined along the way by other Friends. Betsy and Matthew caught them up as they reached the Hoe, Betsy puffing in the cold air. "Oh Sarah, my dear," she panted as they crossed the last stretch of frosty grass together. "Is there danger for us all, dost thou think?" John hastened to reassure her. "We have had threats before and are no strangers to persecution. Do not be afraid." They joined the other Friends, and soon the little Meeting House was full.

John, standing by the oak table in the centre of the room, looked around him. "It seems that most of the Plymouth Friends are here, or at least someone from each household. Let us be quiet and seek the Light to guide us." But even as they waited, the stillness was shattered by a loud banging on the door. This burst open and a body of the magistrates' men rushed in, all armed, some with heavy cudgels and others with muskets. The Friends drew closer together, mothers gathering children to them, but all otherwise making no sound or movement. John spoke for them all. "This is a peaceful Meeting, Friends. May we not proceed?" The leader of the intruders, as tall as John himself, but much broader and heavier, stood squarely in front of him. "We've had our orders," he said roughly. "All these meetings are forbidden from now on and we've had orders to take all the men away." There was a gasp then from the Friends, but still no-one moved. John's gaze did not waver as he continued to look steadfastly at his opposer. "I do not question your orders, but cannot I be taken to stand for the rest, as a token? Some of the men amongst us are elderly, and in poor health." "It's too late to think of that," the man advanced menacingly, "we've got to get you lot to Exeter." "Can we not go home first?" This was Robert Cary. "We need to make provision for our families", "and see to our businesses" added John Light. But there was no mercy. "You're going straight from here, just as you are, so hurry up and get into a line." Arthur Cotton spoke then, leaning on the back of a bench and breathing with difficulty. "Stay in the Light, Friends, we will uphold each other whatever befalls, and our dear sisters and the children, I commend you to the care of each other and to God." Families embraced briefly, with the intruders anxious to be gone and pushing roughly at the Friends, hurrying the lingerers with their sticks. John kissed his children and held Sarah for a precious second, as did Francis Anna, and James Rachel, then with John Harris, Robert Cary, Arthur Cotton, John Light, John Martindale and the others, they were gone

The women and children crowded at the doorway, watching their men out of sight. Then, turning back into the room they sank down on to the benches. Everything had happened so quickly that they all felt stunned. At last, Priscilla Cotton rose to her feet. "We must be brave," she said,"and keep our homes and businesses going - and we must keep the Meeting till the men are back with us again. It is the only way we can support them. Come now, there is much to do."

It was a sad household that returned to Rag Street that day. Sarah insisted that Betsy and her girls came back there as well, for Matthew and Nat had gone and Nat's young bride Jane had returned in tears to her parents' cottage. Sarah and Betsy gathered the children together in the living-room and tried to make them aware, without frightening them, of what was happening. "We must all be brave," Sarah said. "There will be a lot for everyone to do, even you little ones, for father - and your father too" (she looked at Betsy's girls) "will be relying on us. John-Richard, I hope you will manage the shop as best you can." The lad stood up straight and tall, proud of the charge put upon him.

"You can depend on me, mother. I will keep everything going till father returns." "And you older girls, I shall trust you to look after the house for us for much of the time, for Betsy and I will be engaged in caring for Friends, and maintaining the Meeting." Even little Mary looked solemn as she gazed at the serious faces around her, and Sarah, lifting her to her lap, hugged the child. "All will be well," she said, smoothing the soft curls. "We shall all take care of each other and I know you and William will be good children."

Mary nodded, not really understanding what was going on, but still wanting to be part of it. Once the children had gone to bed, Sarah and Betsy sat together, talking and planning. "The worst part," Betsy said, warming her hands at the fire, "Is not knowing how long the men will be away, kept in that dreadful place," and her voice faltered. "Yes, but we can do something about that." Sarah spoke as firmly as she could. "We must get word to the Friends in Exeter, and they will visit the prison and take food and comfort to our men. I'm to see Priscilla Cotton tomorrow morning to make arrangements."

She had tried to sound positive for the sake of Betsy and the others, but as she lay awake late into the night, thinking and planning and worrying - for John especially - Sarah remembered her mother and how heavy the burden must have been for her when Richard was away. But she had shouldered it without complaint, and Sarah knew that she could do no less.

Chapter Twenty-One

IT WAS NEARLY THREE long months before the men of Plymouth came home, on a chill, damp day at the end of March 1661. Exeter Friends brought them to the Meeting House on the Hoe in two farm carts. The women and children had been waiting for them there since early in the day and now the afternoon was far spent. The children watched at the door, and sharp eyes spotted the little procession as it reached the last green slope. Eager hands helped the men from the carts and into the Meeting House. Arthur Cole was gently lowered to the ground first, and the women, with Priscilla going first, led him inside.

There were other casualties. John Light was limping, his leg bandaged, and young Nat, who was assisted by Matthew, had a dressing that covered his head and one eye - so that Betsy cried out when she saw him. The others were exhausted and battered but anxious wives were greatly relieved to see nothing worse.

There was silence with the first embraces, children clinging to their fathers' legs. Then the tears and laughter flowed together, the women holding their men at arm's length, anxiously examining them for signs of injury or sickness. Priscilla was so relieved to have Arthur back that she refused to be downcast. "Thou wilt soon be restored to health, my love," she said, holding him close, "with rest and care, good food and clean clothes." "Yes, they all need the last." Sarah laughed in her relief, for they were all dishevelled and ragged. She held John's hands for a long time, her eyes searching his face where an ugly bruise blackened one eye. Then he said, relinquishing her grasp, but with one arm still around her shoulders, "We have much to be thankful for, Friends. We have had some rough handling as you can see, but God has restored all of us to our families, and though Friends who were ailing before are a little frailer now, yet they are ills that can be mended. Shall we

119

have a Meeting for Worship now to give thanks for our deliverance and for the keeping in safety of our dear ones, and tomorrow we will meet again, for we have news to give you from Exeter, but 'twill keep a few hours more."

And so they sat in silence as the evening dusk crept into the room and peace passed from one anxious heart to the next, enveloping them all. Then, when it felt right, they all rose and made their various ways back across the Hoe to their homes, Robert Cary taking the Exeter Friends to his home for the night, where the horses could be stabled.

It was late as Elizabeth, John-Richard, William and Mary gathered around a John who was now clean and tidy once more. While Sarah bustled between kitchen and living room, preparing a meal for them all. "I am proud of you, my son, and tomorrow we shall go to the shop together that you may show me how you have managed." "Thank you, father," and John-Richard turned proudly and took a platter from his mother to place on the table. "I have good reports of you, Elizabeth, as well. Your mother tells me how much she has relied upon you these last weeks and how accomplished you have become in looking after the house," and their closeness was shown as always in the warmth of the smile they exchanged. "And you two," John picked up Mary and led William by the hand to their supper, ready now on the long table. "I believe you've been really good children all this while," and William grinned while Mary looked solemn, as was their wont.

Much later, the children in bed, there was time at last for Sarah and John to talk together, the first real chance they'd had since the men's return. "Thou art thinner than ever, my love" Sarah said. "I shall never get more flesh upon thee, I'm sure," and she stroked the bony wrists and long fingers. "Ah well, I was never meant to be plump and the Lord has made me strong, and we have come through another persecution." Sarah suddenly remembered something he had said earlier. "Is there news of great import that you have brought back from Exeter for Friends?" she asked him now, as they prepared for bed. "There are matters that need our attention," he answered as he stood for a moment at their chamber window, breathing in the sweet spring scents that thankfully seemed so far now from the noisome stench of Exeter Bridewell. "Our local Baptist friend, Pastor Abraham Cheare was brought into the prison while we were there, and we promised to look to his family and his flock." "I'm sorry that he has been taken again." Sarah's expression was troubled. "He is a good man, and even though not of our faith, he's been of a great help to us." "He has indeed, and it seems now that ill-treatment has spread to all dissenters, even the Presbyterians. 'Tis only the Anglican Church that is free to worship as it pleases. But times of adversity always produce good men and women and we have much to be grateful for." "Oh yes, indeed, and did you know husband that Thomas Salthouse has come back this last month to Plymouth from his journeys around the West Country - they are calling him the Apostle of the West - and he is to settle now in our town, which will be great encouragement to Friends hereabouts."

And so they talked late into the night, until at last, happily weary, they fell asleep, safe in their warm mutual security and knowing that much planning and discussion lay ahead of them.

There was indeed a great deal of news to contend with in the days and weeks that followed, for suddenly Charles stepped up his campaign of revenge on Plymouth, and sent down Commissioners from London to make a purge of the town's officials. With no opportunity of presenting a case in their defence, the Mayor, Aldermen and Councillors, six Magistrates and the Town Clerk were all ejected from office, and replaced by puppets of the King, the new mayor being William Jennens. As if this was not enough, Plymouth's ancient Charters were torn up and new ones made.

It was James who brought all this news to the Friends, coming straight from the Council House - from which he was now excluded, to Rag Street, where many Friends were gathered, and the anger he felt brought gentle reproofs from some of the Quakers. "We cannot control all the workings of our town," they said, " we must follow the Light and live in accordance with it."

But to James that could not be separated from striving against the causes of so much suffering, and he went home that night very indignant and concerned.

The rest of that year and 1662 brought great trials to all those who were trying to follow their consciences. William Jennens undertook his campaign with great zeal and thoroughness. George Hughes, the Vicar of St. Andrew's, who had himself persecuted the Quakers and other dissenters, was imprisoned on Drake's Island, which had by now become a state prison, a notorious place of incarceration and, as well as the Puritans, political opponents of the government were sent there and left to rot. Colonel Robert Lilburne, one of the judges of Charles I, died there, as did John Lambert, the Cromwellian general who had tried to establish a republic in place of the king's restoration.

Sarah often thought that matters were as bad now as they had been during the days of the War, worse in some ways, for it seemed sometimes that enemies were all around and that no-one outside their own immediate circle could be trusted. She knew that John had been greatly exercised about this for some time, and in the spring of '62, he called a meeting of all Friends, asking them to come by night to Rag Street. "It is not," as he explained to Sarah, "that we should be afraid to worship in our own Meeting House. For often when we are turned out from there we can gather on the grass, which is as holy as any building, but there are important things to discuss and we need to do this without interruption." So gradually in ones and twos the Friends climbed the hill to the Luscombe house and all were received and brought quickly inside. When all were assembled, and had shared a few minutes of quiet, John asked Arthur Cotton to speak to them. He was better in health at this time and stood firmly in their midst. "Several of you have realised for some time," he began, "that although the times are difficult for us now, we are not so alone as we were, for the Baptists and even the Presbyterians suffer as we do, and there can be a unity in this suffering. We are already helping each other, as you know, as in the case of our good Baptist friend, Abraham Cheare. And now Nicholas Sherwill whom many of you know as a Presbyterian and important merchant, has been released from Drake's Island." Many of those present nodded at the mention of the name, for his reputation was good. "He is to start what he calls a Unitarian Congregation in his own home, and many of the Puritan vicars who have been driven from their own Churches are doing the same thing. We hear they are coming in from villages outside of the town, from Plympton, Tamerton and Brixton, so be cheered, Friends, for there is this great movement towards freedom of worship here in Plymouth. It may not be here yet, but it must come."

122

Arthur sat down then, exhausted with the power of his message, and the silence with which it was received was deep and searching.

Other Friends spoke and finally John rose to tell them of business matters. "We understand," he said at last, "that a notice has been received from the Government in London asking for contributions for what they are pleased to call 'a Free and Voluntary Present for His Majesty'." He smiled around at his friends. "We still have to search our consciences as to what we contribute to this." He paused and then continued: "But I will send you home, my dear Friends, with news which will gladden your hearts, for we have heard to-day that there has gone to Charles a Peace Testimony from London Quakers, but representing us all, and it says in part - 'All bloody principles and practices we do utterly deny, with all outward wars and strife and fightings with outward weapons, for any end or for any pretence whatsoever, and this is our testimony to the whole world." He waited again, then looking around at the faces turned to him, he said: "If we are faithful now to this and all our testimonies, maybe in many years to come, they will be accepted by all men as guides to live by," and Sarah looked at her own children and thinking of future generations and of this town which she loved so much, fervently prayed that it would be so.

Chapter Twenty-two

THE EARLY 1660s WERE busy family years for Sarah, apart from all that went on around her in the life of the town. In 1662 John-Richard was fourteen and impatient to be finished with school and working all the time with his father. John saw a better future for him than he himself had known and consulted some of the Friends who were merchants in their own right, buying and selling goods at source. John realised that already Quakers were becoming known for honesty and fair-dealing and this trust in its turn caused them to prosper.

Amos Collier, in particular, took an interest in the boy, having only daughters of his own, and started to take him with him sometimes to the villages outside Plymouth, then to Exeter. John-Richard enjoyed these trips and came back excited at all he had seen and done and the transactions in which he had taken part. Then one day, Amos called at the house in Rag Street, asking if he might take John-Richard with him to Bristol. "We shall need to be gone for two or three weeks at least, but I will take good care of the lad."

Sarah was doubtful. It was a very long journey, much further away than any of them had ever been, and the roads were unsafe, with so many beggars and robbers. But as she put forward all these arguments, Sarah knew in her heart that she was afraid of this elder son of hers slipping away from her. Then, as he looked at her, with his father's dark, beseeching eyes, the excitement of a world outside Plymouth coursing through him, she prayed for strength to handle this well. Late that evening as she and John sat together in the garden - for the April air was mild and gentle - he looked at her with concern. "Thou art very quiet to-night, my love, and we had scarcely a word from thee at supper. What is it that causes thee such worries?" She poured out all her troubles to him and he listened with understanding, but still was firm in what he saw as the right thing to do. "He is growing to be a man," he said, "and we must allow him to find his own way. We have tried to teach him the truth by which to live but it is his own light that he must follow. One thing I can say of comfort," he continued, "they will not travel alone, for I believe there are several merchants planning to go together, so they should be safe. It will be a great adventure for him. We must accept that he is virtually a man now. Lads younger than he is were fighting in the war, remember?" Sarah shivered. "Let's hope that those times are well behind us now," she said.

The next morning they told John-Richard that he might go, and Amos too, so plans were made for the following week, Sarah making sure his simple wardrobe was adequate for the excursion, and spending one morning making pasties so that he should go well provided with these. William and the girls were very impressed at the importance of such a journey. "I heard Amos say the other day that the people of Bristol have a strange way of speaking, not like us, and it's hard sometimes to understand them." This from Elizabeth. "I shall manage, I am sure," said John-Richard proudly, "and I will tell you all about it when I return. There are great ships there with goods from -well - everywhere - and shops too, much bigger than ours."

But in the midst of all the preparation to send John-Richard off to Bristol, something else happened to divide Sarah's thoughts and concerns. Matthew came hurrying to Rag Street one morning, dishevelled and frightened. When she answered his frantic knocking, he caught her arm. "It's Betsy," he said. "I can't wake her. I've left the girls with her, but please, Sarah, come quickly."

Sarah paused only to call a few words of instruction to Elizabeth, then she was hurrying alongside Matthew up the street to Castle Lane and the cottage where her dear friend lived.

Her daughters were one on each side of the wide wooden bed, Joan holding tightly to one work-roughened hand, while Margaret wiped her mother's pale brow. They both turned as Sarah and Matthew hurried into the small room. Sarah pulled back the curtains and thrust open the tiny window. But as she drew near to the bed and felt the cold cheek, she knew with a sickening certainty that the life had left that well-loved body, and she felt a grief that she had only known with the death of her own parents.

Matthew and the two girls read the truth in her eyes and fell upon the figure in the bed, the tears and sobs of the girls mingling with their father's groans. For the rest of that day Sarah had no time to think of her own little grief for there was much to be done in the cottage. It was only late that evening when she and John sat together once more in the garden that she could give vent to her own feelings. "I can't imagine life without her," she cried into John's arms, while he held her close and tried to comfort her. "She came to mother when Francis was born, and thou knowest how much she was a sister to me. My dearest friend, and she never thought of herself," and there passed through Sarah's mind one after another the countless kind, unbidden deeds and words of good advice and encouragement which she had accepted without question from Betsy for the whole of her life, and there was desolation in the realisation that they would be no more. "And 'tis of no use for thee to tell me that it is God's will and must be accepted, for that I cannot do - not yet at any rate," and she glanced up at John with a tremulous attempt at a smile, for she knew how well her husband understood her and the rebellious spirit which still sometimes burst forth from her. He held her a few minutes more, then said gently: "Our faith is often tried - it must be so if we are to be Friends of the Truth and followers of the Light - but easing will come to thee and to us all. But now we must look to Matthew and Nat and the girls, for their need is the greater and remember, my love, that Betsy had a good life. She was no longer young - not many years from 50, I think - and she had been very tired of late," and Sarah, remembering all of this, tried to find comfort.

The little Meeting House was full for Betsy's funeral, for she was well-known and loved in the community, and many tributes were paid to her practical kindness and always ready help. Sarah in particular was thankful that the Meeting took place without disturbance or interruption, and as they laid Betsy to rest in the little graveyard, Sarah was able, at last, to feel a sense of peace, of a life well-lived. A drizzly rain fell as the Friends drew close together, the children sheltering beneath their mothers' cloaks. John's firm hand rested on Matthew's shoulder, while he, in his turn, gathered his daughters to him, and Nat - who had been for so long all the family that Betsy had - seemed for a while locked into his own grief.

126

As the others moved away down to Rag Stree where Sarah and Elizabeth Perryman had prepared refreshment for them - a task that had always been Betsy's own - he stayed by the grave-side, with shoulders bowed and head bent. His young wife, Jane, carrying their baby son Benjamin in her arms, turned back to him. "Come, husband," she said gently, laying a hand on his arm, "we must go back and *she* will always go with us."

It was just two days later that John-Richard started on his journey, the whole family seeing him off from the fields at Houndiscombe. It had been decided to travel in a pack-horse train. Friends had reported that the roads were particularly bad after a hard winter and wet spring, so that carts would make a very rough, slow journey. The number of merchants ready to set off had increased since Amos had first asked to take John-Richard, and the pack-horses were laden with goods of all kinds - wool and cloth, leather and many grocery items and supplies. There was one small cart, however, for Amos, John-Richard, and as many boxes and bundles as could be got into it. The boy had wanted to travel on horseback, but he had ridden very little as yet and could not argue with the older men's experience. As the train set off, Sarah's heart was torn between pride and fear for her first-born son, who turned to wave to them with the same excitement shining from his dark eyes as his father had had when he set off for war, and though he was better shod and clad than John had been, with strong boots, well-knitted hose and a warm coat, yet still thin wrists protruded from his sleeves, and he had the same turn of the head and way of flicking back an unruly lock of hair. "God keep thee safe, my son," said Sarah and John together, and having watched the procession out of sight, together with the children, they walked back into the town and the busy days that lay ahead of them.

Matthew had insisted that he could manage in the cottage with his two daughters, but Sarah knew they would need help. So every day she made sure they were well supplied with food and all their household needs and she knew that she must not fail to see that the home, kept always so clean and comfortable by Betsy, was maintained as her dear friend would have wished.

It seemed too that problems were increasing daily for the Friends, some because of unwarranted persecution and some, it must be said, because of the deeds to which their own consciences led them. Men Friends would not remove their hats in court, nor would they give surety for their future good conduct, arguing that they had done no wrong, nor would they give surety to appear at the higher courts - Quarter Sessions or the Assizes. It followed then that they were either held in the cells under the Guildhall for this time, or were fined heavily, sometimes as much as £50. There was no question but that the better off Quakers helped their poor brethren, but even they were hard put sometimes to put the money together, for it had to be paid immediately. Failing this, furniture and household goods were taken instead.

One morning about a week after Betsy's funeral, James came hot-foot as always to the Luscombe home. John was at the shop but Sarah listened anxiously to the tale he brought. The previous evening an elderly Friend, Thomas Rattenbury, had been apprehended as he left the Meeting House. He had been there alone, to repair one of the benches, and the Constable who took him was obviously delighted to find such an easy victim. "Thomas was thrown into a cell for the night," James continued his story while Sarah made him some refreshment though he would hardly wait to take it, "and then this morning, just a few hours ago, he was fined £20. He had not got it, of course, for thou knowest how slender are Thomas' means, and they would not give him time to seek the help of his Friends. No, they have destrained all the contents of his cottage. I met them trundling it all away on a cart, and have come quickly to you. I will go now to other Friends to let them know," and he got up to leave.

Sarah was in tears. "He will be so bewildered," she said. "Such a quiet, gentle man, but do not fear, there will be enough of us to buy everything back for him again," and calling to Elizabeth to look after the younger children, she picked up her cloak and followed James from the house. She hurried down the hill to find John, and for them to make their way to the Guildhall. Events such as this had become regular occurrences now, and as she went quickly to the grocer's shop, Sarah wondered who would be the next Friend to be rescued thus.

Chapter Twenty-three

A MONTH WENT BY and there had been no news of the group who had travelled to Bristol. Sarah was becoming anxious and though John tried to reassure her, he could not still her misgivings. "They have much business to conduct, my love, and we know the journey is long. But our lad has many Friends to protect him. Do not vex thyself."

But busy as she kept Sarah could not help starting up at every knock on the door, at each footfall coming into the house. Sometimes in the afternoons she would take William and Mary for a walk to Houndiscombe and watch for any sign of the returning pack-horse train, but though she strained her eyes till they ached, looking into the distance, and though there were many travellers coming and going, they were never the ones she longed to see.

On one such occasion, a warm May day when the hedges were sweet with crane's bill, vetch and columbine, Sarah tried to hurry the children home for there was to be a meeting at their house that evening, but Mary wanted to stop every few steps along the path to add to the nosegay she was holding in one fat little hand. "Look at these white violets. I'll gather you a bunch of them, shall I?" then suggested her mother, "we can put them into that pretty jar with the flowers on and stand it on the table." This satisfied Mary, and soon the three of them had reached the bottom of Rag Street, and with a helping hand to each child Sarah encouraged the small legs to struggle up the hill to home.

It was to be a special meeting that evening and the Elders had decided that to avoid interruption a home might be safer to use than the Meeting House. The younger children in bed, Elizabeth was placed in charge of the front door to admit the visitors, a task Sarah herself had once performed, while Sarah prepared refreshments, sorely missing Betsy's help, for she was realizing more and more how much her friend had lifted burdens from her without ever needing to be asked, with kindness and with quick efficiency. John was cloistered with Thomas Salthouse, who had made his home in the town now, and spent much of his time visiting and aiding Friends and building up the community. But the purpose of this evening's meeting was to welcome Elizabeth Trelawney, now married to Thomas Lower, a leading Cornish Friend. Unlike most of the Plymouth Friends who were shopkeepers, merchants or yeomen, she was a member of an ancient noble family, being the eldest of nine daughters of Sir John Trelawney, Sherriff of Cornwall. She had been convinced by George Fox on his first visit to Plymouth. Tonight she was to share letters she had recently received from him, and Plymouth Quakers looked forward to the inspiration and encouragement this would bring.

The room quickly filled, and Sarah opened the casement windows, so that the scents from the garden mingled with those from Mary's jar of flowers, and, in spite of all their difficulties a sense of peace soon pervaded the meeting.

Sarah looked at Elizabeth Trelawney as she commenced to talk to them and was impressed by the firmness of her expression and the steadfast assurance with which she spoke. She said that Fox hoped to pay a visit to the West Country before long but thinking it likely he would travel to Topsham, and then into Cornwall, where he hoped Plymouth Friends would join him. Thomas Salthouse had agreed to meet him at Topsham and take him on. Friends nodded thoughtfully. Exeter and Plymouth were places to be avoided at that time. "We would not wish George Fox to be taken again so soon," they said. "He warns us," Elizabeth continued, "of the Press Gangs that haunt the streets of many towns, especially the streets of the poor, and snatch boys - scarcely more than children, to carry them away without redress."

Friends with young sons looked at them with trepidation for this was another horror that had recently come to Plymouth, and they all knew that naval service was something to be avoided at all costs with its cruelty, its deprivation, where no-one was paid and everyone underfed. This was another worry for Sarah to add to her concern about John-Richard. Supposing he had already been press-ganged in Bristol? How could she just sit here in quiet when she wanted to be out looking for him? She glanced up at John, but his eyes were closed and his brow smooth. How could he be so calm! Elizabeth was continuing to read from Fox's letters and enlarging upon them. "Our beloved Friend tells us," she said, "to be watchful and caring of Friends who are leaving the army, where many stayed on with Cromwell after the war but find that now, with their new faith, they can no longer wear the sword."

The meeting thought about this for a few minutes in silence and comments were made as to how such Friends could best be helped. Fox's letter ended with a warning to Cornish Friends that they should desist from the practice - still maintained by some - of robbing wrecked ships. Elizabeth's smile was wry. "I must certainly pass that advice on. I wouldn't wish my father to hear about it." The meeting soon drew to a close and Robert Cary took their visitor to his home for the night, before she returned to Cornwall.

The next day turned wet and for almost a week the town hung in a shroud of heavy dampness. Sometimes the rain poured down and at others it was no more than a thick mist with tendrils dripping from trees and bushes, and from cloaks and hoods and even from strands of hair that crept from these. This weather did not raise Sarah's spirits for she knew that the roads outside the town would be even more difficult to cover and John-Richard was still not home.

But other problems seemed to crowd in upon Sarah that week. At eleven years old, Elizabeth was growing rapidly into a young woman - tall and fair as Sarah herself had been at that age and already there were questionings in her mind as there had been in her mother's, and at times the girl seemed to inhabit a world of her own, being thoughtful and almost withdrawn.

She was skilled with her needle, as her grandmother had been, and on this wet, dismal day Sarah came upon her in her room, finishing a shirt she had been making from one of William's for a poor Quaker family whose husband and father had died after a period of imprisonment in the Clink under the Guildhall, the cold and damp having finished a chest already weak. But it was not the small shirt that was in the girl's hand as Sarah entered the room. That lay on her bed. She looked up guiltily at her mother then her eyes dropped to the sewing she still held, but crumpled now, in her lap. Sarah saw it was Elizabeth's own cap, and she touched the strings that fell from it.

"Have they come loose again?" she asked. "I think the damp must rot the thread." Then, wondering at the girl's blush, she took the cap from her. "Oh Elizabeth, what are you doing, my child?" She sank to the bed beside her daughter. "Thou knowest that as Friends we try to live simply, which means that we do not decorate our garments," and she fingered the pleats that Elizabeth had started to put along the edge of her cap. "I'm tired of always being so -, so plain, mother." She twisted her hands in agitation. "It's not much to ask is it? - just a pleat?" Sarah tried to think of the right things to say, mindful of how she had often felt restless and resentful at this age, but although Presbyterian her family was not then Quaker and the war which followed had brought her a kind of release, for values changed quickly and she had had Will and then John to help her.

All these thoughts went through Sarah's mind in those next few minutes and she felt a great sympathy for this daughter of hers. "I do understand," she said gently. "I will speak to thy father and see what perhaps we can do, but you do know my child why this plainness has become our way of life. It is because we know how wrong are the excesses and extravagances of this worldy life, lived by so many from the King down." "Yes, mother, I do know." Her words were quiet and Sarah hugged her tightly before she left the room and went to her own chamber. She crossed to the carved wooden chest which stood under the window. Sarah knelt before it and lifted the lid. As she turned over the linen she came to some sheets and covers that she had embroidered and decorated many years ago in preparation for her marriage to John, and sitting back on her heels, she remembered how her mother had given her the chest and encouraged her to work to fill it, when it had seemed so long to wait till her wedding. Elizabeth was younger than she had been then, but perhaps she could find some comfort this way. She was still thinking and remembering when John came in. He knelt beside her. "All alone up here, my love," he said. "Elizabeth has started to prepare supper. She is a good girl." "Oh, she is." John was surprised at the vehemence in her voice, and more so as she told him quickly why she was there. "It must be hard sometimes for the young to accept all the ways that seem right to us, so I thought perhaps if I could give her something to prepare for, something prettier, not so plain, it might help." John nodded. "I think thou hast chosen wisely," he said, "though I hope it will be many years yet before a marraige chest is needed for our daughter."

The next morning Francis came to the house. It was early. John had not yet left for work, so that Sarah's heart missed a beat as she let the visitor in. "Is there news, brother?" she asked, and Francis' expression, always serious, seemed to become more so. "Well, yes," he answered in his slow way, as Sarah led him through to the living room where John was gathering up some papers. "One of my clothiers has just arrived back from Exeter," he said, "where there was news of great troubles in Bristol." He paused then reached out a hand to his sister. "I'm afraid it involves the Friends from Plymouth." "John-Richard?" Sarah could only whisper the name as John's arms went around her and stopped her from falling.

There was quiet in the room for a minute with John and Sarah staring agonisingly at Francis who was still standing just inside the door and looking uncomfortable at the attention focussed upon him. "Tell us, brother Francis, all that thou knowest, for we are very anxious." John's voice was calm, but his arm tightened around Sarah's shoulders. Francis nodded and took a deep breath. "Yes, as I said, Robert Fox arrived back just an hour ago, and I came straight here to tell you. It seems that before he left Exeter other Friends reached there from Bristol." He paused and Sarah prompted him. "And what had happened there? What was the news of - of our people?"

Francis took another deep breath. "There was a cruel attack on the Friends in Bristol. A Meeting was broken up, and - and the Plymouth Quakers were there and they - " "John-Richard?" Sarah whispered. "No, he was not involved. Apparently there had been trouble before and Amos was very concerned for the boy so had sent him earlier in the day to some elderly relations of his." "Thank God," Sarah breathed. "Yes, they kept him for the whole week the Friends were held in prison, then, once they were released, it took a while for them to complete their business. In fact they had to pay a great deal in fines and lost much. I think they're still trying to do what they can, but the important thing is that they should be home within two weeks and I believe your lad has conducted him-self very well, but you'll hear about that when you see him. Now I must get back." John saw Francis to the door, and returned to find Sarah still sitting where he had left her. "Well, it's a great relief to know all is well, my love." "He is not yet back," said Sarah, getting to her feet and gathering up dishes from the table. "I shall not be content until he is safely home with us, and I shall not be eager to let him go again." "Thou shouldst have more faith, my love," and he smiled at her with understanding. "Now I must go to work too," and picking up his papers, he was gone.

For the rest of that day, as Sarah went about her household tasks, her mind was filled with thoughts of her family, and especially at this time of John-Richard, and she realised more than ever before, how completely a woman's life is bound up with her children. Men love their families, she thought, but they do have lives apart from them. She remembered how her father, Will, Matthew and even John had gone off to the war. She had not - did not now - query their judgement in doing so, but she knew that for herself, and for all women she supposed, children were, in their dependency, all in all, and she thought how terrible it must be for those Quaker women who had been dragged from their families. Would she ever have the faith and the strength to cope with that? She prayed she would not be put to the test.

The weather matching their mood it seemed, brightened and became mild and sunny with promise of an early summer. No more news came of the travellers but Sarah tried to be content and to accept John's assurances that every day brought them nearer and if ought else of ill had occurred, then those tidings would surely have reached them. She spent as much time as she could spare with her younger children. Elizabeth seemed more settled and contented, and Sarah talked to her of her own mother whom she so much resembled in character. She encouraged John to take her to the shop and out with him on business, as Richard had taken her, but Elizabeth was shyer than she had been, and was not so easy with strangers. But she spent her free time happily with her cousins and with Betsy's daughters, Margaret and Joan, especially the latter who was the same age as Elizabeth herself, and Sarah was always glad to see the two girls in the garden together or setting off for a walk on the beach or to look for flowers in nearby hedgerows and fields. Sarah was preparing William to start school though, like her brother James as a child, he was always keener to be out at play than practising letters in his horn-book, while to Mary life at four years old was a happy time surrounded by love, and some spoiling, even in a Quaker household.

It was almost exactly two weeks from the arrival of Francis with news from Exeter and Bristol that the party long looked for returned. It was dusk and Sarah was preparing the evening meal, listening for John's return and anxious, as always, that another night would pass without John-Richard. Then she heard the front door open and the sound of voices calling and laughing. She ran into the passage-way and her son ran towards her. "Look who has come home, my love," John said, unnecessarily, as she hugged the boy and then held him at arms' length to examine him closely. "I'm sure thou hast grown these last months, but thou art very travel-stained," she said, and hugged him again. It was a happy family who sat at the table that night, joined by Francis, Anna and their boys. John-Richard was the centre of attention as everyone plied him with questions and listened to his news. His parents exchanged amused glances as he told of the business he had conducted with tradesmen there, and how Plymouth's local cheese and butter had been well received. "And while Amos and the others were in prison, I managed on my own, and, mother, I have a present for thee in my bag." He ran from the table into the hall just as a knock came on the front door. John-Richard opened it to admit Amos, whom he showed into the living-room. Sarah and John were pleased to see their old friend and greeted him warmly. While they pressed refreshment upon him he told them of the final success of the undertaking, how helpful and how reliable their son had been to the older Friends in Bristol while so many of the rest were being held. John-Richard came running back into the room with a wooden box in his hands. "Look, mother, I got this for thee, for us all to try." They crowded round as he lifted the lid, and looked at the tiny black leaves inside. Elizabeth wrinkled up her nose. "What is it?" she asked, "it looks like dead dried leaves." "It's a new drink," the boy said proudly. "It's called tea, and you put some in a pot with boiling water, stir it, then wait for it to..." He paused, and Amos finished for him, "to infuse," he said, "and then pour it out. The leaves can be dried and used again. 'Tis regarded as a great luxury, so look after it well, for as yet it is hard to come by and it came into Bristol on a Dutch ship from the East." Sarah duly made her first pot of tea, and everyone sampled it. The children, except for John-Richard who was in duty bound to support his own gift, each took

135

a sip, then pushed their mugs away, while John's comment was "I do not think it will ever replace ale," and Sarah decided she'd reserve judgement for another time.

The rest of that year and the next continued without much change in the lives of the Plymouth Friends. They learned to cope with persecution and when troubles came to any of their number there was immediate support by those who for the time being had escaped. The biggest cause of imprisonment was the refusal of Quakers to take an Oath. When brought before a Magistrate and required to tender an oath of allegiance to the Crown they would not, saying instead that they could only make a statement of loyalty. Sometimes this was accepted, but more often the hapless Friends were thrown into prison, sometimes for as long as two years, and then real deprivation followed. Towards the end of 1663 Matthew was taken in this way, and for more than a year languished beneath the Guildhall. He bore his incarceration bravely but was concerned for his two girls. So they came to Sarah and John and became part of the household in Rag Street.

They all visited Matthew as often as they could and took him whatever comforts he was permitted to have, and Sarah assured him that his cottage was being looked after and his girls too. "Indeed," as she said to John one night, "our Elizabeth and Joan seem delighted to spend so much time together" - for now they shared a room. John looked quizzically at his wife. "And Margaret, is she finding comfort?" "Thou knowest she is, for our John-Richard is very protective towards her," and they looked into each other's eyes, remembering all those years ago when the two of them, under Mary's watchful gaze, had found peace in the troubles of their youth.

But 1664 would soon be upon them, and that year was to bring changes and happenings that they could not now foresee.

Chapter Twenty-four

DR ROGER ASHTON was now the Vicar of St. Andrew's, and he supported the increasing hardening of the attitude of the authorities to those who refused to worship at the parish church. Their power was increased by the passing of the Conventicle Act, which forebad meetings of more than four people, so that Friends had to be ever vigilant. Often they met in the open air and could disperse when warning was given. Parish priests also had a legal hold over Friends when they refused to pay tithes. "Why should we contribute," they said, "to the upkeep of steeple-houses in which we do not worship, and cannot, in all conscience, support?"

The Quakers suffered two sad losses in 1664, with the deaths of Elizabeth Trelawney and Priscilla Cotton. It was true that Elizabeth did not come often to Plymouth, but her support was always available. The loss of Priscilla, however, was greatly felt, for she had been one of the founders of Plymouth Meeting and was still not yet forty years old. At the Meeting to lay her to rest and to give thanks for her life, Friend after Friend paid testimony to her constant, loving-kindness and practical help in so many difficulties, and they remembered how on her death-bed she had given wise counsel to them. "Friends, the Cross is the power of God. When thou flee the Cross, thou wilt lose the power, but as thou wait in the Light thou wilt come to know the Cross in all of life." All that Friends could do was to follow her teaching and to look after Arthur, which they did gladly.

The Dutch wars were under way by 1664, and though the people of Plymouth saw no fighting they heard the Dutch guns as de Ruyter passed the port in his sweep up the Channel. This meant that the press-gangs became even more ruthless in their search for seamen, and they commandeered money and food whenever and wherever they could. Sometimes it seemed to Sarah and her family and friends that there were dangers everywhere all around them, and they needed a very strong faith indeed to maintain their endurance.

Matthew was home again in his cottage, but his time in prison had weakened a constitution never strong and never really recovered from his war service. He became less and less able to work, until, by the end of '64, he had not the strength to leave his home. Margaret and Joan cared for him devotedly, and the Friends held Meetings in his small cottage, so that he still felt part of them.

Francis, in his role as head of the family business, made sure Matthew was well provided for, and Sarah, ever conscious of the debt she owed to Betsy, visited him frequently, and made sure that the girls were coping well with the house and their father. John-Richard was always only too willing to carry messages to them and to walk along the beach with Margaret when they both had an hour to spare.

James' duties as a miller took him often to the countryside beyond Plymouth, from where he would bring back stories of how the people lived and the problems some of them faced. Some evenings he would come to Sarah and John's home full of anger at some injustice he had witnessed. "Thou are a noisy Friend," John would laugh to him and say with mock seriousness, "and how much flour hast thou given free to-day?" knowing that his brother-in-law could not bear to see children hungry or the sick uncared for. James took to visiting the Lilburne brothers who were both held in the prison on St. Nicholas Island. John Lilburne, the Leveller, who after a stormy political career had become a Quaker, had fallen sick and died soon after James' first visit to him, but Robert lingered on till August '65. He was one of the regicides, his name being the 28th of the signatures on the King's death warrant. He had been sentenced to death but was instead kept in perpetual imprisonment. James took him food and other comforts when he was allowed to take a boat across to the Island to visit him, though this was not often. Then James asked for a special meeting of Friends to be called, and there he pleaded that approach be made to the authorities to allow Lilburne to spend his last days in Plymouth among Friends. "He is a brave man," James begged, "and even before the time of Friends as an army commander he showed much compassion to the Anabaptists and extreme sectaries in his army."

The Friends agreed to make representation, but this was, as they feared, refused. However, when he died they were permitted to bring him back to the town where he was laid to rest in the Quakers Burying Place - the old graveyard bordering the Hoe.

Scarcely was this done when news came through to Plymouth of the dreadful plague raging in London. Plague itself was not a new phenomenon, either in Europe or in England, but, as 1665 wore on, it became evident that this was a worse epidemic than ever known before. The worst danger, of course, was the great risk of infection. All who could, left the capital - especially in the early days; though neighbouring towns and villages were not eager to receive the refugees.

Friends in Plymouth did not know how to help Quakers in London beyond holding Meetings to commend them to God, and sending supplies of food, blankets and healing balms to special places in the countryside beyond the wretched, poverty-stricken suburbs and the Metropolis itself. Parishes like St. Giles-in-the-Fields, where the plague had first broken out, were deserted now, and every other house seemed to bear its scarlet cross and to be silent except for the raving cry of a plague victim who still lived. It was a dead waste-land, whereas in areas where the plague still flourished, there was noise, the shouts of fear, and of warning, and the smell of sulphur, of fumigation and of desperate attempts to kill the dreadful poison, to stop it spreading, mostly a losing battle.

The goods which Quakers left at the designated places were collected by other Friends and distributed to the most needy. Word travelled south of the selfless bravery of many Quakers who stayed within the city, working in the pest houses and in the stinking alleys and lanes, until they themselves took the dreaded disease whose symptoms they recognised only too well. Then, when they could no longer work they would shut themselves away, sometimes crawling to an outhouse or shed, anxious not to spread any further the evil pestilence, and waited where they lay for the release of death.

These were the stories that reached Plymouth Friends in stages, from those that got out of London, and such news brought great sorrow to the West Country. But it was not until the following year that an opportunity came to meet the tragedy head on.

The children came hurrying home to Rag Street one aftternoon excited about a new ship they'd seen in the Sound. "We heard some men talking about it," William said, "and it's a prison ship. What do you think it's doing here?" "I do not know, now come along." Sarah was busy with the evening meal and it was only when John came home a short while afterwards that she realised something serious had happened. "It's the Black Eagle," her husband told them, "and Friends lie aboard her." "Oh John, where are they from?" "We are not sure yet. James is down on the Quay trying to obtain more information. I must go back myself. I only came to let you know." And Sarah had to be content with that till much later that evening, when John finally returned. Sarah made him sit to his supper while she listened to his news, Elizabeth and John-Richard also anxiously awaiting what he could tell them.

"Well," John said, as Sarah put a large slice of mutton pie before him and spread a thick slice of bread with butter, "it appears that there was no Certificate of Health so the Harbour Master wouldn't let anyone ashore. Then they discovered that fifty-five Friends, both men and women, were taken from Newgate where they were under sentence of transportation, and were put aboard the Black Eagle at Greenwich. Plague broke out on board." "Oh John, how terrible," Sarah gasped with horror. "What happened then?" "The ship lay seven weeks in the river and half the prisoners died, the others must be in a very bad way." "Well, what can we do?" "A great deal, my love. Early tomorrow we'll hold a special meeting to arrange for provisions and medicines to go out to the ship. There is no time to waste if we are to save them."

And so, at dawn, Friends gathered at Rag Street and decided what each could contribute. Offers of help were quickly forthcoming and a depot was set up on the quay. Arthur Cotton and Robert Cary went straight there to receive the goods. Sacks of flour and sugar and jars of ale and oil were carried down right away. The women took honey, butter, cheese and salted meat from their store cupboards, while some, including Sarah and Elizabeth Perryman, baked all that morning - pies, pasties and bread. They gathered together blankets too, and jars of soothing balms, with linen cut into strips for bandages. By midday the quay was a scene of great activity. Apart from the group of sober clad Quakers in the midst, many of the townspeople had come to watch, shouting warnings of the pestilence that lay in the Sound. Children, seeing this as a holiday, played on the beach and got in the way of the busy men and women. The weather was warm and Sarah thought as she hurried to the shore laden with heavy baskets, how the Friends who languished on the Black Eagle must be suffering. The men had managed to acquire a fishing-boat large enough to carry all the supplies, and two men - but not a boat of great value for it could not return, the risk of infection was too great. It took a while for the harbour authories to allow the expedition at all, but at last James and John Light emerged from the office right on the front with the required permission. The Friends gathered round them. "We have to take the boat out ourselves," said John Light, "and leave it as close to the ship as we can, then come back in another boat that will follow us." The men nodded. "We just have to decide who'll go," said James. "I am for one." They all volunteered, the women watching anxiously, for they knew there could be danger from too close contact, and yet knowing too that this was the only chance they had to help their Friends.

Finally, all was settled. James and John went with the loaded boat, and Robert Cary and Francis followed behind to bring them back. As they set off, the beach became strangely quiet, all faces turned to the water that lay between them and the Black Eagle. Even the children were still and mothers held tightly to them, everyone willing the enterprise to succeed.

Chapter Twenty-five

THE FRIENDS DID REACH the "Black Eagle" safely, and changing to the other boat, returned to the shore without harm. From a safe distance they watched figures descending ropes and lifting the boxes, bundles and casks and making them fast, to be pulled aboard. When this was done the boat was tied behind the ship and those on board - and there seemed to be pitifully few of them - waved to their benefactors, and the expedition was completed. "We couldn't see much more than you did," said John as he helped to beach the small fishing boat they'd returned in, and walked up the shingle with Sarah, "just a few figures scrambling and lifting."

"I hope there are enough still sufficiently fit to help the others," sighed his wife. "I put some messages amongst the food, just to tell them that Plymouth Friends are with them in spirit, and we will uphold them in our Meeting."

At all events, less than two weeks later watchers reported early one morning that the "Black Eagle" had disappeared from the Sound, and Friends prayed for her safe arrival on a friendly shore. (By a strange turn of events, the prisoners were finally brought back to England. The "Black Eagle" was taken by a Dutch privateer, was sailed around Ireland and North Scotland to Bergen in Norway and finally to Holland. There the Quakers were released, and with the help of the Friends of Amsterdam, they returned to England.)

So life went on in Plymouth with most people there glad to be far from London and its dangers. But as the year turned to '66, they realised they had troubles of their own to face. Since the restoration of the monarchy, Charles had not completed his vindictive revenge upon the town that had for so long resisted his father's forces. But now he turned his attention westwards. He sent troops to the Hoe and virtually destroyed it, while the townspeople stood helplessly by. As usual, it was James who brought the news first to Rag Street. "I have told as many Friends as I can gather for the moment," he said. "Thou must all come to the Hoe and see what is happening," and he hurried off again. It was true that already many townspeople were gathered there, the women anxious at so many soldiers and the children excited at all the activity. "Look, Mother," William ran back from the front of the crowd to tell them, "They're pulling down Drake's fort and St. Katherine's Chapel." It was true, as heaps of rubble and burning wood soon revealed, with dust and smoke rising in clouds. Then other shouts went up. "Drake's bowling green, it's all churned up, his spirit surely will not rest now." But the destroyers had not yet finished, and, as the crowds saw what was next was vandalised, they stood silent in horror.

On the slopes of the Hoe there had been cut into the turf two giant figures. They had been there as far back as records went, and bore the names of Corineus and Goemagot - commemorating the legendary fight between Corineus the Trojan and the giant Goemagot. No-one took much notice of the figures - they were just there, but they were part of Plymouth's heritage and were periodically renewed by the Corporation. Now, as they watched, shivering, the King's men quarried away the slopes, and removed all traces of the figures.

Even men of religion - whatever their denomination - had never queried the pagan presence amongst them, and now the supersitious crossed themselves, shook their heads and warned of terrible things to come.

When all was cleared it soon became evident what Charles' next intention was. A few weeks later the people watched again as all the accoutrements of building work were hauled to this now cleared site. James - who always had his ear to the ground - and some of the older Friends from their business contacts, brought home the news as they heard it, though John warned them that rumours were always rife at such times and they must wait to see what would really happen. When William and his friends burst in with tales of what they had seen and heard, Sarah was reminded of how James himself with the sober Francis trying to keep him in check, had acted in just such a way when Charles Church was under construction. But this new undertaking was no Church, it was to become a great Citadel, built, so the information went, to protect

Plymouth from dangers from the sea. The Mayor called a meeting in the Guildhall to explain this, reading a notice purported to have come from the King himself. But the townspeople were suspicious and murmers of disbelief crept around the hall, gathering momentum as he read on. "When has Charles ever cared about our welfare?" said Arthur Cotton, sitting with a group of Friends including the new wife he had just married, and John Cary nodded in agreement. "It'll be something to make life more difficult, especially for us," he said. Sarah looked up at John to see what he was thinking, and as always he tried to bring peace to the argument. "Let us wait," he said, "before we judge, and hear what other news there is. James is hot-headed enough for us all, 'twill do no good to meet trouble in advance."

But they could not wait in peace for long. As the year went on into the next, the fortress was constructed. When Sarah and John walked up to the Hoe to note its progress one balmy autumn evening, they found a crowd there pointing to the guns which were being manoeuvred into place. "There are as many pointing over the town as point out to sea." John Cary gesticulated with the stick he now used. "Is that to protect our town from enemies, or is it so that the King can, at any time, turn them on us?" Old heads were shaken in foreboding, younger ones were raised in anger, while the children ran about pretending to shoot each other.

James and some of his friends were striding across the Hoe and walking around the walls of the Citadel, when John, Sarah, William and Mary caught up with them. James was exclaiming excitedly, "Look what else they're doing. The moat and drawbridges are distinct from any defences, it will never fall easily." John tried to calm the Friends and led them to the Meeting House for a time of quiet. As they went, Francis said thoughtfully, "I heard to-day that people are talking of Samuel Pepy's writings and the understanding they show. He reminds us to reflect at this time upon Oliver and what brave things he did." And more and more this was what the people thought, for there was now much reaction against Charles for his salacious private life, his waste of the treasury, intrigue with France, and his persecution of non-conformists. Most of them knew that although Charles was Protestant by oath, he was, in secret, a Roman Catholic.

144

But other news was coming from London too, in this year of 1666. Throughout the hot summer the plague raged uncontrolled. The remnants of the local and national government still in the capital, met in desperation to see a way out, till finally the Lord Mayor issued a Proclamation, and this Plymouth's Mayor got news of and told the townspeople in another special meeting in the Guildhall.

"They have decided," he said in sombre voice, "to use fire to smoke out the plague, for it is in the very air." Plymothians looked at each other and some shook their heads in disbelief. The mayor continued. "Every group of twelve households is to be responsible for lighting and tending a fire to burn without stop for three days.*

The fires were lit from 5th-8th September, and spectators told of the city in flames, which could be seen from a great distance like hell itself. When next the Mayor of Plymouth called a meeting, it was to report that rain had come a month later, and London lanes and streets were filled with steam and smoke, but plague death figures were still terrifyingly high. Plymouth Friends again sorrowed for those still in London. Would the terror ever finish?

Then, almost suddenly, as autumn turned into winter and the weather became colder, the deaths slowed down. Survivors were afraid at first to believe the figures that were posted but it soon became evident that the progress was indeed established. After a few weeks more men, women and children came blinking from the darkness in which their lives had been held and London crept back into the daylight, and "Ring a ring of roses" was no longer a song of death.

---

* The plague in fact was carried by fleas and lived in clothes, in sewers, cellars and middens, even behind wainscots.

Chapter Twenty-six

ALTHOUGH '66 WAS such a difficult year in many ways for Friends, yet, after that the persecutions in Plymouth seemed to ease, and they were able to run their businesses, bring up their families and organise and develop their Meeting with much less harassment than hitherto. The Quaker movement had come into being as a spiritual revolt from organised religion, from the idea that any man or body of men could be the keeper of another's conscience, and in its early years there was no organisation, just in Plymouth and all over the country little bands of men and women often called "Seekers". From the beginning there were meetings too in West Devon at Modbury, Kingsbridge and Totnes, all run separately. It was George Fox himself who realised that some kind of unity was needed, to provide mutual help and support, and in 1667 and '68 he travelled the country urging the establishment of such a network. In 1668 he came west and his diary entry for 22 June records: "Next day several Friends accompanied us into Devon and Cornwall where we visited meetings till we came to Land's End. Then journeying up again by the South part of this county, we came to Tregangeeves where at Loveday Hambly's home we had a general meeting for all the county in which all Monthly Meetings were settled." It was felt to be a good thing for all the meetings in one area to gather each month and settle their affairs.* Then Quarterly Meetings were established on a county basis, the burden and expense of travel was shared, care of each other taken, and even discipline exercised when sometimes young and inexperienced Friends strayed from the laid down guidelines. All meetings were held in the guidance of the inner light, and everyone was listened

---

* Plymouth's Minute Books start in 1669 and are continuous from then to the present day.

146

to - decisions were not made by a mere majority vote, but by seeking the divine will. Meeting for Sufferings had a special function - to record and to relieve where possible the misfortunes and persecution of Friends all over the country. That meeting's correspondent in Devon was Arthur Cotton. In the early days of the movement women worked and ministered alongside men and always remained of equal value, but gradually as the century proceeded, women's meetings were established and they and the men fell into their own areas of work, for the women it became mainly work of a charitable, almost domestic nature.

But these developments came gradually and Sarah's time during these years was fully occupied with her family and their concerns. Matthew died quietly and peacefully - as he had lived - in 1667, and a few days after he had been laid to rest, John and Sarah were not surprised to be greeted after supper by a serious and rather nervous pair of young people - their elder son, John Richard, and Margaret Bovey, Matthew and Betsy's elder daughter. John teased them for a moment. "What problems can you two possibly have?" he asked with mock seriousness, "that takest the smiles from thy faces?" But Sarah was remembering how she and John had stood thus in this very room, before Richard and Mary, seeking their permission to marry, John conscious of the seriousness of the occasion, and she herself excited and eager to show her parents that there was no reason at all why their wedding should not take place. She looked at Margaret now, seeing in her rosy face and already plump comeliness so much of her dear Betsy that she longed to take her in her arms, but knew she must wait. So she and John, trying hard not to smile, looked suitably solemn. John-Richard took a deep breath. "We want to be married," he said, his voice cracking slightly. "We are both quite old really. I'm nineteen and Margaret" (and he took her hand in his own) "is eighteen." John nodded as if this was information he had not known before. "And now that Matthew has died, there is the house and I would be there to look after Joan as well - till she marries that is." He stopped for breath and Margaret whispered shyly, looking up at these older people from under her dark lashes. "She already has a good friend - 'tis John Cary's grandson." "Right," John said now, looking at Sarah for her reaction, "but I think we'd better settle thy case first."

"I take as true," John said now, "that thou lovest each other well and can both accept what is important to the other?" "Oh yes," the young people answered together, John-Richard firmly and with head held high, and Margaret more quietly, but both with beaming smiles. Sarah's heart ached for them as they stood with hands tightly clasped, and she could not be quiet any longer. "I am sure we know all else that is necessary, for John-Richard works for thee, husband, and there cannot be any secret as to the security of his position, nor as to his being a good and steadfast worker."

John relented and held out his hands. "Your mother and I have no doubts, and we are glad to welcome thee into our family, Margaret. The way thou has cared for thy father bodes well for thy nurture of a husband." Sarah embraced them both, tears mingling with her smiles, and the four of them sat late making plans and settling on a date for the marriage. No-one could find a reason for waiting, and it was only a few weeks before the Meeting House on the Hoe saw this marriage held midst the warmth and blessings of all their Friends.

Sarah stood beside John and watched the young people make their promises, then, looking around at all the Friends gathered there, at Francis and James and their families, she realised how all the children were growing now to young man and womanhood. This was the first couple of their generation to marry, but others would not be long in following them she knew, all born into the Quaker faith. And this was her son, her firstborn, moving away from her to start - if God were willing, and in the fullness of time - another line.

She felt John's hand reach for her own, and knew that his thoughts were similar to hers.

The day was too damp for the wedding meal to be taken out of doors, but Rag Street managed to hold all the guests, and it was a time of simple but deep shared happiness.

Later than evening while the young people still chatted together, John and Sarah walked slowly back to Rag Street from what had been Matthew's cottage. It was well-stocked with household items and John-Richard, like his father and grandfather before him, delighted in carving wooden utensils for Margaret's own special use and pleasure. Sarah and John admired these while they put down the last of John-Richard's belongings that they had carried there, plus boxes of preserves and supplies of Sarah's cheese and butter. Now, on their way home again they paused at the edge of the quay as the pale autumn sun lightened what had been a damp grey day. "Shall we rest here for a few minutes," and John moved to the low, stone wall. Sarah followed him with an anxious frown. "Art thou very tired, my love?" her tone was concerned. "It has been a long day I know, and thou should'st have waited for the young people to carry those heavy bundles." He put an arm around her shoulders and after a few minutes, as they sat quietly, he breathed more easily. "There, 'tis nothing, just the hill and the damp seemed to clog my lungs for a moment, but I'm well now. 'Tis good to catch the evening air for a little, is it not?" Sarah drew closer to him. "We shall miss our son, the first of the family to leave the nest." She concentrated on this thought, afraid to accept the weariness she'd seen in John of late as anything other than the normal tiredness of a busy life. "I'm sure we shall see as much of him as ever. His new home is no distance away," her husband said now, "and thou knowest we are a close-knit community. And do not forget my love, we shall have William and Mary for many years yet, and perhaps Elizabeth too," and with that Sarah had to be content as they walked slowly up the hill to home.

In the days that followed, Sarah occupied herself busily as always. Just a week after the wedding, she was called one evening to the Cotton's home across the Hoe, where Arthur's second wife Margaret was lying in childbirth. By morning Sarah was holding a beautiful baby girl, named Priscilla in memory of that Priscilla who had been such a strength and support to the young meeting, and as she walked home later through the grey drizzle, she realised that marriage, birth, and even death were intertwined with all their lives and she shivered. Then, pulling her cloak more tightly around her, she walked quickly to her home and those whom she loved within it.

In these years leading up to 1670, there were national events of great importance to Friends, reports of which trickled through to Plymouth surprisingly quickly. Sometimes news was relayed from town to town by merchants and other businessmen, and sometimes by Friends themselves travelling in the Ministry. Thus did they hear in '66 of two aristocratic scholars who had joined the Society and who were to leave their mark upon it and upon the life of the country for many years to come. These were Robert Barclay and William Penn. It was not long before Penn, who exulted in his new life, set forth to the New World and set up his "Holy Experiment" there in the rich lands of what was to become Pennsylvania.

Sarah had two main reasons for concern at this time - her husband, of course, and her elder daughter. It was true that the mild spring of '68 brought ease to John's breathing and colour to his cheeks but, in spite of all her watchful care of him, his strength, the strength that she had known and loved in him as a boy and young man, and which had sustained her through so many difficulties, seemed destined never to be regained. John-Richard was a great help and took on much of the work and now the responsibility of the business, and though Sarah was always anxious that her children should not leave school too soon, William was now fourteen and eager to leave his studies behind. He had been running messages and doing odd jobs in the shop for several months, and Sarah remembered how her brother James and John-Richard had been eager to become working men.

On this occasion she was busy preparing the evening meal. She liked to have it ready when John came in though nowadays, she sighed to herself, he usually had to sit a little to recover his breath before moving to the table. It was a mild, spring day and she thought that perhaps they could sit in the garden for a little after their meal. Elizabeth came in now with Mary, whom she had taken for a walk along the beach. "Look, Mother," the young girl, now nine years old and growing more like her grandmother every day, Sarah thought, held out her apron to her mother. "I've gathered all these pebbles. Aren't they pretty? Can I put them on the shelf in my room?" "Yes, my love, but don't be long. Supper is almost ready and father will be home soon." She watched fondly as Mary skipped up the stairs, her cheeks rosy and her brown curls bobbing under her cap. Sarah turned back to Elizabeth, who had already gone into the kitchen and was gathering platters together to bring to the dining-table - for she knew well the household routine. She had not spoken since she came into the house and as always Sarah wished she could understand better her elder daughter. She did not seem unhappy, and helped her mother without demur. Yet increasingly she seemed withdrawn from them all, in a world of her

150

own. Sarah did not wish to worry John about the girl, so kept her concerns to herself.

Suddenly there was a knock on the front door and Sarah hurried to answer it, worried as always that something had happened to John. But it was Francis who stood there and as she welcomed him in, she remembered how it had been all those years ago when he had left his studies and books and gone to work for Richard and she knew now how much he would have preferred to remain a scholar, but accepted that the business needed him.

He was holding out a parcel to her. "It's the cloth you wanted for dresses for the girls. I thought I'd bring it to you." "Oh thank you, Francis." Sarah held up the grey material. "I will be glad to make a start on them. Will you eat with us? We are just waiting for John." "Thank you, no. Anna and the boys will be waiting for me." They walked together to the front door. "Art thou happy?" Sarah asked him, on impulse, "and content with thy life?" His smile was kind and surprisingly understanding. "Why should I not be, sister? I believe God lays down our lives for us, and I am very blest in satisfying work and a good wife and family, and I still have time to read and study - hopefully that helps to spread the Light." He hesitated at the door. "I am always here if thou shouldst need help or counsel," and he took her hand in his before leaving the house. She watched him stride down the hill, forty years old now, his grey locks still thick below his tall hat. He had put on very little weight over the years, and Sarah could not help but wish that her husband was as fit. As though her thoughts brought John closer, she saw him turn the corner at the bottom of the road at that moment just as Francis reached it, and the two men stood together for a moment talking. Then Francis continued on his way and John started the climb up the hill. Seeing Sarah standing in the doorway he waved to her, while she hurried down the hill to walk back with him, slipping her arm through his and suiting her steps to his slower ones.

Chapter Twenty-seven

SARAH MANAGED TO keep John well through 1668 and into
'69, giving him all her care and devotion. John-Richard and
William, together with two hired men, worked hard in the business, John-Richard travelling more and more, selling and buying
their goods, so that their father, beyond checking the books and
paying visits to the shop when he felt well and able, could leave it
all in their increasingly capable hands.

The summer and autumn of '68 were warm and sunny, and as
the people of Plymouth lifted their faces to the balmy western air
and opened their doors and windows to freshen their homes, Sarah
devised plans for John to benefit from the good weather. She borrowed a cart from John Harris and drove him out into the countryside. They went often onto the moors and one day they paid a
visit to Horrabridge, to the old farm where John had grown up.
His cousin Jane and her husband Paul ran it now, and John had
paid only infrequent visits there over the years.

They set off early in the morning, Mary, excited at the outing,
sitting between them as the cart rattled on, and pointing out the
sheep and cows fat on the luscious grass. She wanted to pick flowers from the hedgerows rich with wild roses and the last of the
strawberries and Sarah, remembering her outings with Richard so
long ago, said that they would stop when they reached Roborough
Down to rest the horse and partake of some of the refreshments
she had packed in the big basket. As they drew near to Horrabridge
and the cart trundled down the last rutted lane, John reached over
and took the reins. They drew up before the small farm - the house
was little more than a cottage with chickens pecking in the yard,
its winter mud dried to dust. Two small boys and a little girl played
on a patch of grass at the side of the cottage, with an iron hoop and
a see-saw made with a plank of wood balanced on a barrel. The
children's shouts stopped as they saw the visitors and they stood

close together, staring with big eyes, then running into the cottage, as Sarah, John and Mary got down from the cart. A woman came out into the yard. She seemed to be a few years younger than Sarah's age, her full figure wrapped in a sacking apron, tendrils of damp hair escaped from her cap, and she smiled in surprise as she saw Sarah and John. "Why cousin John, 'tis good to see you. It has been a long time, and Sarah too, and can this be little Mary? Come into the house." She led the way into the small kitchen. The others followed her while Mary ran off to play with the children, the small girl shyly taking her hand and the ginger-bread man Mary took from her apron pocket.

The kitchen was cramped but neat, and hot from the cooking fire and the sun pouring through the small lattice. Jane had been cutting vegetables for the mutton stew bubbling in the iron pot hung over the fire, but she quickly cleared a space at the scrubbed wooden table and pointed to a long bench. "Please sit down and rest yourselves," she said now, and "I'm sure you'd be glad of some refreshment," and she placed a jug of ale on the table with a wedge of cheese and a loaf which smelt new and appetising. Sarah moved to help her. "You cannot be far from your time," she said. "Sit with us for a few moments." Jane eased herself onto a stool. "No, I've just a few weeks to go. Paul is up in the hills with the sheep. He should be down for his meal before too long," and trying to settle her ungainly bulk she continued to cut up her potatoes and carrots. Sarah uncovered the basket she had brought with her. "I thought a few pasties might be useful," she lifted them out, "oh, and some marchpane for the children." "'Tis good of you, cousin, they do love sweet things. Now tell me all the news from Plymouth, for it's long since I was there." She glanced at Sarah's drab grey gown with its wide, white peaked collar, and John's equally sombre attire. "You are still with your group of - ?" she paused, and John smiled gently at her. "The Friends," he finished. "Yes, we grow ever stronger - in numbers and in faith."

The three of them talked for a while longer then Sarah, taking a small packet from her pocket, showed Jane how to make a pot of tea, laughing as their hostess wrinkled her nose at the unaccustomed taste. "You will get to like it," Sarah said, then, as she saw through the window how the sun had moved westward, she gathered up her basket and white cloth and put a hand on John's shoulder. "We should be going my love, for the boys will be home."

They called Mary from her play with the children, and gladly accepted a basket of early apples from Jane. "I'm sorry Paul is not back yet, he would like to hear about the Friends," she said as she walked with them to the cart and gave a carrot to the patiently waiting horse. "Don't worry," John helped Mary up. "We'll come and visit you again if we may," and with waves and good wishes from both sides the visitors set off on the journey back to Plymouth.

Sarah glanced at her husband with relief. There was colour in his cheeks and he seemed relaxed and rested. "We must have more outings like this," Sarah thought, and, as if to echo what was in her mind, John, taking the reins with a flourish, said, "We won't wait too long before we come again. It'll be good to talk to Paul about Friends, it may be that a Meeting could be started out here." "Yes, if it seems right, but we'll have to see," Sarah was cautious. "Thou hast enough to do, husband, with caring for Plymouth Meeting."

The drive home was as pleasant as the one out had been, John pointing out to Mary the birds and flowers they passed, but somehow as they came back into Plymouth, the bright afternoon seemed to have clouded for Sarah. The evening was still soft and mild, but her own serenity seemed to be disturbed.

The house in Rag Stree was empty, but John-Richard and William came in soon after their parents. John rested in his great chair, while Sarah with Mary's help, quickly set about the supper preparations.

"Have you seen Elizabeth?" she asked her sons. "I thought she would be here when we returned?" "No mother, she has not been into the shop, and we have been busy all day." Sarah was uneasy. Elizabeth seemed to have withdrawn more than ever into herself of late, and though not disobedient, was often away from the house when her chores were finished without telling anyone, and would come back with only vague accounts of a walk or time spent with her friends, usually Betsy's daughter Joan or John Light's granddaughters, Prudence and Patience. Sarah carried the rabbit pie to the table and called the others. "It smells very good, my love. The country air's given me an appetite." John took his place, the boys on either side of him, and only then did he seem to notice Elizabeth's absence. "Our daughter still out, it's getting late, isn't it?" Sarah took a deep breath, she longed to share her worries with John, they had never had secrets from each other, not in all their long years

154

together, but she wanted to spare him from any of the anxieties she was sure awaited them, so she said now, "Oh she won't be long. I know they were only going along the beach." There was a moment's silence and John gave thanks for their meal, Sarah started to serve the pie. Suddenly the door opened and Elizabeth was there. All faces turned to look at her and John smiled. "We were beginning to wonder what the beach had to hold you more strongly than us and your supper. Come and sit down." Elizabeth looked at her mother, who took in the overbright eyes and flushed face, with tendrils of hair escaping from under her cap, and felt her heart ache for this daugher whose growing up was not to be without its difficulties. "Yes, come and sit down," she said now briskly, "or the food will be cold, we can talk later."

Sarah strove to keep supper a pleasant, relaxed meal, and John seemed not to notice the underlying strain. When the meal was finished, and the family had shared the customary quiet of Meeting, Sarah encouraged John to go to bed. "Thou hast had a long day, my love," she said. "Elizabeth and I will finish our tasks, and I shall not be long." "But the day has been as long for thee, dear wife, and as tiring." Yet, nonetheless, he did not take much persuading and before the mild summer evening had quite turned to darkness, Sarah and Elizabeth were sitting together on either side of the hearth, Sarah in her husband's great chair, as though its very purpose as belonging to the head of the household would give her the strength to be firm.

Her daughter had taken her own stool, and faced her mother now with a set face, but with a wariness in her eyes that reminded Sarah of how, as a child, Elizabeth had often, when brought to task for some small demeanour, been defensive and ready with excuses. She looked up at Sarah now. "What is wrong mother, I was not very late home, and I had finished all you asked me to do." Sarah reached out a hand to her. "I am not yet blaming you, my child, but I - we - have been concerned for some time. You seem so distant from us." "Father has said nothing. I do not seem to have displeased him." Sarah bit her lip. "You know your father is not well. I do not want to worry him, surely we can settle any difficulties ourselves. Can you not talk to me?" She sat back in the big chair praying for the right words to come to her. "You do not understand, mother. You and father, it is so easy for you. You have the

Meeting and the simple way and it is enough." "But it's your life too, my child, these things are yours too." Elizabeth stood up then, pulling her cap from her head and flinging it to the ground as though rejecting all it signified. "But it's not enough, I want - oh, other things, pretty things, and oh, some gaiety in my life."

Sarah's hear smote her. "I do understand," she said, "and do not forget, I was once young like you, even though those days seem far distant now and it was before the coming of the Light that changed all our lives. So there was for us, your father and me and our friends, a whole new way of living, albeit one which we gladly embraced." Elizabeth started to pace the room, stopping at the window, then swinging round to face her mother. "But you had a choice, I never have."

Sarah rose too and faced the girl, taking her hands in her own, seeing in her tall, fair slimness, a mirror of herself at that age. "I cannot argue against that my child. We have tried to make a good and happy home for you all, as I myself knew, back before the war, and I suppose we did not query that it would be right for you too." "Oh mother," the girl was weeping now, and as Sarah's tears joined hers, she gripped her mother's hands tightly. "I would not hurt you, but you have often told me how you questioned all matters when you were a girl, and looked to grandfather for knowledge and advice." And as Sarah remembered how patient Richard had always been with her impatience, she knew that much time and understanding must be given to this daughter of hers, and that she must bring John into all new developments. But she could not do it all at once. She wiped Elizabeth's tears now, and tried to keep her voice firm. "I am glad we have spoken thus, now it is clear between us, we can seek the right way to help you." Then, remembering the high colour in her daughter's cheeks when she had returned to supper earlier, she said, "But to this afternoon, it did not seem to me that you had been walking with Joan or the other girls. Can you tell me who your companion was?"

There was silence in the room for what seemed to Sarah a very long time, and the fading light cast shadows across her daughter's face. She heard the girl's quick intake of breath, and then the words, so soft that she had to strain to hear them. "It - it was Samuel Rowe, his family have not long lived in Plymouth, only since the siege. His father is a Cornishman. He fought with the Royalist

156

troops and was taken prisoner and allowed to stay here afterwards."
"Where he has settled and brought up a family," Sarah finished for
her. "Yes, I see, he was not the only one to do so, but I do not
know that name. Where do they live?" Elizabeth was sitting again
by now, and with eyes downcast, twisted the corner of her apron
between her fingers. "Across the other side of the quay," she murmured, "just beyond the fishermen's cottages." Sarah's hand went
to her mouth as she gasped, thinking of the few hovels, for they
were no more, that straggled towards the shore, and her heart ached
as she saw the defence that sprang to Elizabeth's eyes. "His father
fishes sometimes with the other men, but there is not much work
now, and there are younger children. They are very poor, mother,
you would be sorry to see how hard their mother struggles." Tears
ran down her cheeks, and her mother held out her arms and gathered the girl to her. "Oh my love, my love, do not distress yourself
so. Come," and she drew her down beside her in the big chair,
then when the sobs eased she said, "But what about Samuel, what
is his place in this family?" "Oh mother, he is very good. He works
hard at anything he can find to do to help support them all.
Sometimes there is work for the soldiers and, as you know, the new
fort is still not finished, so often he labours there." She paused for
breath and Sarah smiled, in spite of her anxiety. "He certainly has
a good advocate in thee, daughter. Tell me, if he works so hard,
when do you see him, and how did you meet?"

Elizabeth blushed. "It was on the beach," she said, "a few
weeks ago we were both gathering cockles and winkles, though we
had not noticed each other. Then I dropped my pail and spilled
all the shell fish. He came to help me pick them up, and we sat
for a while talking - on that big flat stone where you sit sometimes,
mother." And as the evening held the two of them in its darkening closeness, Sarah remembered Will and how they had sat
together and shared each other's hopes and fears all those years
ago. "What had you to talk about?" she asked quietly now. "Oh,
Sam talked of all the things he hopes to do one day." Sarah could
feel the excitement coursing through the slim body so close to her.
"He talks of going to London, there are such things to see there,
and after the great Fire there will be building going on for a long
time and plenty of work. He is quite grown-up, you know, almost
seventeen, just a month older than I am, and, oh mother, I do love
you and father and everyone else here, and Plymouth which is my

157

home, but there is so much to see beyond this place and I ache to see it."

Sarah rose from her seat and walked to the door with Elizabeth. "I am trying to understand all you have told me, but it is late and we must both seek our beds. Good-night, dear child, we will talk again," and as she watched the slim figure run lightly up the stairs, Sarah wondered if perhaps some of her own young outward striving, never realised, was seeking its outlet now in Elizabeth.

She lay awake long that night, her mind tumultuous with thoughts but as she lay close to John, thankful for his peaceful breathing, she encircled him lightly with her arm, and knew without any doubt at all, that whatever her youthful ideas might have been, she had now within the circle of her life and loved ones all that she could ever want or need.

Chapter Twenty-eight

MATTERS SEEMED EASIER between Elizabeth and Sarah for the next few weeks. Sarah tried desperately to seek the best way of helping her daughter without worrying John about it, though she knew that somehow, and soon, she must involve him.

On a warm autumn day when for once she had the house to herself, and had just put a batch of mutton pies to cool, she suddenly knew what she must do now. She picked up her biggest basket and lined it with a white cloth. Then she put some of the pies carefully inside, together with a slab of cheese, two newly-baked crusty loaves, a pat of butter and some apples. Then, remembering the young children Elizabeth had mentioned, she added marchpane and a pot of honey, and taking her cloak she left the house and walked quickly down to the quay and across the beach, pausing to rest for a few moments on the big stone, for the basket was heavy. Then, on she went past the fishermen's cottages to the forlorn dwellings beyond.

Sarah saw that the first of these had been abandoned to seabirds and lichens, its wooden door hanging disconsolately, and the whole building sagging at a drunken angle. She picked her way across the shingle to the other cottage and stopped a few yards from it, wondering what to say and do now that she was actually there. She knew that John would have been concerned that she had come alone, exposed to possible danger from people very poor and probably hungry. But she tried to remember that there was that of God in all men and women that she must reach out to, and she moved her basket to the other hand and covered quickly the last few steps.

The cottage was partly hidden by an outcrop of rock which sheltered it from the worst of the westerly gales. Smoke was coming from the tiny crooked chimney, and as she hesitated a small girl came running through the dark doorway, followed by a tiny toddler. For a moment Sarah was not sure whether this was a girl or boy, for the child was covered from neck to his bare feet in an old, well-washed shirt and as he toddled out after his sister he tripped and fell on the rough shingle, for the cottage had no garden. Sarah ran forward but a woman came quickly from the cottage and gathered the child up in her arms, comforting him. Turning, she saw Sarah, and for a moment the two women stood looking at each other. Then the mother called to the little girl who had disappeared behind the rocks that sheltered the cottage. "Meg, I need you to look after Joshua - in the house, or he will follow you and fall again." The child came to her mother and caught hold of her apron, staring at Sarah with big, dark eyes. Sarah picked up her basket and walked the few steps that separated them. She felt unsure of herself, but seeing Elizabeth's face in her mind, knew she must bridge this gap.

She smiled at the woman. "Children always seem to be falling down at this age, don't they? Is he all right - Joshua, isn't it?" and taking a piece of marchpane from her basket, she held it out to the child. After a moment's hesitation he stretched out a tiny fist and took the sweatmeat. His mother hesitated. "I don't know," she said, but the warmth of Sarah's smile seemed to convince her, and when Sarah offered a piece of the marchpane to Meg, she led the way to the cottage.

"Come in," she said, that was all, but Sarah obeyed, looking around her as she did so. The single room was small and dark, but Sarah could see that it was swept clean, and the table, though crowded, had an orderliness about it. There were simple cooking utensils, and a few vegetables - "Not very fresh," thought Sarah to herself, "but all the poor woman could get, I expect." Then she realised that it was up to her to offer some explanation.

"Thou dost not know me, Mistress Rowe, but I am Sarah Luscombe. We live across the other side of the harbour, in Rag Street, in fact, and I believe your son Samuel is acquainted with my daughter Elizabeth." Ann Rowe put the toddler down on the floor to play with his sister before answering, and when she turned round she was frowning. "My Samuel is a good son, he works very hard for us all - his father tries but work is hard to come by, and he gets very, well, discouraged, but Sam will do anything. He has very little time to himself, but I have wondered. Of late he he has seemed distant sometimes, even from me." She looked at Sarah's

160

dress as if seeing it for the first time. "You are one of those sober families, are you not?" "Yes, we're Quakers, there is quite a community of us here in Plymouth. We are fortunate in that we help each other, and all have more than enough for our needs, so - we try to help those for whom life is more difficult, and I wondered-" she lifted her basket onto the table, "I'd been baking and had made too much." Ann Rowe hesitated. "We manage," there was independence in her voice, but she looked at her children and Sarah knew she would accept help for them. Sarah took out the provisions, feeling she had done all she could for the moment, when there were footsteps on the shingle outside and a large frame filled the narrow doorway. "Mother, I've had a good day. I've some plump herrings, and - "

The lad who came into the cottage seemed to bring new life into the small room. The children ran to him, clinging to his legs, while his mother's eyes were filled instantly with love and pride. Samuel Rowe was tall - as John had been at his age, remembered Sarah - but broader, and with strength it seemed in shoulders and arms. His clothes, though poor, were clean and well patched, his hose darned and his boots scuffed but still strong. His eyes, like those of his mother, were a very bright blue - the dark ones of his brother and sister must have come from their father, Sarah thought, and the boy's dark auburn hair matched that of the loose tendrils escaping from under the mother's cap. He looked enquiringly from her to Sarah.

"This is Mistress Luscombe," Ann Rowe said, "from up in the town - her daughter Elizabeth, it seems you know her." The boy's face, already ruddy with wind and fresh air, blushed deeper. Sarah could see that he didn't know what was expected of him and for a moment she felt sorry for him. "My daughter speaks highly of you, Samuel," she said gently, "and of how hard you work. I thought perhaps I should come and meet you and your family. But I must go now," and she picked up her basket ready to leave. The boy and his mother spoke together. "Thank you," they both said, Ann adding "for the food," and Sam, "but we can manage. I look after us all." "Yes, your mother has told me," Sarah smiled at him. "You must come and see us, ask Elizabeth to bring you." "Let me carry your basket," he said, and when she hesitated, "just across the beach, the shingle's very uneven. I won't be long, mother," and they were gone, the children watching them from the doorway. "Of course," Sarah said, "that's how you and Elizabeth met, isn't it, when she tripped and dropped her pail of shell-fish?" Sam blushed again. "Yes, it was fortunate I was there." He stood back for her to walk round a tiny rockpool. They didn't speak again till they reached the end of the harbour. Then Sam gave Sarah's basket to her. "I am glad to have met you," he said, then shyly, "Elizabeth is very like you." On impulse Sarah said, "Will you come back to the house with me now?" But the boy shook his head. "Thank you, no, but later I should like to," and he turned and was gone, running back across the beach.

Sarah walked on up the hill to home, her thoughts in turmoil. She liked what she had seen of this boy, in spite of his background, for she sensed there was a depth to him she could not yet fathom and she realised that the way both he and his mother had spoken did not seem to belong to that poor cottage. There were mysteries here to solve, and as she went into her own house, Sarah felt that the solving of them would be worthwhile.

When Sarah reached home she found the family all there before her, so she was able to busy herself right away with preparations for supper without having to answer too many questions. They were all used to seeing her around with her big basket taking food to the poor of the town so this was just another such occasion. As she moved quickly between the kitchen fire and dining-table, she noticed thankfully that John seemed better, stronger, and as they sat around the big table, healthy appetites soon devouring the rest of the mutton pies and the rabbit stew, she thought how fortunate she was in her comfortable home and fine family, and she knew that she must do what she could to help the Rowes, and maybe Elizabeth as well. Her daughter was quiet and through the meal darted glances at Sarah from under her lowered eye lids, but it was only when the two of them were working together in the kitchen after supper that Sarah was able to say quietly, "I met Samuel this afternoon and his mother and the younger children. I went to their cottage." She heard Elizabeth's quick intake of breath before she turned to look at her, and she saw the girl blush then look worried. "But mother, I did not know, was there any trouble? Was Sam's father there?" "No. I didn't meet him, but I enjoyed talking to Mistress Rowe and the children." "And Sam?" the girl whispered.

162

"Yes, and Sam. He came in just as I was leaving, he walked back along the beach with me, and he seems a fine young man." Elizabeth put down the platter she was holding and threw her arms around her mother. "Oh, he is," she cried, "he's so good to them all, they rely on him so much." "Yes, my love, I could see that, in fact I've some thoughts about it. Come, let's finish these and we'll have a talk."

So it was that sometime later, when William and Mary had both gone to their beds, John was sitting in his great chair with a pile of the shop's accounts on his knees. He looked up from them as Sarah came back into the room. "Ah, my love, hast thou come to join me for a while?" "Yes, husband, I have, and Elizabeth too, for we would speak with thee." She drew the girl forwards and they sat together facing John.

"This sounds a serious matter," he said, his smile belying his words. "Is the meeting just to be the three of us then?" "Yes, it is," Sarah replied, "for the moment at any rate." She took her daughter's hand in her own, and with a look of encouragement to her began, "Elizabeth has a new friend, that we would like to tell you about. His name is Samuel Rowe." John looked puzzled. "Rowe," he said. "That is not a name familiar to me. You say he is a Friend here in Plymouth?" Sarah looked up at him. "Not a Friend within the Meeting, but a - a companion that Elizabeth has come to know. I met him yesterday and most of his family." John's interest was aroused now, and he listened intently as Sarah continued, telling him of the poor circumstances of the family, of how they had come to be in Plymouth, and last - and here she tried to explain most carefully - of how Samuel himself seemed to be a fine hard-working lad who had taken the whole support of the family onto his own shoulders.

John listened, gravely looking at the two anxious faces before him. "He sounds a fine young man, as you say my dear, though I do not see what future there can be for Elizabeth in this friendship." Sarah paused for a moment, feeling that what she said now, and how she said it, could have a great bearing on what lay ahead, perhaps for all of them. "I have been wondering John, as the business is doing so well, and you are all working so hard, that perhaps you could find a place for Samuel. He would be very quick to learn, I'm sure." She felt Elizabeth draw in her breath quickly, and turned to her. "I have not had time to discuss this with you, daughter, but it seemed to me that it might be a good thing." "Oh yes, mother, I'm sure it could be," and both women looked expectantly towards John. "You must understand," he said thoughtfully, "that this has all been rather sudden for me, I can't take into my employ every worthy but poor young man who comes my way. However, perhaps I could talk to this Samuel Rowe. If you are likely to see him, Elizabeth, perhaps you will arrange this, though I have to say that nothing may come of it. And now, my loves, it is getting late, I think we should all seek our rest." Elizabeth kissed them both goodnight, embracing each of them tightly, though no more was said.

But when John and Sarah were within the privacy of their own chamber, she turned to him with great thankfulness. "Thou art a good man, my love. I am so grateful to have thee." John held her tightly. "The good fortune is mine, my dearest wife, and has been through all the years we have been together. But if it is that young man you are thinking of, well I do not yet know what can be done. We shall have to see, and we know it is not a good thing for Elizabeth to get too attached to someone not of our faith." But Sarah's certainty that John would find a way would not be quenched, and that night the two of them found a depth and a closeness that Sarah was to remember for a very long time.

But for the next few weeks she had no opportunity to support any help for Sam, for John-Richard's wife, Margaret, went into early labour, and it took all Sarah's skill and care to save both mother and baby. All through the difficult time, Sarah thought of Betsy, Margaret's mother, and felt her helping and guiding her. But at last Margaret was well enough to receive at least some members of the family into her cottage bedroom and to show her little daughter, Catherine, so that her dark hair and big brown eyes could be admired, and her tiny features recognised as belonging to this or that relation.

Sarah stood beside the bed in the small room, with John-Richard on the other side, proudly holding his young wife's hand, and when John came hurrying up the stairs, Sarah turned happily to him. "Look, my love, our first grand-child, a beautiful little girl," and together they looked at the tiny baby with great love and pride. Margaret's sister, Joanna, came into the room then, carrying a bowl of water and towels. "If you can manage for a while," Sarah said to her, "I'll go home for a little. It seems a long time since I saw Rag Street."

She and John walked slowly up the hill to home, arm in arm. "Has Elizabeth been looking after you, my dear?" she asked. "Yes, she has done very well, well-trained by her mother. And talking of Elizabeth, I have seen Samuel Rowe." Sarah stopped suddenly. "Oh, I had forgotten Sam, with all the concern about Margaret. Tell me, what did you think of him?" and she waited anxiously for her husband's reply.

Chapter Twenty-nine

"LET US GET HOME first," John took her arm again, "it seems so long since you were there, and I want to make the most of time with you till you hurry off to Margaret again." "I shall not neglect you much longer, my dear, for I think Joanna can manage now." Nonetheless, Sarah did not ask again about Sam but continued up the hill with John. Much later when they had time together, John told her all that had happened. "Do not worry about Elizabeth, for the moment at any rate," he said as their daughter went up to her room, "for she has been a part of all our discussions. I have seen Samuel, and talked long with him. He's a strong-minded young man and very proud -" John smiled at the recollection, "- reminded me of myself at his age, though the red hair is all his own. At all events, he is to start with us next week. I've told him it will at first be clearing up and generally helping, he would have some time then for his own fishing and other work. But if he proves willing and capable, well, perhaps I could teach him the business. At any rate, I hope it will keep Elizabeth more contented for a while." "So do I," Sarah replied fervently, "we don't want her going off to London with him. Thank you, husband, thou hast done well. And hast thou met any of the rest of the family?" "No, only Samuel. I gathered from some of the things the boy let fall that the father is rather feckless, and is fonder of strong ale than he is of work." Sarah nodded. "We will do what we can, husband, and seek guidance for what we cannot." And with that the two of them found a contented rest.

The next few weeks were busy ones for Sarah - with the new baby to fuss over, and Sam to get to know, while she kept a careful eye on John, thankful that he seemed to be maintaining better health. This improvement lasted through into the new year, one which was to prove eventful for them all.

166

In the Spring news came from Swarthmoor Hall in Ulverston that George Fox was to marry Margaret Fell, the widow of Judge Fell, who, though he never became a Quaker himself, yet always supported his wife in her faith and gave shelter in his home to many persecuted Friends. Plymouth Meeting decided to hold a special Meeting for Worship to give thanks for this union. John and the other Elders sent letters to the couple, hoping that they might visit the west-country if at all possible - Plymouth hopefully, Exeter perhaps, or even Bristol - and plans were made for a great gathering. But they knew this could not be till later in the summer and meanwhile Plymouth would have its own meeting followed by a celebratory meal - out of doors, if the weather held, and in the Meeting House itself if, as was likely, the spring was chilly. Elizabeth and Sarah worked together cooking and baking for the meal and one day Sarah took the opportunity to make a suggestion to her daughter. "I wonder," she said, "whether Sam might like to come - not to the Meeting, I wouldn't suggest that - but perhaps to the dinner next day. I thought he might like to meet some of the other Friends. You know they're friendly, helpful people." "I don't know, mother," Elizabeth put down the bowl of pastry she'd been mixing. "He likes to keep to himself, though he works hard, father is pleased with him." Sarah smiled at her immediate defence of Samuel and put an arm around the girl's shoulder. "Yes, my love, I know what a good worker he is, and I've come to like him very much the more I have seen of him, and he is certainly a great help to Father, lifting and carrying all the heavy loads. It's just a thought I will leave with you."

Then suddenly the faintness that had attacked her frequently during the last few weeks overcame her again, and she told Elizabeth to "carry on with the pies, love, I must just sit down for a few minutes." As she did so, in her own chair, resting her head against its carved back and closing her eyes, she knew that she could no longer deny what was happening to her. She was with child, and with God's blessing would give birth later in the summer, and her mind went back to the time last autumn when in the early worries they had shared about Elizabeth, she and John had drawn so close together.

As she rose to her feet again and went back into the kitchen to continue the baking, smiling at Elizabeth who turned anxiously to

167

her, she thought how strange it was that their love for this daughter had led to the creation of another child.

She kept the knowledge to herself for a few days longer, pondering it in her heart and mind, though knowing that she must, very soon, share it with John.

The next afternoon she wrapped her cloak around her, for the spring air was still chill, and walked down to the beach, to the long flat stone which had been the scene of so many of her hopes and fears through the years. This new secret was to her a mingling of both and she wanted to be clear before she presented it - like a gift - to the husband she loved so dearly. Although it was only now that she had admitted to herself what had happened, the knowledge had been creeping up on her over the past weeks. But could this really be happening to her - to them? They were grand-parents after all, this child would be younger than little Catherine. Then she thought of how she had held that latest member of their family - the warmth and sweetness of her - and knew that she would love the coming child as dearly as she loved all the other children and John - she knew - he would feel the same.

But John was almost forty-two, she herself would be thirty-nine when the baby came. Well, many women had late babies and managed, and she was fortunate in having a good family and friends and the means to bring up another child - the means, the business, John - her thoughts moved from one consideration to another then stopped at John. He needed all her care and attention. How could she look after him properly and a new baby? John's health was better at the moment, certainly, but it was fragile she knew. Her mind raced for a moment then she tried to be completely still, there on the beach - quiet and still, until she felt a sense of peace steal through her. If God had given them this blessing, then he would also give her the strength to manage. She got to her feel now, calm and sure, and walked as quickly as she could across the quay and up the hill to her home.

She was glad later on that evening when she broke the news to John that she had had this time to prepare herself. She could see in his eyes the jumble of his thoughts and feelings, and was ready for them, both the joy and the concern - especially for her - and she felt a cold chill of fear when he said, "I am glad, my love, that whatever happens to me, you will have friends and family around you and I must make preparations so that all will be well." Sarah threw her arms round him. "It is only you I want, my love," and she buried her face in his chest. John stroked her hair. "And I hope too that our time together will be long and happy, but we must be provident," and for that night alone they shared their secret with no-one, but thought and talked and planned about it, and prayed that all would be well.

Soon, however, they told their family and Friends, and the Meeting to give thanks for the union of George Fox and Margaret Fell, asked as well for blessings on John and Sarah. The shared meal the next day was a great success with tables spread in the Meeting House itself, all the women bringing food and ale - pies, tarts and bread, cheese, honey and butter, great pots of stew and even one of tea, for this, though still a delicacy, was arriving in small quantities at John's shop quite frequently now.

The day was fine and sunny though kept cool by a strong wind blowing from the sea. Friends walked across the Hoe, bringing their contributions, the adults greeting each other as they met and the children running, skipping and playing, the older ones happy at a day's holiday from school and the young people walking together in groups, some quiet and shy, others laughing and jostling one another. When Sarah came outside the Meeting House to pick up some platters left on the grass, she saw both William and Mary amongst a group of these young people and realised that at fifteen and nearly twelve they would soon by fully grown, and away on lives of their own, and she gently touched her swelling stomach with a feeling of comfort that there would still be a child to care for.

As she turned back inside, when one of the other women called her, she saw coming to the Meeting House from a different direction, two figures walking close together.

They were Elizabeth and Sam, and she was struck by the contrasting picture they made, her daughter tall and slender in her plain grey gown with fresh white collar and bonnet, and the boy, taller still and broad, his red hair and ruddy complexion bright above his plain but well-darned shirt and hose, and she wondered what lay ahead for these two.

Chapter Thirty

"I'M GLAD THOU hast come, Samuel." Sarah put out her hand in welcome to the boy, and reached to take from him the basket he was carrying. "Let me take it inside for you," he said. "'Tis heavy," and following as she and Elizabeth led the way into the Meeting House, he placed it on the floor beside the long, already-loaded, table where Joanna and Margaret and some of the other women were working. Then he turned away shyly. "Master Luscombe will not be long, he is just closing the shop. Can I do anything to help you?" "No, this is a free day for you, or at any rate half a day, so go with Elizabeth and meet some of the other young people. It will soon be time to have the meal." They did as they were bid and Sarah, glancing from the doorway, saw them talking to William and Mary, both of whom Sam already knew, and to Francis' boys, Joshua and Thomas and James' son Oliver. Samuel towered above them all, but at least he stayed there talking to them, Sarah thought. "Yes, maybe matters were going in the right direction after all."

Everyone enjoyed the meal, partaken after a brief silence and a shared prayer. Sam sat at one ond of the long table with some of the young people, but Sarah, as she passed dishes and filled tankards, noted that he was quiet and neither ate nor talked much, but his eyes watched Elizabeth as she helped her mother. Suddenly, just as it seemed that appetites were satisfied and the talk lessening, there came a loud, urgent banging on the door. Friends looked at each other anxiously. Was there trouble outside the Meeting House, there had been little persecution of late but the older Quakers knew it could start up again at any time. They waited for a moment, the men standing now, quiet, preparing themselves, the women looking to the children, gathering the small ones close, so that within those few moments the whole scene changed.

Then the banging came again, and James, who was near the door, turned to the others. "We must open it, Friends, there is nothing to be gained by waiting." He pulled open the heavy wooden door, while breath was held, or quiet prayers murmured, but only a young boy stood there, panting from running, his hair falling over his face and by his clothes seeming to be from one of the fishing families. "Sam, where's Sam, he's wanted quick - now." The boy's eyes were searching the Meeting House, as James turned swiftly to call Sam, but he was already at the door. "What is it, young Nat, what's happened?" "'Tis your father, down on the beach, he's had a fall. I was sent to fetch you. I'd best get back," and he was gone, his bare feet flying across the grass. Sam only paused for an apology to Sarah and a quick squeeze of Elizabeth's hand before he was gone too, his long strides easily overtaking Nat's shorter ones. For a moment there was a stunned silence, then a babel of noise within the building as everyone seemed to be speaking at once, with anxiety for what had happened down on the shore, and a relief that many felt that there was not more trouble for the Friends. Elizabeth turned nervously to her mother. "Do you think it's bad? Should we try to help?" and Sarah looked up at John, the same question in her eyes. They were joined by James and John-Richard. "I think some of us should see if help is needed," said the ever-practical James. "I'll go down with John-Richard and a couple of the younger lads - Joshua and Oliver will you come? - and we'll see what's happening." They set off after the others, while John said a prayer for them all and the women set to clearing the table and packing up the remnants of food.

"Will they let us know what is happening?" Elizabeth's hands were busy but it was clear that her thoughts were down on the beach. "Yes, my love, of course, and we'll finish here and go home to wait. There is still food to spare, we'll put a basket or two ready in case it is needed." They walked back across the Hoe with Mistress Light and Mistress Harris, and then took the path to Rag Street and home. The Spring evening was darkening and Sarah and Elizabeth were glad to rest for a while in the comfort of their own home. But Elizabeth soon became restless and searched the windows for someone bringing news. At last the front door opened, but it was only to admit John, who had been back to the shop to check some goods which had arrived. He looked anxiously at Sarah, for although he was glad to see her taking a rest, this was such an unusual occurrence that he was always concerned at what it might mean.

He came and sat beside her, and a few minutes later the door opened again, this time to admit John-Richard. Elizabeth flew to him. "What has happened, where is Sam?" "Give your brother a chance to get in. Come and sit down." Sarah was going through to the kitchen. "I will fetch some ale." William and Mary had joined them by now and they all waited anxiously to hear what John-Richard would tell them. "At first it was thought there had been a fight," the young man began, conscious of his position as information-giver, "but it appears more likely that he was drunk and fell and hit his head on a jagged piece of rock. At any rate he's dead, they tried to revive him but it was no good." Elizabeth and her mother both caught their breath. "The poor family," Sarah's hand went instinctively to her stomach and the child within her. "We must see what we can do." John-Richard continued, "There were neighbours there when we arrived - from the other cottage - and they've carried him home. Our people are doing what they can to help and Uncle James has told Mistress Rowe that we will sort matters out tomorrow and will see that they are not in need." "Perhaps we should go down now with food at least." Sarah got to her feet, but John put a restraining hand on her arm and was glad when his elder son confirmed what he was thinking. "I think we should leave them together for this night," he said, "they have Sam. Tomorrow will be time enough to go down, and they will be glad then of your help, I'm sure." At the mention of Sam's name, Elizabeth's hand went to her throat. "Is he managing?" she asked quietly. "Oh yes, he is coping with them all. I'll warrant he has been the mainstay of that family for a very long time." It was obvious that no more could be done that night. John-Richard returned to his own home and the inhabitants of Rag Street sought their beds.

The next few weeks saw the lives of the Rowe family drastically changed, for time could not be wasted. With the death of the father and husband, the cottage, poor place that it was, would be lost to them, so a home was the urgent need. John, after a hasty consultation with his family, suggested what seemed the best possible solution. He had been for some time considering opening a shop at Plympton, for he already had customers from that far away.

There was a premises available and John-Richard would manage it. Sam and William would help John with the original business where Sam was already proving very valuable, and he, with his mother and young brother and sister, would move into John-Richard's cottage. The journey each day, with the long hours that would be involved, especially at first, would be too much for the new manager, so he with Margaret and young baby Catherine would move into the empty cottage adjoining the Plympton shop.

The evening that all these matters were settled, when Sam had joined them for supper, the family gave quiet thanks for the way that God had led them into this right ordering, and Elizabeth, glancing at Sam, felt a great flood of thankfulness flow through her, that he seemed to share with them in this knowledge of how they had been led. It was a tiny beginning, but she hugged to herself the hope that it gave her.

There was plenty for everyone to do, the women cleaned and prepared the new home at Plympton and there were expeditions by horse and cart which took on quite a holiday atmosphere, with the early summer sunshine and hedges full of wild roses. Sarah was persuaded by John to let the young people, with James to organise them, carry on with the work, but she looked after Catherine for Margaret and as soon as her cottage was cleared, helped to prepare it for the Rowe family. Their possessions were pitifully few but the house in Rag Street yielded extra stools and benches, and Sarah took from her store chests blankets and coverlets. At first Mistress Rowe was reluctant to accept help, but gradually was persuaded by the kindness of those around her. Sarah knew that the ice was broken when she came upon her in the new home one day, sitting quietly weeping while her younger children stood silently by, unsure of what was happening.

Sarah went straight to the woman, smoothing back her auburn hair, and kneeling, put her arms around her. "All will be well, Ann" she said. "You will always be amongst friends now," and turning to Mary who had come with her, she said, "Take the children to play in the garden. There is some marchpane for them in my basket." And the two women sat quietly together exchanging confidences. In fact from that day on a warm friendship developed - albeit slowly at first - between Sarah and Ann and gradually they found much that they could share. It transpired that Ann came from a sober Saltash family, none of whom now remained. She had married the dashing young Royalist soldier, Jeremiah, and followed him to Plymouth, waiting for him to be released from prison at the end of the war. However, the marriage was not a happy one, for Jeremiah had no liking for honest toil, and drank away most of the little he earned. But Sarah guessed that what had been hardest for the young wife to bear, had been the lack of all sensitivity and understanding, so that it was to Sam she increasingly turned for advice and even conversation. "Perhaps I relied on him too much," she said now to Sarah, "making him a man before he was a boy, but when the little ones came and Jeremiah seemed to get worse, it was the only way we could manage." "I'm sure you did what was right," Sarah got to her feet as Mary came back with the children, "but you will have many new friends now, and we can all look forward to my new baby." As she walked home with Mary, Sarah had a lot to ponder over, mostly matters of hope, but she had just a thread of unease, that if Samuel was so committed to his family, what room would there be for her poor Elizabeth, even supposing other problems could be overcome.

But, that concern apart, it was a calm and happy summer for Sarah. This pregnancy was the easiest she had known, and though she missed Betsy, the rest of her women-folk rallied around and made things easier for her. She and John spent much time together, and he kept fairly strong, though she tried to put out of her mind the knowledge that this was because he did little in the business now except to oversee that all went well - just as her father had done all those years ago. John relied much on William and Sam while he and Sarah took short walks together and sat in the garden or on the beach, and whenever he tried to talk of the future and how things might be for her, she hushed him gently, saying "Let us live and enjoy one day at a time, my love, and leave the rest to God."

So it was that when she woke one morning and knew that this day would not be as any other, she did not tell John but encouraged him to go to the shop. "You have neglected it of late, husband, go to-day, then we can spend time together again without concern."

When he had gone she called Elizabeth to her, sent Mary to fetch Joanna and Mistress Harris, and quietly made her preparations.

174

Chapter Thirty-one

THE SUMMER WAS so long and balmy in that year of 1669 that the people of Plymouth hardly noticed when September came to the town. Sarah felt quite excited as John helped her up into the cart, and handed baby Thomas to her.

This was her first real outing since Thomas had been born a few weeks earlier and they were off to visit John-Richard's new home in Plympton. Sarah felt warm and happy as John tried in vain to encourage the horse to increase his usual plodding pace, and she held the tightly swaddled baby close to her as they jogged along. Her labour had been long, but after a few days of weakness it was soon forgotten, and once Thomas had been placed in her arms, with John proudly embracing them both, she was very thankful and content, and glad too that already he looked like his father with a thick thatch of black hair, and, Sarah insisted, a very sweet smile.

She looked at John now, and at his hands on the reins - such thin hands, with the wrists protruding as they always had from his cuffs. He felt her glance and placed one hand over hers. "Let us really enjoy this day," he said, "for God has sent us a warm and pleasant one." It was indeed a pleasant drive. Thomas slept and Sarah absorbed the beauty of the day and the closeness of her husband and child. The hedgerows were full of blackberries and elderberries and Sarah realised that for the first time for years she had not made preserves and cordials from the fruits. "But there are more important things," she thought, as the cart drew up at the end of the cobbled street outside the Luscombe's new shop.

Margaret came hurrying out to greet her and to take Thomas from her. "He gets more like his father every day," and she pulled back his covers to see the tiny face, eyes open now, as his mouth stretched in a wide yawn. Sarah's heart warmed at the words, as she stopped to admire the refurbished premises before following her daughter-in-law inside, while John was quickly engaged with John-Richard on matters of business. Margaret proudly showed her mother-in-law all that had been done to make this shop as up-to-date as it could be. It took up the whole of the ground floor and was light and airy, with goods well displayed. It had a large window, completely open now, for at night it was closed with shutters, let down by day to form a counter. Sarah ran her hand along the counter admiring the smooth surface. "Yes," said Margaret proudly, "John-Richard did that. He worked so hard on it." Sarah remembered, "he always liked to work with wood." "We're selling many more items now," Margaret went on. "We've got arrangements with some of the farms around here, and have ham, bacon and sausages from them. We thought, you see, that some families haven't got much in the way of facilities to make their own, so as long as we keep the prices down, they're glad to buy from us."

Sarah nodded in agreement, "and I warrant that if they can't pay they still have the goods." Margaret smiled. "Well, sometimes," and Sarah remembered how in the old bad days her brother James had given many a sack of flour to the poor. "And here,"Margaret pointed to some stout barrels ranged along one wall, "are herrings soused in vinegar. "I think they keep their flavour better than the dried ones." Sarah looked around at the variety of goods - at the scented herbs hanging from their hooks, and boxes of rushes ready to be laid on cottage floors, candles and rushlights, and even a collection of wooden buckets by the sacks of potatoes. Sarah took the baby as Margaret led her to the back of the shop. "We've put a store here so we can keep a lot more goods than the shop will hold. Now let's go next door and have some refreshments. Thou must be tired."

She turned to the village girl who was minding the counter. "Master Luscombe will be in shortly. He's only just outside," and as she and Sarah went out through the open doorway, James arrived with a cart-load of flour. "Uncle James always knows when it's time to stop for ale and pasties," she smiled at him and he, chuckling at his new nephew, followed the women into the cottage next door.

This too had been made as comfortable as possible, with two rooms downstairs and a kitchen, with a tiny dairy and a room where

176

the beer was brewed and potions distilled, behind them, while upstairs there was a sleeping chamber. Looking around Sarah could see many of Betsy's treasures and knew they were being put to good use. There was a small but beautifully figured spice cabinet that had been carved by Ned, and an embroidered wall-hanging that Sarah's Mother, Mary, had given her old friend, and Sarah saw now even the sampler with the crooked stitches that Sarah herself had made for Betsy all those years ago. Margaret called her now to the table where ale, cider and mutton pasties were laid out, plus a newly baked cheese-cake. "This all looks very appetising," Sarah took the chair offered to her, and laid Thomas in the carved wooden crib that had been used by little Catherine. In answer to Sarah's query, Margaret now said, "Kate is with Joanna to-day, they are great friends. But I have made thee tea, mother. I thought thou might prefer it." As they sat comfortably together, James having gone outside to join the other men, Sarah thought, as she so often did, how fortunate she was in John-Richard's choice of a wife, for she had brought to the family the same sense of comfort and understanding that her mother had given to them all.

She sighed now, hardly realising she had done so, till Margaret asked her gently, "Does something ail thee, perhaps thou hast come too far so soon after Thomas' birth?" "Oh no, 'tis not that, it's just that seeing the happy settled home that John-Richard now has with thee and Catherine, I worry about -" She paused, and Margaret said very softly, "About Elizabeth? I do not mean to interfere or cause thee pain, but I have wondered of late, sometimes she seems happy, but at others, well -" "Restless?" Sarah interrupted her, and then sighed deeply. She took a sip of her tea, glad to talk to Margaret. She could not worry John, but things were not right, she knew, with her daughter. "She had seemed more contented just a month or two back, and happy with her friendship with Sam." Margaret nodded. "He seems a straight and honourable lad, and John-Richard says he is a good worker." "Oh yes, all of that is true, but somehow I feel he is just waiting to move on. I know he has to support his mother and the little ones, and I had hoped that would make him feel part of our community, but I fear now it does not." They were both quiet for a moment, and then Margaret said thoughtfully, "I am sure that he loves Elizabeth, and she him. I have seen the way they look at each other and how close they are when they are together, as if they are already one." "Yes, it is just like that," there were tears in Sarah's eyes now. "I feel sometimes my poor Elizabeth is being torn apart. Sam seems to have no interest in our faith, so how can we ever entrust her to him? No, my great fear is that some day they will run away together. They used to talk of London." Margaret put her arms around the older woman and held her close. "Hush now, mother, do not be anxious. Things may not be as bad as they seem. I will speak to Elizabeth and see what is in her heart. Now, I can hear the men coming back," and she gently wiped Sarah's face and straightened her cap.

The drive home was quiet, Sarah was wrapt in her thoughts, as she held the baby close to her, while John looked weary and did not seem to notice her silence. A fresh wind had sprung up, and Sarah looking at the sky knew that the summer of 1669 was finally over.

Chapter Thirty-two

BACK AT RAG STREET, life for the family settled into a routine that, on the surface, seemed regular and comfortable, but undercurrents worried Sarah very much. The slight hope she'd had that Elizabeth was becoming more content had faded. The girl did all that was asked of her as she always had done, but no more. Sam too worked very hard for John and nothing was ever too much trouble for him. He and Elizabeth spent their free time together but it didn't seem to make either of them happy. Sarah saw the restlessness between them and sensed the tension. But, apart from talking sometimes to Margaret, which offered some little comfort, there was, for the moment, nothing she could do.

John caused her continuing concern and became thinner and less and less active, but his descent was so gradual and so without complaint that she accepted it almost with resignation.

Thomas flourished and was a contented baby, and the rest of the family seemed happy and well as 1669 became 1670. Even Sam's mother had settled well with her children into their new home. Sarah visited her sometimes but could not persuade Ann to mingle with the Friends.

Sarah welcomed news that came to them from the world outside Plymouth, and, especially as far as Friends were concerned, tried to see these happenings as part of God's wider plain, and she was glad too when John was able to take an interest in these matters. Sarah's two brothers, James and Francis, were the Meeting's contacts - supplying between them the practical, political concerns and those of a more spiritual nature.

They had had much news lately of two new Friends, William Penn and Robert Barclay, both aristocrats who had become Quakers. William was the pride of a well-established family, the son of an admiral, and became first a lawyer then a soldier. But in

179

1667 when he was still only 23 years old, he was convinced by a sermon he heard in Oxford, and so joined the Quakers. "He seemed to have been in trouble right away," said James one evening while they were all sitting together in Rag Street, "and has been in and out of prison for his outspoken beliefs ever since."

"Yes," commented Francis, "'Tis said he spends all his time while incarcerated writing books and pamphlets. Last year in the Tower of London he wrote - what was it? - oh yes, 'No Cross, No Crown'. I believe it has been a great inspiration to Friends. We expect a copy here as soon as possible." John's eyes lit up with interest at this. "We must have a Meeting, more than one I'm sure, to study what our Friend has written." "It is said," James went on thoughtfully, "that the King listens to him on matters of state as he does our Friend Robert Barclay, though that does not save them from persecution. Penn talks too of the New World - perhaps a time will come when this country can no longer hold him."

The conversation changed then to lighter matters, and great interest was expressed in the coffee that was beginning to arrive in the South West. "We haven't got any yet," said John, "but I believe John-Richard has a supply at Plympton." He looked fondly at his son. "They are much more go-ahead out there. I believe that the Grammar School they're building is well on the way to completion. 'Twill be in time for my grandson's education. But Friends, I'm sure there is coffee enough for you all to try it," and with a blessing and a moment's quiet, he sent them all to their homes.

Sarah, beset by a need to maintain a continuity to their lives as though to ward off any violent changes that might lie ahead, was determined that John should enjoy the early spring and see as much as possible of the countryside around Plymouth. Horrabridge was now too far for him to be jostled along country lanes, but there were many estates closer to home being developed and laid out with beautiful gardens, and so the two of them, with Thomas between them, took quiet expeditions off to Culme at Mannamead, Little Efford and Freedom Fields, and once they took a picnic and drove as far as Saltram House where the Parker family were establishing a fine home. As they paused and gazed at the work being carried on, John turned to Sarah with his gentle smile. "I cannot see, my love, why one family should need such a great house, and all the splendour that goes with it," and she with a squeeze of his arm, and only a hint of seriousness, replied, "Ah, but they have not yet learnt, husband, the simple ways of Friends," and she turned the horse towards home.

Although all his children were very dear to him, John took an especial delight in this youngest son of his, to which Thomas responded with all the warmth of his sunny nature, and although there was never a shortage of family members to care for him, it was to his father most of all that he would reach out to be picked up or played with, and it smote Sarah's heart grievously the day that she realised that even the baby's weight as he grew more plump and bonny was too much for John to lift. Thereafter she was always quick to anticipate the need of both of them and scooping up Thomas, would gently lay him on John's lap or beside him in the great chair.

One day in early May, when the weather had suddenly turned too chilly for out-of-doors excursions, John sat in his chair, a book on his lap, facing the window where he could see his garden and beyond it the sweep of the Sound. Thomas was at his feet on a rug and playing with wooden animals carved many years ago for the older children. Sarah was busy baking in the kitchen, looking in now and then to the living-rom to make sure that all was well. She felt at peace to-day, her family either here with her or not far away engaged on their various activities. Even Elizabeth had seemed happier the last few days, and as she worked, Sarah offered up a silent prayer of thankfulness for all her blessings.

Then, suddenly, as she wiped the flour from her hands and rolled down her sleeves, she heard her name called, just once - "Sarah". She flew to the room, and as she paused for a moment on the threshold, she knew that the scene that greeted her would remain etched for ever on her memory. Thomas must have crawled across to his father's chair, then pulled himself up by the arm and was standing, his fat legs in their baby gown, swaying in uncertainty, but his wide grin as he turned to his mother was full of pride at his own achievement. A tiny wooden pig lay on John's thin leg, while he, one hand outstretched towards his son, smiled at them both, then fell back, his head resting on the carved back of the chair and his hand falling to his side.

Sarah rushed across the room and taking Thomas sat him back on the rug with a "Good boy, Thomas, clever boy, now play with your toys." Then she threw herself down beside the still figure of her husband, willing him to respond to her, chaffing his cold hands and kissing frantically his white cheeks.

At last she knew that all life had gone from that beloved form, and she threw herself across him, gathering the thin body close to her and giving herself up to sobbing that seemed as if it would tear her body in two. She stayed thus as the evening shadows crept into the room and when Thomas, wondering why no-one was playing attention to him, crawled to her, she gathered him too within her embrace, hardly pausing in her paroxysm of grief, and thus they were found when William, followed closely by Mary and Elizabeth came in soon afterwards, expecting the usual warm welcome of a happy home.

Although Sarah had known that John's increasing frailty could not sustain him much longer, and had tried to prepare herself for the inevitable, yet his death when it came rendered her completely devastated, and she would not be comforted. She listened to the words of comfort and acceptance of her brothers and the other Friends, but although her mind tried to respond her heart could not. She went through the motions of the funeral preparations, allowing no-one to touch his body save herself, and at the Meeting in the Meeting House first, then at the grave-side in the Hoe burial place, her whole body was expressionless and rigid, as though she was holding herself together against assault. She would allow no-one near her, not Elizabeth, Mary, Margaret, nor her sisters-in-law, or any other of the women. When James tried to remind her gently that her children needed her, she just shook her head, and pulled Thomas closer to her, for only in him did she find any assuaging of her grief. It was quiet, shy Francis who came to her rescue, at a family gathering, when they were so anxious for her, even fearing for her sanity. "I think we have to let her be," he said. "She knows we are here, but she has to grieve in her own way. The ice will melt, and she'll come back to us," and he put an arm on each of William and Mary's shoulders. "You know she has always been there for you all and she will be again. If you young people need any help, just come to one of us." And so it was. There were plenty of willing hands to keep the house running, and John-Richard was well able to oversee both shops, and so Sarah somehow got through those weeks as spring turned into summer. Often she would go down onto the beach with Thomas, and find her way to the big flat stone, where she did not so much think as allow all the images of the past to pass before her eyes, and she realised that she was not just mourning for John, but for all those others who had touched her life and passed on - her parents, Mary and Richard, young Will, Betsy and Ned, and neighbours and friends no longer there, and she knew that this terrible grief was in a strange way for them all.

Sometimes Sam's mother Anne would shyly approach her as she sat on the beach, and quietly sit beside her, hardly a word passing between them. Sarah seemed glad of this unobtrusive company and when they parted she would take the other woman's hand and with the pressure of the fingers something of compassion passed between them. But mostly Sarah tried to hold the image of John within her, his face always before her eyes. Once she woke up terrified in the night because his face had slipped from her mind, and she could no longer recall it. She ached for the comfort of his presence, the wisdom of his support. She cried out to him to come to her and to God to let her feel John close to her, but she never did, and her grief - and as she saw it, her betrayal - was absolute. She wandered about the house at night, unable to sleep, touching all the things they had shared, everything belonging to him, trying to reach him. Then suddenly, as she stood at her bedroom casement one night looking out to the sea, with the bright stars above, there came into her mind the promise they had made to each other all those years ago when he went off to the war. "Wherever we are we'll think of each other at this time every night, and that will bring us close together." It was John's voice she heard saying these words, and she knew he was still saying them, would always be there for her. She fell to her knees and wept, but this time the tears were healing ones, and that night she slept deeply for the first time for many weeks.

The next morning Sarah greeted her family with a smile, and, as she embraced them all, she knew, and they realised, that she was back with them and that together they would face life without John.

Chapter Thirty-three

SARAH WOULD NEVER have believed that she would laugh again that summer, or would take pleasure in the sunshine and in the sight and sound of the waves breaking on the shore. But she did, and was almost surprised when she realised one morning that the days were cooler and it was already October.

That afternoon she had arranged to visit Ann at her cottage. She left Mary playing with Thomas in the garden and promised that she would not be away long. As she reached Ann's gateway, the children Joshua and Meg came running to meet her, greeting her like the friend she had become, and Sarah thought how they were growing, how bonny they looked, as did Ann when she came to the door to welcome her. There was a lightness about her step and a bloom to her cheek, almost belying the fact that she was mother to a great lad like Sam. Ann and Sarah sat together companionably, Ann pressing her guest to try some freshly baked strawberry preserve tarts.

Then she put the plate on the table, and folded a pleat in her apron, and after a moment she looked up at Sarah. "I've - I've something to tell you. I hope it will not displease you." "I'm sure it will not," Sarah's smile was encouraging. "Do tell me what it is." "Well, I have become friends, good friends, with someone who now wants to marry me." She touched a stray tendril of auburn hair. "I know it is not long since Jeremiah died, but Peter is lonely too. He has a small boy of nearly four, and his wife died in childbirth last year. He finds it hard to manage, and I've been doing some washing and cooking for him, and well -", she paused, and Sarah - just for one moment - almost envied the comfort which obviously awaited her friend.

Then she reached out and hugged her. "I'm so glad," she said. "Now, tell me all about this Peter." "He works for Master Light the clothier - I believe *he's* one of your people." Sarah nodded. "Yes, he's one of our Elders, one of the founders of our Meeting, in fact." Ann smiled. "Yes, Peter says he's a good man and a very thoughtful employer. Peter started by doing odd jobs and making deliveries, but he is learning the business now, and is considered a good worker." "I'm sure he is, now tell me your plans," and Sarah listened attentively, offering any help she could. It was only as she got up to leave that she asked Ann - "Where will you live? I'm sure it will be quite acceptable for Peter and his little boy to move in here." "Thank you, that is very thoughtful of you. But Peter has a home, it's a cottage in the yard behind one of Master Light's mills. It will be roomy enough for us all. Though -" and she hesitated, "I expect Sam will want to find his own home one of these days." "Yes." Sarah could say no more, but waving to Ann and the children, turned for home.

She knew the thoughts that lay unspoken between herself and Ann - Sam and Elizabeth - Elizabeth and Sam. This could be a home waiting for them - but there were too many difficulties, and she sighed as she reached her own front door.

The rest of that year was busy for Sarah - she deliberately made it so - with caring for her family and the needy in the community. She carried John with her always in her heart, in all her work and at the Meeting, and sometimes she would steal a few minutes and find her usual place on the beach where she could feel him all around her, and each night before she slept she would stand at her casement and talk to him as though he were in the room with her, telling him about her day, especially if she had problems to deal with, and try to think how he would have dealt with them.

Then in the first week of 1671 she helped Ann with her simple wedding preparations and afterwards her move to her new home. She liked Peter Curnow, and knew he would take care of his new family. Sam moved with them, but Sarah knew he was not happy. Elizabeth had talked to her just two days earlier, opening up to her mother as she had not for a long time. "He doesn't feel he is needed any longer - to look after his mother and the children, and he's done it for so long." They were sitting at the dining table as they talked, having just cleared it after the family supper, and Sarah reached across now to touch her daughter's hand. "Perhaps he will be glad to be relieved of that responsibility and, and - look to his own life, and I hope he is glad for his mother to find some happiness. I do not feel that Jeremiah brought her much comfort." Elizabeth got up from the table, and Sarah could see angry spots of colour on her cheeks. "It does not seem that happiness is there for all of us," she said, and rushed from the room.

Sarah felt helpless, as always, in the face of this problem, and had to lay it aside. The weather became very cold that winter of '71, and in February snow covered the Plymouth streets. Young Thomas took a chill and lay for several days with inflammation of the lungs, so that Sarah was wholly concerned with him.

Mary helped her diligently in the sick room, and Margaret spent time in the house. It was only when the fever finally broke, and Sarah, wiping the still little face, and smoothing back the ringlets of damp, dark hair, felt his forehead suddenly grown cool, and turned to embrace Mary in her relief, that she could begin to think of the rest of the family. When Margaret called them to a meal later that evening, Sarah was almost too tired to eat it, and when she did ask where Elizabeth was, for she had not appeared at the table, Margaret tried to reassure her. "I'm sure she will be home soon. She has been helping this week wherever she's been needed, she has been to Plympton looking after Catherine the last few days. Now please try to eat something, mother." Elizabeth came in a few minutes later, looking tired and strained. She glanced enquiringly at Mary, who was carrying dishes in from the kitchen and when her sister turned to her with relief alight in her face, calling out, "It's all right, he's going to be all right, the fever has broken," Elizabeth said quietly, "Thank God", and going to her mother she hugged her tightly, then went straight to her room.

The household overslept the next morning, all exhausted with nursing and anxiety, so that Sarah, rushing from job to job, did not realise that Elizabeth was not there. She attended to Thomas, and got William to work, while leaving Mary to her tasks. It was only much later in the day when the younger girl went into her sister's room to put away some clean linen, that she saw the note lying on the chest. It was addressed to Sarah, and Mary put it into her apron pocket to give to her mother later, for she was busy cooking in the kitchen. She did not hurry with it, not thinking for a moment that it was important, but finished the jobs she had to do in the other chambers.

Finally, she held it out to Sarah. "This was in Elizabeth's room. I suppose she couldn't find you before she went out earlier and left you a message." Sarah put down the pan of milk she was warming for Thomas and took the letter from Mary. As she saw the one word "Mother", an icy band clutched her heart. "Sit down," Mary said anxiously, leading her to a stool. "You look exhausted. You have worked so hard of late." Sarah unfolded the sheet. "My Dear Mother," she read, "I am sorry to cause you distress, but I can stay at home no longer. I am going away with Sam. Please do not blame him. He has tried to dissuade me, but I must go and he will take care of me, so I would beg you not to worry and try to forgive me. - Elizabeth."

She passed it to Mary to read, then paced up and down the room, desperately trying to think what to do. She stopped and caught Mary's hands, looking into her frightened eyes. "Now, I must go and find out what I can. Take care of Thomas, and if William comes in, tell him, and give him something to eat. I'm going down to the shop. William may still be there, and perhaps John Richard." Mary had already gone to fetch her mother's cloak. "Wrap it tightly round you," she said, "it's very cold outside." The next few hours were a nightmare of anxiety - for all the family, but especially for Sarah. Everyone gathered together in Rag Street - her brothers, her sons and their wives, and sisters-in-law, even some of the children, with the men who worked in the grocery business.

Francis and James between them took charge, and tried to build up a picture of how and when the fugitives had left. Seeing them all sitting round her big dining table, Sarah thought for a fleeting moment that this was one situation for which she had never expected to see them gathered here. But there was no time for such idle thoughts. James was speaking to them now. "It seems," he said, "that Sam was to take the cart to Modbury early this morning, and to come back this evening. There's been no sign of him. I've sent to his mother to see what he took with him. We already know that Elizabeth has taken a bag of clothes with her." At that moment, Ann and Peter burst into the room, Ann rushing to Sarah. "Oh, what has happened?" she cried. "It seems that Sam has taken all his possessions with him, but there's no note or message." Then Francis spoke to them all. "Now, Friends, we must try to be still, there is nothing more we can do to-night. We'll send to Modbury

187

in the morning, and see what the news is from there. Now, let us have a Meeting for Worship and seek God's peace." So the room became quiet and all - men, women and children - stretched out hands to each other and their hearts and minds to God.

Most of the family returned to their homes, but John-Richard, Margaret and little Catherine stayed with Sarah, William and Mary, in case any news should come through the night. But it did not, and none of them slept very much.. Sarah hugged to herself the white collars and caps that Elizabeth had left behind, as though she had given up all links with Quakers, and so with her family, and when Sarah tried to talk to John that night the only words that came were, "Forgive me, my love, I have failed her and you."

The next day brought all the news there was, but this was pitifully little. The grocer's cart arrived back from Modbury, the driver telling John-Richard that Sam had left it there to be returned, saying that he had work to do further away, and he was gone before more questions could be asked. Of Elizabeth nothing had been seen. She could have been waiting for Sam, the family decided, anywhere in the area.

They all tried to comfort Sarah, but there was nothing anyone could do save contact Friends wherever they could between Plymouth and London, which they all felt was their destination, asking them to look out for the pair.

Sarah felt numb for those first weeks, then worked harder than ever to fill her days. She knew that there was nothing anyone of the Friends could tell her that she wasn't already aware of, and the only person who could comfort her was Sam's mother Ann. They wept in each other's arms, assuring each other that neither was to blame, and somehow because of not having to pretend, each could be open with the other and gained from it.

Life settled down, as it had to, even for Sarah, for that year of 1671 and through the next few years, until the spring of 1675, and in all that time, not a word was heard of the runaways.

Chapter Thirty-four

BY 1674 PLYMOUTH Friends were quite seriously outgrowing their Meeting House on the edge of the Hoe. The Society had developed rapidly in its first twenty years and of late persecution had mercifully been very much less so that meetings could be open and made known. However dangers still lurked, and there was as yet no legal right of assembly so Friends decided that whatever new property they acquired it should be held on a lease. This meant that, although the contents of the building could be legally destroyed, the house itself had some protection.

At the end of this year, Friend John Light, the clothier, acquired the lease of two dwelling-houses, a garden and outbuildings at the junction of Bilbury Street and Treville Street, situated well down in a busy area of the town, though towards the outskirts of it and not far from Charles Church. The lease was determinable on the death of the survivor of three people - Nicholas Harris, son of John Harris of Pennycross, Patience Light and Mary Croker.* The ground rent was twenty shillings per annum, which the Meeting could provide, but the cost of conversion into a suitable Meeting House was a more difficult matter and this had to be met by subscription. Lists were made and careful records kept, and Sarah's brother James was one of the committee allocated to this work. At a gathering in the existing Meeting House James explained the situation to the Friends, reading the document which so far declared. 'The Account of what Friends payd in towards building the Meeting House.' "Now Friends,' he said, gently but firmly, "We gave been guided to this undertaking, but it will require sacrifices on all our parts to pay what is still needed. However, no Friend should be

---

* This 'Three Lives' system was a very common method of holding property at this time.

189

reduced to penury to make his contribution, so give what thou canst and we will make an account."

In turn each Friend came to the table where James sat, and made a pledge of his or her contribution. The Women's Meeting, well established by now, promised £5, while from individuals or families came contributions varying from £60 from John Light himself, to £30 each from Richard Smith, George Croker, Edward Jewell, Arthur Cotton, Francis Jewell and Sarah Luscombe, while amounts decreased to £5 from John Harris, James Fox and Ephraim Goodyeare. This was only the first day of the appeal and James went home that night well pleased. "Friends have been generous," he said to Sarah, "for these are great sums of money , and certain monies have always to be kept in case of fines to be paid."

Finally by the beginning of 1675 £373. 13s. 6d. had been collected and the work of conversion began. This amount proved insufficient however, and a further £100 was borrowed from John Light as an interest-free debt. With nothing more to delay them the work went ahead, Friends themselves helping with labouring and 'fetch and carry' tasks, and later the fitting out of the simple building which all were confident would indeed be a place where the presence of God would be truly felt.

Benches and the well polished table were brought from the old Meeting House, and new benches carved in love and devotion by John-Richard, William and others of the Friends, while the women tended to the small garden and planted sweet smelling flowers to grace their Meetings.

It was Spring once again, and a soft balmy one, that afternoon there was to be a special Meeting for Worship, the first to be held in the new Meeting House, and it would be a time of thanksgiving and celebration. Letters had been received from George Fox and Margaret Fell, and from other Meetings in Devon and Cornwall and beyond, and it was felt that Quakers everywhere would be sharing in the worship. Indeed Sarah felt a special closeness with Margaret Fell, for she had written to her some months after Elizabeth's disappearance, wondering if - with eight daughters of her own - Margaret had ever faced similar problems. The other woman, though not having been confronted with such a dilemma, yet could offer some thoughts which were of comfort to Sarah's poor, aching heart, and the two women continued to exchange letters. When, the following year, the Fox's had visited Exeter for a great rally there, Sarah had accompanied her family to this event, and the two women found in close, personal contact, an even deeper freindship.

Now, as she tidied herself for the meeting in Bilbury Street, Sarah called to Mary to be quick for they should be gone. Mary was the only other occupant of Rag Street apart from Thomas and Sarah herself at this time, for William was now married and living in the cottage vacated four years ago by Ann and her children. William had married a gentle Quaker girl of John Harris' family and they had a two-year old son, Nathan. "No problem there," Sarah thought now, thankfully, as she tied her cap and called Thomas from the garden. If only - but she had learned that regrets served no useful purpose even if there was an ache in her heart that would never be eased. Mary came down the stairs now ready for the meeting, and turning to look at her Sarah thought, as she often did, how like her own mother, Mary - for whom she was named - she had become. There was a plump, soft warmth about her that attracted all the children who came into contact with her and indeed to all the children of the Meeting she was a big sister or aunt.

She seemed in no hurry to marry, though she was now seventeen, although Sarah knew that young Peter Fox would have been happy to change that situation, but meanwhile she was glad to have her younger daughter still with her.

Friends tried to remember their testimonies of simplicity and humility, but could not restrain feelings of thankfulness and just a little pride as they looked around their new Meeting House that spring day. Everything shone with their efforts, as the sun poured through the windows on to the bent heads and serene smiles, giving an extra glow to the great vase of daffodils and bluebells in the centre of the table. The spacious room was well-filled, and Sarah looking along the benches of her own family growing as it seemed every year, with John-Richard and Margaret now having two small boys to keep watchful eyes on in addition to the rapidly growing Catherine, now nearly six, lifted up her heart in prayer for them all, with as always a special plea for the one who was missing. Now, with a deep thankfulness for Thomas sitting beside her and already so like John in his dark slenderness and ready smile, she lifted one small grandson on to her knee and held him tight.

191

Many Friends gave ministry that day, and it was dark when Sarah and all her family finally shared a meal at Rag Street. Supper was ready and Francis had risen to his feet to give thanks, when there came a knock on the front door. "I'll go, mother." Mary slipped out into the passage-way, while dishes were passed around the table. Sarah looked up as Mary came back, leaving the door open behind her. Her face had a strange expression. "Who is it, my dear?" "It's - it's some more Friends come to see you." Mary stood aside and Sarah stepped out into the hall. In the fading light she could not see clearly the figures standing there, only that one was very tall, and was holding a small girl, while the other, a baby in her arms, looked achingly familiar. They both were dressed as Quakers, and for a moment as she stood afraid to move, Sarah was back all those years when her father had come back from the war and she had not known him. Elizabeth held out one arm to Sarah, while the other still clutched the baby. "Mother," she whispered, still hesitating, till Sarah with one quick movement enfolded them both, and they clung together, crying and laughing at the same time.

Then James came from the living-room. "Canst thou not bring our Friends in, sister, and we can eat together." Without another word she drew the visitors in. There was a gasp from the family assembled there, then they all crowded around, someone taking the baby from Elizabeth. "It's a boy," she said, "Richard, just six months old," and she turned to her companion. "This is Sam, Friends, with our daughter, Sarah-Ann." Francis came forward then, the others looking to him for guidance. "Thou art dressed as Quakers," he said. Sam spoke then for the first time, standing his little girl on the floor, where shyly she hid behind her father's legs. "Yes," he said gently, his arm around Elizabeth's shoulders. "We were married as soon as we got to London. I got building work and we found a room to live in. It was not easy but we managed." Elizabeth looked up at him and the love in her eyes was plain for all to see. "Then one day we found a Meeting at Cheapside, and Elizabeth persuaded me to go along. It was the best thing I ever did - well, almost. They welcomed us, and helped us, and finally received us both into Membership." "But after a while," Elizabeth interrupted eagerly, "for they already knew our story, they showed us that it was right that we should come home and seek your forgiveness - and this we do now."

192

There was no doubt of their welcome. All four of them were received literally with open arms, and drawn to the table where food and drink were pressed upon them. Suddenly, James clapped Sam on the shoulder. "Your family," he said. "I take it thou hast not yet seen them?" "Oh no, we came straight here." "Then they must be sent for, at once. William, wilt thou go?" A little while later, Peter, Ann and their children arrived and came into the living room, shyly at first. Then Ann, seeing her son, ran to him and was gathered up in his arms.

It was long before the household in Rag Street took to its beds that night, Elizabeth, Sam and their children being found a place there, for much had to be said and so many questions asked and answered, Richard and Sarah-Ann being greatly admired, Sarah particularly drinking in the fair bonniness of her grandson, so like Elizabeth herself at that age, while Sarah-Ann, a beautiful, graceful child of three, had her father's tumble of auburn colours. Cousins were introduced to cousins, and likenesses compared.

Later that night, when all were finally in bed, Sarah spoke quietly to John, with a full heart. "She has come back, my love, with a family, a wonderful family, so we can both rest easy this night."

Chapter Thirty-five

IT WAS LONG BEFORE Sarah in the year of 1675 could become accustomed to having all her family around her, for not only was Elizabeth back, and married - in the manner of Friends - to Sam, but there were her grandchildren, Sarah-Ann and Richard, of whose existence she had not even guessed. It was decided that they all stay, at any rate for the time being, in the house in Rag Street, for there was plenty of room. Mary loved having two more children to help look after, and Thomas was delighted with new friends to play with and share his secrets.

At first it was difficult to find work for Sam, for he could not move back into the grocery shops. They were fully manned at this time, and although maintaining a good business there was not room for another family member. Indeed, Sam would not have wished it so, and for the first few days was content to explore his old haunts, to walk the beach and to generally renew acquaintance with the town. Both he and Elizabeth said how sorely they had missed the sea, and took their children with Thomas in tow to all their favourite spots. On a bright afternoon they found the big flat stone and sat close together on it, Elizabeth holding Richard while Thomas and Sarah-Ann explored the rock pools. "It's so good to be back," Elizabeth said, resting her head on Sam's shoulder, and sniffing the air appreciatively. Sarah-Ann came toddling across the shingle, carrying a beautifully coloured shell, its inner side pearly and incandescent. She held it out to her mother, delight sparkling on her rosy face. "Look," she said, "shining". Sam jumped to his feet and picking her up, held her high above his head till she squealed in delight, while Thomas came running up, "Me too, me too," not wanting to be left out although a big boy of six. Sam swung him round and round, till all collapsed in a laughing heap. "'Tis not seemly behaviour for an old married man," said Elizabeth in mock admonition, "and a Quaker one at that." Sam dusted the sand from his clothes, and the little party set off for home. "I know Thomas is surrounded by love," Sam said as he took Richard from his wife, "but he must miss a father. Maybe I can give him some 'rough and tumble' in recompense." Then as they started across the beach he added, "Can we walk past the new Citadel, my love? I should like to see how it is progressing." A few minutes later they paused. "It is certainly a great construction, but only made for war, I fear. I should not like now to be working on it. To rebuild homes, as we did in London, seems of greater import."

Sam was quiet that evening, and while the rest of the family sat together in happy conversation when all their tasks were completed, he wandered out into the garden, where Elizabeth found him much later. "What art thou doing, my love, sitting here in the dark?" "I'm sorry, wife. I just wanted to think. I had not realised it was so late," and with his arm about her shoulders they walked back into the house.

The next day there was to be a meeting in Treville Street for Sam and Elizabeth to tell the Plymouth Friends about all they had seen and done in London, and to pass on greetings from Quakers there. The Meeting House was full for this special occasion, for there was much information to impart from the great city, which few of them had ever seen. Elizabeth answered many of the women's questions as to the care of families, when so many homes had been lain waste, and then Sam spoke of all the rebuilding that had taken place since the fire, and was indeed, still going on. Sarah saw Sam's eyes light up when he talked of this work. "The architect Christopher Wren," he said, "has worked so hard and so - so -well, artistically. For example, I know that as Friends we do not go into steeplehouses, we like our simple Meeting Houses, but of the eighty-six churches burnt, he has already rebuilt fifty-one, and some of the designs are quite beautiful." Some of the older Friends frowned in concern at these words, but Sarah knew what he meant. Beauty could be appreciated for its own sake, and she smiled encouragingly at Elizabeth who was looking anxious at this reception of her husband's words. "I learnt so much," Sam said now, "about how houses should be built, how wood and stone ought to be used." He paused. "I should not want to live in London," and here he looked to Elizabeth for confirmation, "for there is much evil living there with greed and gluttony and foppishness amongst the rich, and hunger and sickness the life of the poor, but still, I thank God that I was able to learn about building," and he sat down abruptly with such conviction in his face that the Friends could not but be convinced of his sincerity.

When the Meeting finally closed, and the other Friends dispersed, Elizabeth and Sam had another look around the Meeting House and all the work done on it, while Sarah stayed behind for a moment to speak to James. "I think Sam has learned well in his time away, dost thou agree, brother?" James smiled at her. "I think there is a plan somewhere in thy head. What does thou want me to do?" They walked for a while, and Sarah went home well satisfied. James called at the house the next day and suggested that Sam might care to look at some cottages occupied by employees of the mill, but that were urgently in need of renovation. There was no doubt about Sam's willingness to do just that, and as he hurried away Sarah felt sure with God's help that his new career was about to begin.

In the weeks and months that followed, it was evident that this was so, and Elizabeth was happy in the knowledge that Sam had found what he wanted to do. "We are so fortunate," she said to her mother one night. "To have each other and the children, and to be back with you all, and now to feel that there really is a place here for Sam." "Well, of course there is," Sarah put her arm around her daughter's shoulder. "Why should thou doubt that there is?" "We were not sure whether the Plymouth Friends would welcome Sam. You could not know how the last four years had dealt with him - with us." Then as Sarah held her close, she added, "I thought about you every day, and father too, and wondered what he would have thought of us." "He would have understood because he loved you as I do, and the rest of the family. I will tell you something, my love, that I have not shared with anyone else, but every night before I sleep I talk to your father, in the silence, like a Meeting for Worship, and I feel him very close. I tell him about the day that has ended, especially concerns and worries, and I know that he hears and understands and helps me. So have no fear, all will be well."

There was a tiny room, not much more than a cupboard, which led out from the kitchen in Rag Street. John had kept his woodworking equipment there and there were the gardening implements. Sam cleared it out and gathered together the tools he needed and declared himself in business. James' son John, born in 1658, and unable to settle in his father's business, ("He'll never make a miller," James had often said), now attached himself to Sam and became his willing assistant. There seemed to be a dearth of builders in the town except those working on the Citadel, and the two men soon had as much work as they could handle. Sometimes it was a simple job, repairing a door or window frame, or cobbles that had become dislodged or uneven. But when it was a home - even a small cottage - that needed completely restoring then Sam and young John became absorbed and gave nearly every waking thought to the project. Elizabeth would go looking for Sam sometimes, and would find him on the site measuring, lifting, carrying and asking John what he thought, and before he saw her she would watch him, proud and happy for his contentment, and in the evenings she would smile conspiratorially at her mother when he laid out plans and drawings on the big dining table, and would puzzle over measurements, running his hands through his thick red hair until it stood up like a fiery halo around his head.

'75 became '76, and Mary finally succumbed to Peter Fox's overtures and agreed to marry him in the summer. They found a cottage near the beach. It had once belonged to a fisherman's family but had been empty for several months and was in a bad state. "Just the job for us," said Sam, and willingly took up the challenge. Gradually the little house took shape, becoming sturdy and strong, and Sarah, visiting it often, would see it as a comfortable home for Mary and Peter. It was just within her view as she sat on the beach, and she could imagine in years to come, bringing more grandchildren across the shingle to play among the rock pools and to gather pebbles and shells. That's if she still had the energy, she thought one day just before the wedding. She was turning out her chests and closets, sorting out hangings and linen for the bride, as she had for all her children when they married, and she could hear the shouts and laughter coming from the garden below where Thomas and Sarah-Ann played happily with a spinning top. Thomas was very protective of the small girl. More like brother and sister, Sarah thought fondly, than her son and grand-daughter. She was glad too to hear Elizabeth busy in the little kitchen, knowing that their evening meal was being prepared without her help. She had never thought that she would be happy to relinquish so much of the house-keeping reins to her daughter, but she had to admit as her 46th birthday approached that there was something comforting about this and it brought a sense of relaxation that she had never known before. It gave her time to think and write, and she had become a great correspondent of late, writing frequently to Margaret Fox and to some of the London Friends who had shown such kindness to Elizabeth and Sam. She was writing a journal too, all the things that she would later tell John about. And she spent time with Francis, her elder brother, whose quiet but perceptive understanding she had grown to value greatly over the years, realising how they had all under-valued him as they were growing up. She gathered up a pile of mending now, and went down to join Elizabeth, to confer with her about the meal they would prepare for their Friends after the forthcoming marriage ceremony.

That was a happy occasion filled with sunshine and love, and marred only by a sense of unease felt by all the Friends present. It came from without the peaceful Meeting House and indeed one or two of the younger Friends remained outside the building throughout the Meeting, keeping a watchful eye on all who approached. There had been odd incidents in the town of late, nothing very serious, some of the Friends' property had been daubed, flour sacks split open, and Sam had reported building materials taken from a derelict cottage he and John were working on. The work on the Citadel was almost finished and it was rumoured that the King himself was coming to inspect the work. "It may be," said James, "that those who are against our way of life may see safety in a Royal visit and are starting a campaign of persecution once again." However the Meeting for Marriage passed peacefully, as did the gathering at Rag Street afterwards, and it was doubly sanctified for Elizabeth and Sam stood with Mary and Peter. "For we were wed in London, with none of our families around us," said Sam. "Now we can give thanks for you all."

Though Friends remained vigilant, the rest of the year passed with no more than slight irritations and disturbances, and the Plymouth Quakers were beginning to think that their alarms were unfounded as 1677 saw the end of the work on the Citadel and the arrival of two more grandchildren for Sarah - another son, Isaac, for Elizabeth and Sam, and a little daughter, Susan, for Mary and Peter.

Chapter Thirty-six

THE EVENT OF 1667 which Plymouth people were to remember, in different ways and for varying reasons, was the visit of King Charles II and his brother James, Duke of York. It was said that they had come to inspect the new Citadel and to see that the work had been carried out according to the King's instructions. Friends continued with their daily lives as quietly as always, not joining the crowds who flocked to see the royal party. Hearing that his majesty had attended a service in St. Andrew's Church, Francis remarked wryly to Sarah, "'Tis not likely that our Meeting for Worship will attract him."

But it certainly was at this time that a severe outbreak of cruel persecution of Plymouth Quakers took place, beginning during a Meeting for Worship at Treville Street. Richard Samble was preaching, and he was summarily evicted from the building, and fined the heavy sum of £2. Andrew Horseman, the Mayor, accompanied by Justices and Constables arrived with great noise and clamour, banging on the door, then pulling it open and marching inside. Friends turned, startled, mothers gathering children to them, though many of the little ones were curious rather than frightened, for their short lives had till now been peaceable.

The Mayor took command and dispersed the Meeting none too gently. He was to leave armed men outside the Meeting House right through that summer and into a cold autumn, so that Friends had to gather in the street; and again, in spite of a change of Mayor, this treatment went on throughout a very severe winter.

That first day, all those who were present came in ones and twos and by devious routes to Rag Street where James and Francis and the other Elders sought to both comfort and exhort them, while Sarah and Elizabeth found refreshments for them all.

"Be of good heart, Friends," Francis rose to his feet in the crowded room, stooped now and looking suddenly older, Sarah thought, as she carried a laden tray from the kitchen, "but 'tis not surprising for it was his 50th birthday that he had not long since."

"We must be ever vigilant," Francis continued. "Do not leave your homes and businesses unattended, and keep your children always close. We do not know if to-day's attack is an isolated one, or the start of a long campaign against us, nor indeed whether it is widespread throughout the country. If any Friend suffers more damage than they can cope with, then be assured that there are many of us to give help. If there is anything to report, the word will be passed around for if more than a few of us try to meet in each other's homes, then all are put in danger. Now, Friends, shall we have a short Meeting for Worship to seek God's comfort."

And so they gradually returned to their homes, strengthened in resolve and purpose. But this was sorely tried in the weeks and months that followed, for the abuse hurled upon Friends by the Officers and soldiers of the garrison, as well as by the rabble, included the throwing upon them of stones and hot coals of fire, jostling them on the streets, and bedaubing them with excrement. Friends got to know the most dangerous of the constables, such as Nathaniel Pentire, who looked constantly for even small groups of Friends that they could arrest and bring to the Quarter Sessions, and the names of Arthur Cotton, John Light and Thomas Salmon were often recorded. Indeed, Arthur Cotton was gaoled that year for too vehemently asserting the right to use their Meeting House, and overall Friends often felt very isolated, as townspeople who had hitherto been friendly towards them, now shunned them or joined in the attacks upon them.

This cruel treatment continued into the next year when it developed into a tragedy for Sarah and the Jewell family. She had taken Sarah-Ann and Thomas for a quick run across the beach, for they had long been kept close to the house, and as they were returning home they heard shouting coming from the direction of the town. Sarah's first instinct was to hurry the children to the safety of home, when a figure came running along the street towards them. It was Mary, her bonnet strings flying and her cheeks rosy with exertion, but her eyes were fearful. "Oh, mother, mother," she gasped as she reached them, "it's Uncle Francis, he has been beaten and he is lying upon the ground."

Sarah thought quickly. "Take the children into the house," she ordered. "Elizabeth is there, then raise any of the men you can. I will go straight down." The scene that greeted Sarah as she turned the corner made her heart pound, but concern for her brother dispelled fear for herself, and she hurried to the crumpled figure lying in the filth of the cobbles. The crowd of about a dozen rough fellows, armed with cudgels, drew back sheepishly at her approach, and she fell to her knees beside Francis, lifting his head and shoulders into her lap. He was just breathing, but his eyes were closed and his face ashen, while blood poured from an ugly wound on his head. As she attempted to staunch this with her kerchief, running feet brought Sam and Francis' own sons, John and Thomas. The attackers had by now all run. Sam picked Francis up in his strong arms, and with help from the others carried him to Rag Street, which was the nearest of the Friends' homes.

Francis' wife, Anna, was sent for and every loving care and attention given to the injured man. But he did not regain consciousness and as Sarah gently closed his eyes and knelt beside the weeping Anna, the injustice of this gentle brother of hers, always a man of peace, dying in such a cruel way, almost overwhelmed her.

Family and Friends rallied round as they were so used to doing. James, more angry than any of them, for like Sarah he had always known the quiet and gentle strength of his brother, made complaints to the Mayor and Council. They were nervous at the death of so well-known and respected a businessman, even though he was a Quaker, and had ready their story. "Master Jewell was holding a Meeting of at least six persons," the Mayor declared, "and refused to stop when asked, so my men tried to insist, whereupon he fell upon the slippery cobbles." James turned away in sorrow and disgust, for he knew this was completely untrue, and as he said to Sarah later that day when she was trying to comfort Anna and helping her to prepare for the son and his wife who were coming to look after her, "We know that is a wicked travesty of the truth, for there were no other Friends about, and he was coming quietly home from his work. But 'tis no use to argue, for we cannot prove what happened, and 'twill not bring Francis back."

James and Arthur Cotton both wrote to William Penn, who was still a friend of the Duke of York, to see if he would intercede for local Friends. Penn did his best and for a while things were easier, though they never knew if this was due to royal intercession, but 1679 was a difficult year with much persecution still, and it was not until 1680 that Friends were able to breathe more easily and feel the tension go from their lives.

Not only were they now left unmolested, but Friends were becoming more and more highly regarded as fair and just members of local trade and industry. Their reputation for strict honesty, adherence to what they regarded as a fair price and their refusal to haggle, brought them much custom and a degree of prosperity. So good was their reputation that sometimes rogues affected to be Quakers in order to gain the confidence of victims, and warnings against such imposters were put out by the quarterly meeting. They were respected too because they seemed able to bridge the gap between the harsh strictures of Puritanism and the lax morals of much of Restoration life, so the standards which they set by example were of great value within the community, especially as the law, excluding any dissenters from public office, meant that the movement could take no part in political affairs as such.

Then in 1681 a new body of Protestant believers arrived in Plymouth. These were the Huguenots, the first group of whom crossed the Channel, to escape Catholic persecution, in an open boat from La Rochelle, reaching Plymouth on 5th September. As soon as their arrival was known, Friends offered help to these frightened, hungry people and although they could not speak each other's languages, yet the Plymouth people could offer them kindness and mercy and help to make their lodgings more comfortable.

Like the Friends, and unlike the other non-conformists - Baptists, Congregationalists, and Unitarians - who had by now ceased to meet openly - the Huguenots formed two worshipping congregations at Plymouth and at Stonehouse. Probably their inability to speak English helped them, the Council had no fear that they would gather local people to their services, so left them alone.

It was at about this time that Sarah, conscious of the needs of Elizabeth and Sam's increasing and growing family - two little girls had been born to them in 1679 and 1681 - felt that it was time for her and Thomas to leave the well-loved house in Rag Street, where she had been born and had lived all her life till now, and find a small quiet home somewhere near at hand.

She was 51 years old now, and though she hoped to have many more years to give service to the community and to her children and all her grandchildren, the pressures and responsibilities of a big household were something she was finding increasingly irksome, even with Elizabeth undertaking much of the work. No, she would seek a quiet, cosy home that she could make comfortable for Thomas and herself. As the years went by, this lad had become ever closer to her, and now at twelve was growing more and more like his father, tall, thin and dark, with the forelock that fell continually into his eyes, and sleeves that always seemed too short for his long arms and bony wrists. She would describe him to John when she talked to him at night, telling him how proud he would be of this their youngest child. Thomas was quick at his lessons, but showed no interest in the family grocery business, though John-Richard was always ready to introduce him to its systems. The only stab of concern that he ever brought to Sarah's heart occurred sometimes when they stood on the beach together or on the green of the Hoe, and he would look out to sea and wonder what lay beyond. "One day, mother, I should like to journey, oh - so far away, perhaps to the New World like Friends William Penn and George Fox, and see what lies out there." And she, knowing that she must not make him feel tied to her, would say as casually as she could, "Perhaps one day, my son, it would be a great adventure, I know."

Meanwhile, Sam had found a little house for her, at the side of the Hoe quite near to where the old Meeting House had been. It belonged, as that building had done, to the Harris family, and they were only too willing for Sarah to have it. Sam and Elizabeth had tried to persuade her not to move from Rag Street, but once they realised that her mind was made up, they helped her all they could. Sam put all his effort and ingenuity into the house, making sure that the kitchen and the little dairy beyond were as up to date as he could make them, that the casement of her chamber and of the living room looked out across the Sound, and that within there were ample cupboards and shelves to hold all her possessions and treasures from which she could not bear to be parted.

The family impressed upon Thomas that he would now be the head of the household and must take great care of his mother, and the pride which this charge gave to the lad made Sarah's own heart swell with contentment and happiness. Yes, they would do very well in this little home of their own - and when the time came - as she knew it must - for Thomas to seek his own way, then she would still be happy here with her family nearby. Margaret, Mary and Elizabeth helped her carry the smallest of her goods across to set them in place. The next day a cart carried up her furniture, not too much, for she had left most of the heavy pieces for Sam and Elizabeth, but she took John's big chair and her own smaller one, some of her stools, her linen press and chests, and their beds. Sam had come across a good double-sided table, like the one Betsy had all those years ago, and John-Richard had worked on it till it was satin-smooth and glowing. She walked around the rooms of the house in Rag Street, for the last time as their mistress, saying farewell to each beloved aspect, and then into the garden, from which she had already taken cuttings and plants for her new small patch - and said a small farewell to John - "though I shall look to the same sky and sea each night to speak to you, my love," she said.

Then she shut the door behind her and walked briskly down the steps to Elizabeth who was waiting for her at the bottom. "Come along," she said, taking her daughter's arm, "and I will make thee a first meal in my new home. I think," she added, smiling, "that my family will have to visit a few at a time, for my little house will never hold you all at once."

Chapter Thirty-seven

FOR THE NEXT FEW years Sarah's life settled into a new and quiet routine. Once she had accustomed herself to it she decided that the little house suited her and Thomas admirably, and, much as she loved her ever-growing family, it was good sometimes to close her door and rest, giving herself up to memories and contemplation. She would often sit on the Hoe too, not far from her home, for the grassy slopes were more comfortable now than the shingly beach, and various members of her family would come seeking her there sometimes for her sake and sometimes for their own. Nothing gave Sarah more joy than for a child or young person, or even someone older, to come and sit beside her and share a worry or a joy, all of which she would in her turn share with John in the quiet time before she slept.

She drew closer to James too, in these years, for with Francis gone they were the last of that generation of the family. Sometimes when James could be spared from his own family or business, or matters of the Meeting, he would call upon his sister, and they would sit together in her living room while she brought him his favourite refreshments, and it seemed to please James to talk of their childhood, of Richard and Mary. "'Tis strange," he said to her one day, "to remember a time before we became Quakers, before we knew anything of the Light Within, or Fox, and all our dear Friends," and he sat back and stretched out his legs, wincing a little at the stiffness in one of them. Sarah put her hand gently on his shoulder. "Thou art right, brother," she said, smiling, "'twas indeed a long time ago. We have come through much together and have much to thank God for. Now, I have discovered a new salve for aging limbs and I will give thee some for Rachel to use on thy poor old legs."

The next time James came to the cottage on the Hoe, he was waving a letter in his hand. "A letter from Friend Penn. He is to sail very shortly now, on the 'Welcome'. This time he will stay and set up his own colony in the New World." James was breathless by this time, and Sarah made him sit and recover before they read the letter again together, and talked of the plans that they knew William Penn had for the New World across the Atlantic. But later, when James had gone home, Sarah walked across the Hoe with Thomas, as tall as she was now, and her heart was heavy as he spoke excitedly, as she had known he would, of Penn's great undertaking. "Just think, mother, it may not be many years before I can cross the ocean too, and you could come as well, could you not?" She shook her head, trying to keep the tremor out of her voice. "I am too old for such wanderings, my son, but come, 'tis time we turned for home. There's a chill breeze coming from the sea."

"I know we should not question God's plans," she said later as she talked with John, "but of all our family circle, the only one who wants to leave us is he that I cannot spare." Then there came to her in the quiet the realisation that nothing could happen for a year or two at least, and that for that time there was nothing she could do, so she must have faith and patience.

Towards the end of 1682 more news reached Plymouth of William Penn's achievements and how he had proved himself to be a statesman of note. When he landed on the banks of the Delaware River he carried with him a Charter for the surrounding land, which was to be known as Pennsylvania. The Charter was signed by the King, who hoped to gain from it himself for Penn had undertaken to clear the debt of £16,000 owing to his father Admiral Penn's estate. "We hear," said James to the Meeting that gathered to digest all this exciting news, "that great plans have been drawn and a city started within the state, to be known as Philadelphia, the 'City of Brotherly Love,' and a great house, Pennsbury, is already being built on the banks of the Delaware." There was a sigh from the Meeting. "A great house? How was that Quaker simplicity?" "Ah, but," James looked round at them, pleased Sarah was sure, to be the one to interpret these happenings, "it is not to be just a family home, for from there Penn will organise his colony, and it will be based on principles of religious and civil liberty." The Friends looked at each other in wonderment - to live in peace, with no fear of persecution, to build homes in a new, rich country. "No wonder so many Friends want to go and seek this new life," said John-Richard. Then, catching Sarah's anxious expression, he added, "But it is not for those of us whose lives and families are well established here." Sarah smiled gratefully at him, but, in spite of her good resolutions to the contrary, she saw the excitement in Thomas' eyes with a tremor of dread.

But the Plymouth Community could not be spending all their time thinking of Penn and his Holy Experiment. Life at home was immediate - children were born, young people married, and some of the older ones died. Robert Cary died in that year of 1683, and a little later Kathleen Martindale passed on, also John Light the clothier, who had been such a great friend to the Jewell family for so many years. As Sarah joined all the Friends in the Meeting House for his funeral service, she felt that with the passing of this old man - he was seventy seven years old, her life had now gone, for he was the last link with her own parents. But as they gave thanks for his long and fruitful life, she could only be grateful and look ahead, and in fact, the very next day she helped Francis' widow Anna plan for her daughter's wedding.

And yet the old and new worlds could not be separated for long, for letters came from George Fox on his return from a visit to William Penn, and once again Plymouth Friends gathered to hear this news, and James told them how 30% of those travellers on the 'Welcome' never reached their promised land, but had died of small pox on the nine weeks' voyage. Friends shook their heads in dismay at this news, but James reminded them that 1400 Friends had, over the last few years, arrived safely in the New World. Then John-Richard had a question. "We hear stories about the natives in this new country. Does Fox write about them?" James read on. "Yes, my Friends, he does indeed. Penn had made friends with them. Many of them live along the banks of the Delaware, and he has bought land from them, treating them fairly, so that it seems they all live in peace." And as they entered their Meeting for Worship there in Treville Street, the Plymouth Friends gave thanks for this 'Peaceable Kingdom' all those thousands of miles away.

But '83 soon became '84, and with it the death of Charles II, who had reigned since 1660, and the end of the Commonwealth. Plymouth had felt more and more secure from any further persecution by the King and so it was a great shock to all her people, whatever their religious persuasion when, just before he died, he

207

called in Plymouth's great Charter of Elizabeth, which his father had confirmed in 1628.

The Mayor called a meeting in the Guildhall to inform the townspeople, and the news was received at first in a stunned silence and then in an uproar of protest. The existing governing body was already subservient to Charles, but now the Corporation was to be drastically reduced in power and numbers. "It is not right." "It is not just," went up one cry after another. "Is he still punishing us for what went on all those years ago?" James was soon on his feet, though his sons tried to restrain him. "We have always tried to live honourably, and to support the cause which seems to us right. What reason does he give?" The mayor raised his hands to ask for quiet. "He is the King, he gives no reasons, and remember he already changed our governing body years ago. But now, listen to me, good men of Plymouth, and I will give you the details. All the Council members and myself are hereby dismissed. There is to be a new Mayor, twelve new Aldermen and twelve new Councillors." Men were on their feet again, shouting. "But we have twenty-four of each at this time." The Mayor tried to speak above the murmurings, and he held up a Parchment. "It is all here," he said, his voice defeated and sorrowful, "a new, revised Charter, the new Officers have already been chosen by Charles," and as he read the names it was realised that they were all known, fervent Royalists, certainly not representative of the town. Then he asked the old Council to stay for a while and any members of the new who were present, so that matters could be re-arranged, while the rest of the crowd left the Guildhall, some to go straight to their homes in stunned silence, and others to gather in little groups, gesticulating angrily or shaking their heads in disbelief.

Of one thing there would be no doubt. When Charles died, as he did a few days later, Plymouth showed little sign of mourning the event, for a town which had elected its own Mayor and Corporation for more than two centuries, had now to lose its pride and submit to puppet rule.

"Better," many of them said, "to join Penn in the New World."

Chapter Thirty-eight

THE TOWN SETTLED AS best it could after the death of Charles II and the coming to the throne of James II. That in itself made little difference, thought Sarah, as she walked one day through the narrow, noisy streets of Coxside and the Barbican and recalled how the industry there had grown during her life-time. There were more storehouses and factories - glove leather was now being made from sheepskins and offal converted into glue, and the wine merchants, Colliers, had recently been established in Southside Street.

She jumped out of the way of a great lumbering cart, then stepped carefully over the droppings of its horse and avoided a basket of rotten vegetables a shop-keeper threw out into the gutter just at her feet. Used as she was to the smells of the town, Sarah wrinkled her nose at the stench of the tannery and the glue factory. She was glad to move into the quieter area of Rag Street, smiling to herself at the bewilderment her parents would have felt at such busy activity in their town.

Then, as she neared her daughter Elizabeth's home, she pondered on the fact that there were now already in some families of Friends, three generations of Quakers. Yes, this century had seen many changes and doubtless there were more to come. She climbed the well-known steps and Elizabeth opened the door to her. "Come along in, mother," she said, and Sarah, pausing a moment to regain her breath, declared, "I'm sure these steps get steeper every time I mount them."

Sarah sat gratefully in what was now Elizabeth and Sam's living-room, while her daughter brought in tea and freshly baked tarts. She looked appreciatively around at the well-kept room. Yes, Elizabeth had made a good home here for Sam and their five children - worthy of herself and of Mary before her - and she remembered how worried she and John had been when it seemed as if their daughter would never settle. She was still smiling as Elizabeth came in with another tray. "What secret thoughts are in thy head, mother? Thou seemst to be a long way from us." "In time perhaps, but not in place. I was thinking, daughter, how well the house is kept, and how my mother, Mary, would be pleased." Elizabeth blushed, but Sarah could see that she was happy with the compliment. The front door opened then, and a moment later Sam came into the room with Sarah-Ann. They greeted both women warmly, and Sarah felt great pleasure as she looked at her son-in-law and grand-daughter. Sam at 33, seemed as fit and strong as ever. He had to bend his red head to come through the doorway, and the way he walked straight to his wife warmed Sarah's heart. She turned to Sarah-Ann now, and took the girls' hands in both her own. She was just thirteen and already very beautiful. Her skin was clear and soft and the plain Quaker gown and cap accentuated the brightness of her blue eyes, so like her father's, and the auburn curls that would not quite be restrained. "Pray God she does not break too many hearts before she finds a haven for her own," was Sarah's fervent wish and prayer. Sarah-Ann went out into the garden then, where the two smallest girls were playing - Abigail, seven years old, and Mary not quite four - and as she watched the slim figure of her eldest daughter leave the room, Elizabeth said to Sarah. "She's such a good girl, mother, and so helpful with the little ones. I don't know how I'd manage without her." "I'm sure she is, she's a credit to you and Sam." Sam looked up at the mention of his name. He was poring over plans laid out on the big table, but he walked to the front door with Elizabeth to see Sarah on her way, for it was time for her to return to Thomas.

It still felt a little strange, she thought, turning to wave goodbye to the inhabitants of Rag Street, of whom she was no longer one. She sniffed the parsley and feverfew her daughter had given her, for they grew better in the Rag Street garden, though her own was becoming established and the sweet scent of lavender greeted her as she opened her gate. She saw Thomas approaching from the other side of the Hoe, and waited for him, admiring as always his purposeful stride and his tall, slim figure, so like his father's. He had become apprenticed to the old family firm of clothiers and woollen merchants run now by Francis' elder son, Joshua, and he seemed to have settled well to the work, though Sarah could not but think that the talk there was locally amongst the woollen trade and the Quakers within it, of a planned venture to the New World to establish an industrial settlement there, had something to do with his choice of career. Still, if he was determined to go, perhaps it would be better with a group of Friends in a Plymouth ship than to sign on amongst strangers, and with no more than a slight sigh now, she took his arm and walked with him into the cottage.

As that year of 1685 wore on, it became clear that these plans were not just idle speculation, but grew from an increasing determination on the part of men with practical knowledge and expertise, and also with a vision of a life lived without fear in a land full of promise. It was true that persecution had eased of late, but it could break out at any time and this King James was still something of an unknown quantity.

The possible enterprise became the subject of prayerful concerns at Meetings for Worship, and at the special business meetings held for the purpose. Sarah attended all she could and spoke to James and the other Elders concerning all that it would entail for those who became part of such a dangerous undertaking. For dangers there would be, she knew - from the voyage itself, with storms and sickness, from perils that might await them on the other side of the world - and here Sarah's imagination ran riot - and, over and above all these things, the sheer distance that would separate Thomas from herself and her loving care of him. But, as her nephew Joshua reminded her, they would be making for Philadelphia, an established and ever-growing town with all the protection that afforded, and people did come back from time to time, carrying letters and messages from other immigrants, and had not George Fox crossed the ocean several times, and 'twas said, was planning to go again. She went over all these things in her mind and again when she spoke to John, and in so doing she came to a clarity and a comfort. She could do no more, it rested in God's hands now.

Sarah kept very busy as the summer of 1685 progressed. She helped her sister-in-law Rachel prepare for her and James' daughter's wedding, and as they sewed together, she said to Rachel, "I feel as if I'm stitching garments most of the time at the moment. There seems to be a great number of babies being born this year, within the family and our friends." Rachel laughed. "Well, 'tis certain that our Meeting grows rapidly." James came in then, and his wife and sister could see that, as usual, he had news to impart.

"Well, husband," Rachel rose to her feet to fetch James a tankard of ale, "What have you to tell us to-day?" James thankfully eased himself into his chair. "It seems that Friends James Fox and Francis Rawle are far advanced in their plans for the New World. They are approaching Penn to purchase a large tract of land to set up a township in Philadelphia County. It has to be convenient to the river for the ease of woollen manufacture. There is to be a meeting this very evening for Friends to hear the latest news."

The Meeting House filled quickly and as Sarah arrived with James and Rachel she saw that Thomas was already there with a group of young people, and sitting close to him, Sarah's vigilant motherly eye noticed a companion often seen with him lately.

It was Priscilla Pearce, niece of Nicholas, another of the Friends very interested in the proposed expedition. Sarah's thoughts chased each other around in her mind, as the Friends settled themselves in silence for a time of worship, before the business began. James Fox explained that there was a ship *Desire* a Plymouth ship and a Captain had been found willing to sail to the New World with a group of Plymouth Quakers. These were the main facts, and a surge of excitement rippled through the Meeting and stirred those sober, grey-clad hearts. "Of course," Fox continued, "there are many details yet to be settled and it will certainly be next year before we are ready to set sail."

The Friends sat long in the Meeting House asking questions, seeking information, and Sarah could see that Thomas was in the forefront of those who questioned and sought knowledge. For the next few weeks the expedition was his sole topic of conversation and his excitement was evident. When he was freed from his work at the mill, he would often walk up on to the Hoe, looking out to sea, as though he were already sailing across it, and sometimes Priscilla was with him. At other times he crossed to Saltash, where in one of the docks there work had already commenced on the *Desire* and the changes needed to her. He liked to listen to the talk of the men, and they soon got used to him and let him come on board the sturdy craft, where everything he saw delighted him. Then he would come home and tell Sarah of all he had seen. He took to bringing Priscilla with him and watching them together, Sarah could see the growing affection there was between them. Priscilla was a small girl, but compactly and sturdily built and there was about her a look of 'no nonsense' that Sarah was glad to see. She would help to keep Thomas' feet on the ground if they remained together (or at least on the sea, Sarah thought with a wry smile).

The three of them sat together one bright evening, the windows of Sarah's cottage open to the soft summer breeze wafting from the sea. Gulls wheeled overhead, and those with time to spare strolled across the Hoe, while others, engaged on matters of business or other import, hurried to and fro. Sarah looked from one to the other of the young people, and felt that she must talk to them seriously and try to find what, if any, plans were already in their minds, otherwise any influence she might have would slip away from her.

"Your Uncle Nicholas," she began now, speaking to Priscilla but looking at both of them, "he is very committed to this expedition, is he not, and I'm wondering whether your own father will join him and, your dear mother having moved on to join our Lord this two years since, how you will manage?" No one spoke for a moment, then Sarah went on, "I'm sure he will provide well for you, but Thomas will be gone too, will he not?" She saw the two young people move closer together, and suddenly felt desperately sorry for them both. Thomas flushed scarlet, then became pale. "Well, mother," he took a deep breath, "there is much time yet, it will be a year before we sail." He hesitated, and Priscilla quickly went on. "There are father's sisters of course, and if he goes I know they would be happy for me to live with them - but," and it was her turn to hesitate now, and Sarah saw her reach out and take Thomas' hand, and he, her son who looked so very young, took it upon himself to try to explain. "What we are really wondering - and hoping - mother, is that by next year - we could be married, and go to the New World together."

The last words came out in a rush, then he stopped and the two of them looked beseechingly at Sarah and she was transported back all those years to the day when she and John had stood before Richard and Mary pleading to be allowed to marry. The difference was, she realised, that these two were even younger than they had been, and as well she had to manage this on her own. There was no John standing beside her, at least not that she could feel and touch for support, but she knew that he would understand and how he would feel, and looking at them both again, she said gently,

"Well now, this is news I did not expect to hear to-day, for thou art both very young." It was clear they were ready for this. "We are both more than sixteen, and by next year, when we sail, we will be seventeen." He spoke as though this was indeed a great age. "Do not fear, mother, I will take great care of Priscilla, and her family will be there to help us set up in the New World. There is nothing for you to be concerned about." He looked more relaxed now and smiled down at Priscilla, whose hand he still held tightly. But Sarah's eyes were serious. "Things are not quite as simple as that, my son. We do not have the money to pay for thy passage and share in the settlement. This is something I knew we should have to discuss before long, and now with a wife, it would be even more difficult. And of course," she turned to Priscilla, "what about your father? Have you talked to him yet?"

Thomas answered for her. "Now that we have spoken to you, mother, we will see Friend Pearce." "I expect you felt I would be easier to convince." Thomas seemed unsure of how serious she was, but he pressed on, "As for the money, mother, I will become indentured and serve my time. It will soon pass, and then I'll be free and we will be able to work and make a home." Sarah felt bewildered, so much seemed to be happening at once.

The very next day she and Thomas paid a visit to Friend Robert Pearce who lived in a small house on the other side of the Hoe. Priscilla admitted them shyly and Sarah looked round appreciatively at the well-kept room. Yes, Priscilla certainly looked after her father well, there was no doubt she would make a good wife. Robert Pearce came out to meet them. "'Tis good to see you, Friends. Come and sit down and take some refreshments with us." They talked of every-day matters for a while, of the Meeting, and then inevitably of the expedition. "Art thou expecting to go with the *Desire*?" Sarah asked at length, "with Nicholas and his family? 'Tis all we talk about at home now, with Thomas so excited." Robert Pearce looked serious - but, Sarah recalled, he usually did. He was a squarely built man of average height, with fair, straggly hair already sparse. He was probably still in his early forties, and therefore, Sarah realised with something of a shock, much younger than she herself. "I am considering the matter," he spoke now with deliberation. "It seems to me to be a worthwhile enterprise, but there is much to think about. If Brother Nicholas and I both go,

214

matters will have to be cleared with regard to the business here, and of course I shall have to decide what is best for my dear daughter," and he laid a hand on Priscilla's shoulder.

Both the young people looked to Sarah, and she was conscious of how much they relied on her. "That is partly why we are here, Friend Pearce," she said now. "To think about the future of both these young people. You must know how friendly they have become of late - or would wish to be with your blessing, of course." Robert remained silent, his expression serious, and Sarah realised how little she really knew this Friend. But she must continue. "They came to me, and now we have come to you, because - " and she drew them forward so that they stood before Robert, "they wish to be married next year so that they may sail together on the *Desire* with Quakers and family to seek a good life in the New World." Sarah had chosen her words carefully and knew she could say no more. Three pairs of eyes were fixed on the dark- clad figure before them, and Sarah realised that whatever doubts she might have had before, she hoped now that permission would be given. Master Pearce remained some time in thought and prayer, for his eyes were closed, then suddenly he opened them and smiled at the anxious faces before him. "It seems to me, Friends, that this could be God's will for us, and though I had not thought to give my Priscilla yet to a husband, that may very well give her the best protection I can, and it has shown me God's way forward for myself. Yes, we shall all go with the *Desire*," He embraced his daughter and shook Thomas and then Sarah by the hand, and they remained a few minutes more in a silent Meeeting for worship and thankfulness.

Next day Sarah and Thomas went to visit James, and as many of the family as could be gathered together. They all knew, of course, of Thomas' determination to sail with the expedition, but not of the wedding plans. They greeted this news with warmth for the young couple, and a welcome into the family for Priscilla, and then Sarah said to James. "Brother, there are practical matters we should discuss concerning the costs that Thomas will incur. He has said that he will bind himself apprentice until such a debt is discharged, but -" and she paused. James looked at his wife and his own sons, then at Francis' sons, who both nodded at him. "I do not think we would want Thomas - with his wife - to start their life together in debt. He is the only one of our family to go, and I think we can make sure he is well provided for. After all," and he looked to Joshua for confirmation, "he will represent the family business and help to establish the woollen industry in the New World." Sarah felt very thankful at these words and as she talked to John that night, she assured him that with God's blessing all would now be well.

For the rest of that year and into 1686 there was much to occupy her time and energy, and it often seemed as if the whole of Plymouth Meeting was concentrated on this great undertaking.

Chapter Thirty-nine

THOMAS AND PRISCILLA were married on a bright spring day in March 1686. It was a quiet ceremony in the Meeting House, quiet but filled with love. As Sarah looked around at all the Friends and family gathered there, she knew that the love that permeated this particular meeting owed at least something to the approaching journey of the two young people at the heart of it. They were not, of course, alone in their plans to cross the ocean, for many Plymouth Friends were to make up this company, but the fact that they were so young and marrying in order to undertake the voyage together, seemed to touch all hearts and cast an extra blessing on the undertaking.

The wedding meal was held in Elizabeth and Sam's home in Rag Street, as so many had been before, and Sarah was glad to let her daughters and daughters-in-law take charge of the proceedings while she walked among the guests, accepting their good wishes and offering her own to other Friends who would be sailing. Afterwards Thomas and Priscilla came back to spend their remaining time with Sarah in her cottage, and she treasured every moment of this. She grew to love Priscilla well, appreciating the sensitivity with which the girl made it easy for mother and son to spend time together.

Often as they talked Sarah would tell Thomas about his father and their early years together, and how she had always turned to him for comfort and strength - "As Priscilla will to you, I'm sure, my love." "I do wish you would come with us, mother - we both do. It would make everything perfect. I don't want to leave you here on your own." They were in Thomas and Priscilla's room where Sarah was going through his clothes chest, sorting what needed to be mended or altered, and what he had grown completely out of. She looked at him as he stood by the window, the sunshine lighting his spiky, dark hair, and her heart ached with love for him. "Thou art tempting me, my son," she tried to keep her voice light, "but I am too old for such journeyings. You go and find a wonderful, free life, and then one day you can both come back and tell me all that you have found, and bring back your children to show me." She hugged him, then turned away quickly so that he should not see the tears in her eyes.

The next few weeks passed much too quickly for Sarah. She wanted to hold each day back so that Thomas would never go, but she knew she could not. Instead she reminded him that she would not be alone, she had the family around her, and he must not worry. She kept very busy making sure that both the young people should go as well-equipped as possible, though the *Desire* was not a large ship and they could not take much luggage.

There was one occasion, however, when the real meaning of the coming journey became only too clear to Sarah. There was a Special Meeting called to make an official farewell to the travellers and during this their names were removed from the list of Plymouth Members. When she heard this, Sarah quickly rose to her feet. "But names are only removed for some action against the leadings of the Society. Our Friends have done nothing wrong that we should disown them." James answered her with a smile. "Do not be concerned, sister. We are not disowning them, simply sending them to start another Meeting - the Plymouth Meeting of Pennsylvania, releasing them from our Plymouth, and new certificates are being prepared for them to take with them," and he read the names of Pearce, Luscombe, Shellson, Fox and the others.

Sarah nodded but her heart was still thumping, and it took a while for her to lose the feeling that the travellers - and especially Thomas of course - were ceasing to exist.

But time was moving on and it was only a few weeks later that the *Desire* was brought round from Saltash and lay at anchor a little way out in the Sound. Using rowing boats, stores and then the passengers were taken aboard and asked to stow away their baggage. The family brought down Thomas and Priscilla's boxes and took them out. Then, when the boat returned, Thomas took Sarah's arm - she had been waiting on the shore through all these activities.

"Come, mother," he said. "Come and see where we shall live for the next weeks and maybe months." "Oh my son, I could not. The *Desire* seems a long way out. I have lived by the sea all my life, but 'tis not the same as journeying on her." Thomas laughed and caught his mother's arm. "I should not call it a journey, just a few pulls of the oars and we'll be there." She let herself be persuaded and before she had time to change her mind, Thomas and Priscilla, one on each side of her, were helping her into the boat. John Shellson was also going out to the *Desire* with the last of his baggage and with him was his wife Naomi. Sarah was very fond of both these Friends, old and respected members of the Meeting. They had been married since 1669 and had a young family who were journeying to Pennsylvania with them. Naomi smiled kindly at Sarah now. "Do not worry about Thomas and Priscilla, we will keep an eye upon them, and I'm sure that this will indeed be a blessed expedition."

Sarah was grateful for that, and as they helped her from the boat and on to the deck of the *Desire* she felt a little better. They took her down to the hold where the passengers would make their temporary home with baggage and bedding, and then showed her the rest of the small craft, and the crew putting finishing touches to all their preparations, then they brought her home again, her mind full of wonderings and imaginings.

It was just two days later that the *Desire* set sail for the New World. Sarah with her family and those of other travellers, plus all the Plymouth Friends, stood on the shore to bid them farewell. A short Meeting for Worship was held there on the beach, then the travellers - all 48 of them - were taken out in boats to the ship. Sarah embraced Priscilla first, then held Thomas close to her as though to imprint the feel of his beloved body upon her own for ever. Then she released him and watched with the others as the figures were rowed to the ship and climbed aboard. Those on the shore waved till they could no longer see the ship - so small, Sarah thought, so small and so frail. That night when she talked to John, it was a silent communion for she could not utter the words, but from a full heart the message rose to him and included with great love their beloved son.

In the weeks and months that followed, Sarah's family tried to ensure that she was never left alone to grieve for Thomas. She was visited constantly and called upon for advice and to care for grand-children and those of Friends. She knew that this was a conscious attempt to help her and was very grateful for it, and for the warm upholding that she was aware of throughout the Meeting. Elizabeth

219

had wanted her to move back into Rag Street - "just for a while, mother" - but she would not. Within her home she had prepared herself for this situation and accepted it as she knew she must.

It was especially in the quiet night hours that she found it difficult to still her fears and, though talking to John helped her, it could not dispel her anxieties. How long would it be before the *Desire* reached the Delaware? Would it arrive safely or be cast up on some rocky shore in a terrible storm, or all the voyagers perish from disease or starvation? And even if they arrived safely, what perils would await them? And her mind ranged from Indians to wild animals, and back again. She knew that happy stories had been brought back of successful settlements, for had not George Fox made several such journeys and she must keep her faith. But if only she could have news. Then she would work out how soon it could possibly be before, if everything had gone well, a returning ship could bring news. And so her tortured thoughts went to and fro until, exhausted, she would fall into a troubled sleep. These were the worst days, the early days, and gradually as summer gave way to autumn, and a new pattern of life was established, Sarah found the aching pain eased a little and she could take an interest in the life of Plymouth again.

She continued to write up her journal and her letters, and became the official correspondent for Plymouth Friends, so that the Meeting looked to her for news of Quakers everywhere, and particularly when George or Margaret Fox were able to write to them. Then Friends would gather at the Meeting House in Treville Street to share the news. As 1686 became 87, concern was expressed concerning Fox's health, for his wife wrote: "He never spares himself, but journeys constantly the length and breadth of the land in the cause of the Lamb, and to bring succour to those in need." There were still outbreaks of persecution throughout the country, although the movement, growing now in numbers and strength, was better able to sustain it than it had twenty years ago.

Whenever post was brought to Sarah her first thought (always) was "Perhaps there'll be news of Thomas and Priscilla," but till now there had been none. Then on a cold February day she recognised Fox's writing, and as she opened the paper to read his words, something else fell out. With shaking hands and a fast-beating heart, she picked it up. This letter - hardly recognisable as such - was cracked and stained, and almost fell to pieces as Sarah unfolded it and saw the precious writing. She went to the window to catch the last of the sun's rays as she read the blotched and fading writing, drinking in every word and hearing the voice of her beloved son speaking to her as she did so.

It was quite brief for he said he had heard that a ship was about to sail for London, and the Captain, knowing George Fox, had promised to deliver it to him, ensuring it would then be passed to his mother. He told briefly of their journey, just that it was long and tedious and "we were storm-tossed many times, but the Friends comforted each other and met in worship when things were at their worst. We all survived, through one crew member was swept overboard." He told of their arrival at Pennsylvania, and the welcome and assistance of Friends already there. It was October when he wrote, and the Plymouth Group were proceeding with their settlement. "There is much wood and our houses grow quickly. Priscilla sustains me with her love and support, and has stood our difficulties well. The Indians we have met are friendly and come to exchange possessions." It was when he sent greetings and love to family and friends in Plymouth, and especially to herself, that Sarah's tears fell and the poor, bedraggled letter was in an even more dilapidated state. She lay it aside them and turned to George Fox's words. He was glad that there was news of Thomas' and the others' safe arrival to send to her, and commended his own love and support. His letter to them, though Sarah found it difficult to concentrate on other matters, told too of his great concern for the slave trade that he knew was becoming ever more widespread, and he hoped that Friends would raise their voices against it, and in the New World that owners would at least treat their slaves with clemency. Before hurrying to share this wonderful news, Sarah offered it up to John. "They arrived safely, my love. God watched over them across the ocean. May he continue to do so." She rushed then to James' house, and was too breathless to speak when she reached the door, just handing him both letters. "Come in, sister," James greeted her, "and rest. When wilt thou learn that 'tis not seemly to run like a young girl," but he smiled at her and brought her a tankard of ale. Then he read Thomas' letter and drew his sister into a warm embrace. "Thank God for this good news," and they sat for a few minutes before James said, "We must tell the others, all the others who sent loved ones away. I will gather everyone in the Meeting House. Come when you are rested."

It was only as she rose from her seat that Sarah realised that James' wife had not joined them. "Where is Rachel?" she asked. "Is she visiting one of the boys?" "No," James frowned, "she is resting upstairs. I am concerned about her, Sarah, she seems so tired of late." Sarah put her hand on his arm. "She is getting older, as are we all, brother. It is probably no more than that. You go on, I'll see her for a moment before I follow you." But when Sarah entered the bed-chamber and saw the thin face of her sister-in-law she knew this was more than the tiredness of approaching old age. She propped up the pillows and wiped the hot, damp forehead, and Rachel smiled her thanks, for her breathing was too difficult for talking. Sarah knew there would be much work for her here in the weeks that lay ahead, in nursing Rachel and caring for James, but the good news she had received would sustain her and give her the strength for all that would be needed.

Rachel did not recover, though with Sarah's devoted nursing she remained with them until the summer. On a warm June day, with the casements of the small room open to the sweet air from the sea, Sarah removed the dish of chicken broth from which Rachel could not even take a sip, straightened the sheet and pillows, and kissing her sister-in-law's forehead, gently called James to the room from the garden where he had been walking disconsolately up and down. She waited for him outside the chamber door, then with her arm around his shoulders, she said, "Go to her, James, it cannot be long." As she went down the stairs, she prayed that her restless, impatient brother would be given a quietness of spirit to help him at this time. She stayed in the house for a few more days, then, when James' son Oliver with his family moved in to be with his father for a while, she returned to her own cottage on the Hoe, glad as always to seek its solitude and the presence of John and Thomas that she felt so strongly there.

It was during the actual funeral for Rachel that news came to the Meeting House that Kate, the daughter of Rachel and James, had just given birth to a daughter of her own. There was great thankfulness for this, and James, turning to Sarah, wept tears of mingled grief and joy. "A daughter," he said, "a daughter. The Lord has given us grandsons who are all truly loved, but this is like the spirit of Rachel returned to us," and so the Meeting for Worship as well as giving thanks for Rachel's life, welcomed this new one into its midst.

Chapter Forty

ALTHOUGH SHE LOVED all her family dearly, and those who had passed on were still very much part of her, Sarah felt a special closeness towards her grand-daughter, Sarah-Ann, the eldest child of Elizabeth and Samuel, named for both her grandmothers. She had come to Sarah already a little girl, conceived and born when her young parents were in London, and Sarah would never forget the day they all returned to Plymouth, clad as she had only seen Elizabeth hitherto, in sober Quaker grey, wanting so much to be accepted. Friends had hesitated just for a brief moment, then with Sarah at their head had reached out to them in great love, and the little girl who had hidden shyly behind her father's legs, was coaxed out with gentle persuasion.

From that day on she and Sarah had a close bond, and Sarah would stroke her auburn curls and look into her bright blue eyes trying to see something of her mother in her. But she could not. "She is Sam's child," Elizabeth said one day when the child was eight years old, "and in that I am well blessed, for I'm sure she will not cause me the heart-ache I brought to thee, Mother. There seemed to be always something against which I rebelled, did there not?" The two women had been sitting in the garden at Rag Street with their sewing, though this was for Sarah an occupation of necessity rather than pleasure. Sarah lay down her work and reached out to touch Elizabeth's hand. "Ah, but my dear daughter, I cannot blame thee for that, for 'twas my own nature repeated. But Sam is a good man, with gentleness in his strength, and it will be wonderful to see how our little Sarah-Ann grows."

Now it was early in 1688, and Sarah-Ann was just sixteen. Sarah had thought that even within a sober Quaker community, she would break the hearts of many young lads, but if she did she was oblivious to it as she was to her own beauty. She was content to help her mother in the house and with the younger children, and her greatest delight was to sit quietly on her stool beside Sam while he worked at his plans and drawings. It was only Sarah who could persuade her to come and walk with her, or to come down on to the beach and look for shell-fish, as Sarah had done all her life.

They were doing just this one windy afternoon, carrying between them a pail of cockles and winkles, when Sarah stumbled on an uneven stone and sat down heavily on the shingle. Sarah-Ann stood the pail down then knelt beside her grandmother. "Art thou hurt?" she asked anxiously, and Sarah, gingerly feeling her ankle, smiled up at the girl. "No, my love, 'twas just a silly slip. Now, help me up, child, and we'll be getting home." "Allow me, Friend, and take it slowly." Both women looked up in surprise at the voice, then recognised their old friend, Robert Harris, but not the young man, also in Quaker garb, who stood beside him and was already reaching out a hand to Sarah. Robert smiled at them all. "This is my nephew Jacob," he said. "He has come from London to make his home with me, and I am very glad to have him." Having assured himself that Sarah had suffered no hurt, he picked up the pail of shell-fish, and the four of them walked across the beach to the Hoe and to Sarah's cottage, where she invited them to take refreshment with her.

She made a pot of tea for herself and Sarah-Ann and brought ale for the men, and told her grand-daughter to fetch some of her newly baked pasties. As they sat together in the pleasant living-room, Sarah welcomed Jacob to Plymouth, and then told them how Elizabeth had met Sam on that same beach when he came to her rescue over a spilt pail of shell-fish. Sarah-Ann's blue eyes were bright at the story of how her parents had met and Sarah, looking from her to Jacob, was struck by the glance between them, a mingling of recognition and of a kind of understanding. For the rest of the short visit she let the others carry on the conversation while she listened and watched the young couple. She looked with interest at Jacob Harris, having learnt he was twenty years old. He looked older, she thought, for his expression was serious and thoughtful. He was tall and slight, with hazel eyes and straight light brown hair. Sarah noticed his hands, the fingers long and slender, and wondered how he earned his living. Robert explained this a few minutes later. Jacob had been working for Friends in London, settling disputes and helping those in distress, gradually gathering knowledge of the law. Both of his parents had died recently and Robert had thought that it might be good for him to come to Plymouth, at least for a while. "I think there'll be much work for him here," he said, "for advice, good advice, is not always available to Friends."

Sarah explained all of this to Elizabeth and Sam when she saw them later in the day. "He seems a nice young man," then, "He and Sarah-Ann seemed to get on quite well, as no doubt you'll soon find for yourselves." Elizabeth looked sharply at her mother. "We'll keep an eye on her," she said. And they did, as the weeks and months went by. The friendship of the two young people proceeded quietly and gently which seemed to suit them both.

Jacob, though, proved to be of great interest to the Plymouth Friends. It was amazing how soon and how quickly they brought their problems to him, and listened to his careful advice. He talked too of life in London, not only of the Quakers there, but of the general unrest, stemming from the King and his court, but felt throughout the city. "James is weak and foolish, I believe," said Jacob to a gathering in the Meeting House. "So we have heard," Friends nodded their heads in solemn agreement. "'Tis said that he makes concessions and promises but too late, for already William with his wife Mary - James' own daughter - are making preparations in Holland."

Everyone waited for the next news. This came by a letter to Sam from old friends of his, to say that William had already left Holland, but even as Sam was hurrying to spread this information, a Brixham Quaker came galloping to the Meeting House with the news that William's ship lay off the Devon harbour. "If Plymouth Friends want to see the arrival of this man who may put an end to our sufferings, hurry now to Brixham."

There was great excitement, even amongst the sober Friends, and before long a huge cart and a team of horses was made ready, and the men and boys who could be spared climbed aboard, while the women filled baskets with food and ale for the journey. Sarah's brother James would dearly have loved to be one of the party, "but my legs would not stand such a journey", but he sent his son Oliver together with Francis' sons Joshua and Thomas, John-Richard and William and as many other Friends as could be accommodated.

When they returned a few days later they had much to tell and there was great excitement in the town.

Every Plymouth Friend came to that gathering in the Meeting House. "We saw him come ashore," said John-Richard. "A fisherman, a great fellow indeed, waded out and brought the new King on his shoulders to the beach, and a loyal address welcomed him to Brixham Quay. He replied but his tongue was strange, we could not understand it." "But what of King James?" asked an older Friend. "He has fled," came the answer. "Yes, he has gone, the Stuarts have gone. Look forward in faith, Friends, and give thanks to God." But another Friend was more cautious. "We do not yet know how this William will treat us."

A few days later there was more excitement, for the town. William's ship was to visit Plymouth. This time it was the Mayor who received the news first, and by the time William's fleet sailed round to Plymouth and anchored in the Cattewater, the Hoe was lined with townspeople, the Mayor and Council in the forefront. Even Friends, not usually given to such parades, went up to see this event. Sarah stood with James and Sam and Elizabeth, and could see a few yards away Sarah-Ann standing with Jacob. He, with bent head and still serious expression, was listening attentively to what she was saying. William came ashore in a small boat and was received officially and taken to the Guildhall, where the keys of the Citadel were surrendered to him. As many of the townspeople as could crowded into the Guildhall, some of the young Friends being among them. "Plymouth was the first town in England to declare for William," Joshua told the others excitedly as they gathered on the grass, "but they're going again," and a few minutes later the procession wound down to the shore and the message came, "they're making their way up through Devon to Torbay and further."

There was a kind of anti-climax in the town after this. No-one quite knew what would happen next. Soon, however, it was evident that William's welcome was not as unanimous as it had first appeared, for strong Jacobite sympathy still existed. The Plymouth garrison particularly was not happy about accepting the new order, but after a few skirmishes, they settled down.

The Friends gathered in their Meeting House in Treville Street, and after a time of quiet in which they sought the will of God, they decided they must continue their work and their lives peacefully and wait for the spirit to be revealed to them.

They had not long to wait before the next matter of moment caught them up in its activities, for just a few months after William's arrival in Brixham and then Plymouth, the Prince of Orange was in February of 1689, crowned King William III jointly with his English wife Mary. When the news reached Plymouth, it was young Jacob who informed the Friends of it, and, he continued, "he has made a promise that - 'the Protestant Religion and the liberties of England I will maintain'."

In the Meeting House Friends looked at each other in wonderment. "Does that include our liberties? Please God it may be so." And it was, for while they were still wondering and hoping a new era dawned in England, for William passed the Act of Toleration - all dissenters were now free to worship as they liked. It took a while for Plymouth Quakers to absorb just what this meant, and at Meeting after Meeting they talked and planned and gave thanks. James, and in fact all the Elders, and those who had lived through so much persecution, stood in a silence that could be felt and almost touched. Then James stood, looking around at all the faces turned to him, and said: "All dissenters can now worship freely, here in our beloved town we can meet openly with Unitarians, Baptists, Huguenots and Presbyterians, who will no doubt all form their own congregations, but *we*, Friends - *we*, have practised our religion through three decades of persecution. We have kept our Meetings," And the cry echoed through that usually quiet room. "We kept our Meetings," and Sarah, her eyes full of tears, spoke to John there and then. "We have come through, my love, all over this land, those whom George Fox led in the Way are free."

Epilogue

THE AIR OF FESTIVAL and thanksgiving continued right through that year of 1689, and Plymouth saw many joyous meetings and services. A joint gathering of Baptists, Unitarians and Friends was held on the Hoe, with each group conducting a part of the service according to their own way of worship. When Friends' turn came, the group of Quakers stood quietly and in silence, while the rest of the worshippers hesitated for a moment uncertainly then, as the stillness seemed to permeate the whole congregation, there gradually came a wonderful sense of the spirit of grace moving like a gentle wind from heart to heart, until, as Friends began to minister, everyone there felt a sense of communion with all around them and with the God they were all, in their various ways, seeking to serve.

Sarah had one moment of sadness at this time. She was sitting with James one evening talking over recent events. They often sat together thus, for James would say to her, "We are both fortunate in our families, sister, and love them dearly, I know, but 'tis good to have one's own generation to converse with and to remember the old days," and their thoughts went back to when they were children and all that the war had brought to the town, and they remembered Richard and Mary, Betsy, young Will, Rachel, Francis and all those others who had left them.

Then Sarah said suddenly, "Did the *Desire* sail needlessly, brother? If they had waited three more years, there would have been no persecution to flee from." James lay a comforting hand on her shoulder. "Hindsight makes us all wise, my dear, and 'if only' achieves nothing. 'Twas not merely persecution they sought to escape, for knowledge of a new world draws men and women to it, especially the young. Does thou not remember how Thomas would stand on the cliffs hereabout and yearn to travel across the ocean?" And Sarah could not but agree.

There were domestic events that year, too, which occupied much of her time. Babies were born to James' daughter Kate, and to Sarah's own daughter Mary, so there was much nursing and visiting and toddlers to be cared for as well. Then in July was held the first Meeting for Marriage since freedom had come to them. It was for Sarah-Ann and Jacob. In celebration the Meeting House was filled with flowers. Sarah brought roses from her own garden, beautiful blooms from pure white to golden and apricot, and deep red to the palest shades of delicate pink. Their perfume filled the Meeting House and wafted outside, for in thankfulness for the peace, the doors were left wide open throughout the Meeting. As Sarah watched the young couple, Jacob still serious but proudly content, and Sarah-Ann, more beautiful than ever with serenity in her eyes and happiness in the expression of her whole being, felt her own heart swell with love and thankfulness, for she knew her precious Sarah-Ann would be well cared for and she would assure John of this later. She helped Elizabeth with the marriage meal afterwards in Rag Street, and to carry the last of Sarah-Ann's possessions to James' house where the two were to set up home. James was to come to Sarah and share her cottage. "Thou might as well," she said to him, "for we spend much of our time in each other's company. We shall grow old together," and he, very grateful for this arrangement, said to her, "Well, at least we shall have much to talk about, even if it is only the difficulties of rearing the young and how much better we were at their age!", and he fetched the Bible for them to read together.

Even the grey days of November were brightened, for Sarah especially, by two wonderful events. She learned that Sarah-Ann would be having a child in the spring - her great-grandchild, and although John-Richard's daughter Catherine had already cast her in this role, she knew this would be someone special.

Then there came to her on the last day of that month, a letter from her beloved Thomas, brought on a returning ship. She read it over and over, then passed it to James for his comments, and for him to make out the words she could not quite decipher. All was going well with Thomas and with the group, and their Meeting was already strong. One or two had given up the attempt to develop the woollen industry and moved into Philadelphia, but the rest were persevering. Two of the young men talked of returning in the spring, to seek for wives to take back with them, and then, right at the end, he told her that Priscilla was expecting a child too, at Christmas. She turned to James with shining eyes. "The family goes on and on. Perhaps they'll come back to see us then, but at any rate there'll be news - more news - when those young men return. Now I must tell the other families, in case they have not heard," and snatching up her cloak, she ran down from the cottage and hurried across the Hoe like a young woman, while James could only shake his head, watch her from the window, and wonder at the strength and determination of this sister of his.